UWHARRIE

Uwharrie

by

Eugene E. Pfaff, Jr.
and
Michael Causey

Tudor Publishers, Inc.   Greensboro

UWHARRIE

Printed in the United States of America

First edition

All persons and events depicted in this book are fictional. Any resemblance between any person, alive or dead, is coincidental.

LIBRARY OF CONGRESS CATALOGING-IN-PUBLICATION DATA

Pfaff, Eugene E., 1948—

   Uwharrie: a novel / by Eugene E. Pfaff, Jr., and Michael Causey.
    1st ed.

      p. cm.
    ISBN 0-936389-30-3
    1. Indians of North America—Antiquities—Collection and preservation—Fiction. 2. Excavations (Archaeology)—United States—Fiction. 3. archaeologists—United States—Fiction. I. Causey, Michael, 1947. II. Title.

PS3566.F28U89   1993
813'.54—dc20   93-26735
                                          CIP

To my mother and my grandmother,
    who first taught me the joy of storytelling.
                                    —E.E.P.

This one is for Ibby Hunt.
                    —M.C.

Part I

JUNE

Chapter One

The yelping of the dogs was very far away now, their echoes splintered by the forest so that the hunter could not tell whether they were ahead of him, or had turned, giving chase in a direction slanting to his left or right.

Well, he thought, they'll turn up, I reckon, in the morning, with brambles in their tails and maybe a split ear or an eye cut from the coon. It wasn't the first time his dogs had gone crazy with the scent, and run wild after their prey.

If he were a younger man, he would have gone after them; even five years ago, at fifty, he might have followed along, running at a trot, until the baying could be located. Sooner or later the dogs would either tree the coon, or trap it against a ledge or in a hollow, and the coon would turn to fight. It would fight off his two dogs; any cornered coon was a match for two dogs. With two dogs, the hunter had to be quick enough to get there before the coon turned to fight, and the dogs were driven off.

He was just getting too old, he thought; his legs seemed to give out on him. He stopped for a while and simply breathed deeply, getting air back into his lungs. Then he turned around to head back home, to a soft bed.

He saw Spirit Rock silhouetted against the sky, reflecting the moonlight, which had an oddish red tinge. Good thing there is a full moon tonight, he thought. Otherwise, it'd be damn hard finding my way back home. The landscape looked unfamiliar to him; he had not hunted around here for years.

Was the trail over that way, he thought, or back to the left? *Shoulda brought my specs. Eyes aren't what they used to be in the dark.*

But then he saw the clearing, the old Indian campsite, and recovered his bearings. He heard the rush of the river beyond, rushing east. If he followed it, it would take him all the way to Clearview.

He saw the light of a fire at the edge of the clearing, against a backdrop of darker trees and undergrowth. Now what the hell could that be? he thought. Some boy scouts with a scoutmaster doesn't know there's bogs and sumpholes all round here, even in dry weather? He shook his head at the ignorance of such an idea. *Damn scoutmasters ought to be strung up, bringing kids out here. This clearing's been bad ground even to hunt near, much less to camp on.*

But he could hear no singing, or the hubbub of voices that would indicate a group. He drew closer so that his vision was not impeded by tree limbs. He saw a lone figure illuminated by the low fire; it looked to be a man in some sort of a costume.

Who the hell is that? he thought, more mystified than ever. Could be a tramp, he guessed, but there was no rail line within ten miles that he knew about. Might be some fool hippie kid wandered off from the park area, got lost maybe. Really lost. He decided to check and see. There was no reason to fear anyone; he had the .12 gauge loaded with double ought. The spookiness he had felt earlier was gone.

"Hallo!" he yelled, and started across the clearing. The figure said nothing. As he got closer, he saw it was a man dressed in strange but somehow familiar clothing.

I'll be damned, he thought. Damned if it ain't an Indian. With buckskin britches and a coat decorated with feathers. He was no hippie, at least. The long black and grey hair, pulled tight to the back and tied in a pony tail, set off a weathered, lined face.

"Welcome," said the figure. The deep voice coming from the motionless countenance startled the hunter for an instant. "I see you have been hunting. I heard the dogs some time ago. I do not think you will catch them, they were crazy with the scent."

"No, I guess not," replied the hunter. Whoever this fellow was, he seemed to know dogs. "You...you from around here, mister?"

"Yes, you might say that."

"I thought you was some scoutmaster or somethin' at first. I...are you lost, hurt, somethin' like that? This clearing is bad ground. Lot of bogholes around here, not safe unless you know the country well."

"I spent time here long ago. I know the bogholes and the dangers very well. But you look tired. Would you like to rest? I have some food and drink, if you are hungry."

The hunter wanted to be on his way, but his legs were weary, and his back was beginning to stiffen up. Maybe a spell of sitting would help. "All right," he said. "I'll just take you up on that, stranger." He sat down near the fire, but kept the gun crossed in his lap.

After a few minutes, the warmth of the fire had relaxed the hunter. The Indian had begun to talk about coons and how crafty they could be, that he had seen one climb onto a fallen tree limb at the edge of a pond and float out on it like a raft to evade some dogs.

The hunter had lost interest in exactly who this fellow was. He certainly knew coons and dogs, and in the hunter's estimation this made him trustworthy. Maybe he had drifted off the Catawba reservation down south.

The hunter wouldn't blame him if he had; it was a poor place to live, and Indians were always leaving and then coming back. It wasn't up to him to press about the stranger's business. Live and let live.

When the Indian offered a jug from behind the log on which he was sitting, the hunter took it without hesitation. Indians and their firewater, he thought. "Is this 'shine?" he asked. "I haven't had a good belt of 'shine in a long time."

The Indian just smiled.

"Yep, I'd rather have good 'shine than the bottled stuff any day. Gives more kick and costs less, too." He sniffed the top of the jug, savoring the yeasty aroma. "Must be mighty strong," he said, and took a drink. The taste was powerful, like grain alcohol, but with an herbal tinge to it, like smoke and tree bark. He swallowed and let the warmth slide down his throat.

He passed the jug back to his host, who also took a drink.

Almost immediately, the hunter felt a bit woozy. "Damn! Has some kick, all right," he told the other. "I'd better leave that stuff alone, if I'm gonna get home tonight." He stood, hoisted the shotgun to his shoulder, and looked at the Indian, who was smiling again. "Guess I'll be on my way," he said. "Much obliged for the...for the..."

His tongue was suddenly thick in his mouth, and he felt hot all over. The Indian seemed to change shape before him, his face first smiling, then scowling. Then the face was white, like white paint, with a black circle around one eye. And he was no longer wearing a buckskin jacket, but a robe of some kind, a patchwork thing of bright colors.

"Got to be...gettin' ...on..." he said.

"You will come with me now," the white face said.

Suddenly, the hunter was frightened; his heart began racing. The trees were whirling now above him, and the moonlight streaked at odd angles.

"Go? Go...where?" the hunter said, panic rising in his throat.

"Across the river," was all the Indian said.

The dogs came back toward dawn, whimpering and trotting with their tails low to the ground. One had a split ear and the other was bleeding from the throat, from where the coon had slashed it.

When this happened before to the dogs, they always tried to find the hunter's scent and follow it. Sometimes they would catch up to him before he had got back to the house. By instinct, the dogs were returning now to the last spot where he had been, sniffing the ground and the bushes for some sign of his scent. When they neared the clearing, they became confused. There was a powerful scent from a spot near a log and the ashes from a fire, but it was not an animal or anything else with which the dogs were familiar.

It set them to howling. They sniffed about in circles, agitated and confused. The shotgun was lying on the ground near the remains of the fire. It should have been covered with the hunter's scent, but the dogs hardly recognized it. They circled the clearing, vainly trying to find some sign of their master. But they didn't find it there, and all the way back to the house they failed to sniff out his trail. It was almost as if he had never been there at all.

David Hale shifted his position behind the steering wheel for the hundredth time, trying to ease the aching muscles in his lower back. He had just completed a grueling two hours with Lester Hawkins at his cabin up on Moore's Knob, one of a series of interviews of area residents he was conducting for the public library's oral history collection. The grizzled old man had told him a great deal about the development of the valley in the last fifty years, but he had rambled on far longer than David had really cared to listen.

The car crawled along at a snail's pace up the narrow, twisting mountain roads. Hale was in no hurry to get back to town, although the interviews kept him out of the library for hours at a time, abandoning it to Gertrude, his assistant.

He didn't guess it really mattered that the running of the library in the small town of Clearview was more and more given over to Gertrude and her lumbago, and the lackadaisical attitude it brought to her work. When he had accepted the job four years ago as a recent graduate of the university library school, he had tried to institute a new cataloguing system and other modern methods, hoping that his provincial hometown library could become a showplace in the state. He had reason to be a self-starter then, ambitious to change things.

But the oral history program was the only surviving remnant of those early days. He was beginning to wonder if he could find the motivation for it much longer.

The road wound snake-like down through the surrounding countryside, until it left the hills, the chain of domed peaks known as the Uwharrie Mountains. The heat simmered above the asphalt in waves that distorted the horizon. David took one last draw on a cigarette, almost flicking it out the window absentmindedly. But it was just that kind of carelessness that could torch the dry, brittle grass, starting a wildfire. Similar incidents had burned off much valuable timberland over the years. He stubbed the butt out in the ashtray instead.

He rolled down the window, letting the breeze blow over him in a futile effort to stave off the early summer heat. He had to remember to ask Jim Barlow at the garage to fix his air conditioning. He angrily turned off the country and western song that was droning on the radio.

He gazed off into the distance at the larger Uwharrie mounds. At one time, they had been the highest mountains in the eastern United States, so old that the Appalachians and even the Rockies were mere youngsters in comparison. But that had been in the Pleistocene Age; now, they were little more than large foothills that rose abruptly from the flat piedmont of North Carolina.

Gazing at the ethereal blue haze of the low mountains, he realized again the almost magnetic force they exerted; perhaps one reason most people who were born here stayed, except the most ambitious, was an inexpressible sense of bonding with the land. Even those that left, as he had, for educational or career goals, seemed to gravitate back within a few years. Certainly, it was a place of "roots," of the *old* underlying and subsuming everything that could be called *new*. The Clearview Library was just such a mix. Half was of stone, dating back to the 1880s and including a circular stone stairway with wrought-iron railing up to a small attic tower where a few local history displays gathered dust. The other half, the reading room and the children's addition, was built recently and smelled of metal, plastic, and leatherette.

The old and the new, blending inharmoniously.

It was with mixed feelings that he had come back to Clearview after library school. Shortly after graduation, he had married Linda, a local girl who had preferred to live in Clearview. And his mother had been in failing health and wanted him close by.

But all of that was behind him now. With his mother's death, and then the divorce a year ago, he found himself in a gentle trap, with the reasons for that trap gone. His job, and the familiarity of the rural setting in which he had grown up, were now the psychologically soothing anchors that held him to Clearview. But the anchors had begun to weigh down upon him. At twenty-eight, he'd had a glimpse of himself at forty or forty-five, still going through the motions. He was beginning to realize he wanted to be something more than a small-town librarian. Clearview was a bit too obscure for his liking.

With this seed of anxiety in mind, he'd taken more and more time from the regular business of running the library to scour the countryside, upgrading the collection of tapes and interviews in the oral history collection. The handed-down tales of other generations—even ghost stories and myths—interested him in a way everyday reality could not. And besides, if he could build even a small reputation as an oral historian, perhaps publish a book, he could parlay that into a more rewarding position at a university or metropolitan library.

That, at least, was a half-formulated plan.

David turned off the highway onto a short stretch of tar-patched concrete road that led him to the stoplight and the township of Clearview. Compared to the mystic blue and cloudlike quality of the mountains in the near distance, Clearview was prosaic, unpretentious and moribund, undistinguished from other small rural towns in the Southeast. It was comprised of a main street, two blocks long, and a number of quieter, parallel streets on either side. Here on Commerce Street, which served as the main street, were two rows of businesses in that mixture of old brick-and-wooden frame buildings that mimicked other towns further down the highway. The post office was in the same one-story structure that housed the sheriff's office and other municipal offices. Then a gas station. A combination real estate office and notary public which attorney Oswald Jenkins ran as sidelines. Mabe's cafe, with the only look of real activity this late weekday afternoon. The hardware store. Fleming's Drugs and Sundries. Further down the block, a rail crossing and siding with a rusty flatbed car which had been there as long as he could remember.

He turned from main street to the left, past the Grain and Farm Supply. The library, a converted residence and the oldest building in town, jutted up against the medical offices of Dr. Elias Burke, family practitioner.

The engine gave a shudder and stopped in a parking stall that, surprisingly, was unoccupied, although it was marked *D. Hale* in white paint.

CHAPTER TWO

John Wolfe Singer parked his pickup in front of the roadhouse and walked with deliberate steps into the dark, cool interior of the building, straight to a small corner booth in the very back. There were only a few other customers this early in the evening, the sun not yet down, although later there would be a big crowd of locals, noisy and boisterous as they drank beer and played pool.

Singer, oblivious of the other customers, stared at the wall in front of him. Although it was his custom over the past few months to stop here several times a week for a beer and a steak, he avoided conversation whenever possible, giving his order to the waitress with only a few curt words. He had once been more gregarious, slapping backs and buying rounds at innumerable roadhouses such as this one. But that was all finished now. He had been removed from the normal order of things.

The nights he stopped here were for convenience sake only, after a day of driving his pickup over the roads between Clearview and Ulah. Sparrow-in-Snow had said he must learn about the landscape, feel the forest and the low hills again as if they were his birthplace. Which the shaman, in his last visit, had said it was.

Singer now regarded the roadhouse as a strange, almost foreign place, and was anxious to eat and leave, to return to the old shack in which he lived, high on a slope above the valley.

The waitress was a fortyish woman, still very pretty, and full-breasted with a trim waist. Her name tag identified her as "Betsy." As she made her way to the corner booth, the eyes of several men at the bar followed her. Singer was engrossed in private thoughts and did not notice her for a moment.

"The usual?" she said, with a smile.

"Yes," he said, coming out of his reverie, "the usual."

"Sirloin ground, green beans, rolls. The cook ran flat out of corn this afternoon. We have hominy, if you want. Or we can give you hash-browns. And we have blueberry pie, or apple. Comes with the meal, no extra."

"Hominy. No pie."

"Coffee and beer both?"

Singer nodded.

Betsy wrote down the order on her pad and put it into the pocket of her apron. She stood for a moment, hesitantly, then said: "Are you okay? I, uh, well, you look like you're, I don't know...not really there, you know?"

Singer raised his eyes and forced a semblance of a smile to his lips. "I'm fine," he said. Then, after glancing at her name tag, he added, "It's all right, Betsy. I'm just tired today."

"Yeah," she sighed. "The heat has been awful for so early in the summer. Well, you try to take it easy." She seemed pleased with his answer, relieved. "I thought you might be having some problems. You always sit over here in the corner all alone. You ever want anyone to talk to, why, I'm always here. You remember, huh?" She patted his arm, letting the gesture linger, and then walked back to the counter.

"I'll remember," he called tonelessly. And he did remember. Some nights alone up on the mountain, he remembered all too well the women in other towns. The softness of their breasts, how they had opened themselves to him. It got lonely up on the mountain, the nights that Sparrow-in-Snow did not visit. With the visits he was no longer lonely, but something else. Perhaps something worse.

As he ate, and drained his beer in long gulps so that he could savor the coffee, he forgot about Betsy and her softness, and of the life he had lived when he was a 'town man.' It was like a long-ago dream. Now, he was of the mountain, and what the mountain brought to him was his destiny. It might drive him insane, he might journey with Sparrow-in-Snow to a place from which he could not return, but that was the way things must be. His long-dead great-grandfather might have said it was written in the stars, or on the wind, that he would meet that destiny in a place of rocks and trees, of clean air and fresh water. And sometimes, darkness.

He shrugged. Singer knew he no longer had a say in the matter. It was not up to him. The shaman had convinced him of that.

Singer finished eating and left the roadhouse, driving through the town, with its smell of gasoline exhaust and whites, as quickly as he could. He reached the base of the mountain, turning onto the narrow, curved rut of a road that led to his shack, before the odors were completely out of his system, and he felt stronger.

The library always had a few clients who waited until the last moment to check out an armload of books. After dispensing with them and locking up, David checked his watch and saw he was late for his appointment with Arthur Walters. Walters, a professor in archaeology at the state university and a long-time local resident, had called a few days earlier, speaking of 'an interesting proposition,' whatever that meant.

Even though David was fond of the older man, who had served as his unofficial advisor at the university, he was not enthusiastic about the meeting. The professor probably wanted some reference work done for him at the library.

Hale started the old Volkswagen and drove past the rail siding, into the residential part of town, two blocks of 'townies,' as the outlying farmers and timberland owners called them. The homes were neat, but not new, mostly painted an off-white with square yards and carefully-trimmed grass and shrubs. Most had that gentile extension, a spacious front porch. And screen doors.

Just outside the municipal limit sign, David drove down a long driveway bordered by a stretch of white fence. It was a two-storied country house with tall pines bordering the yard; a garage apartment behind the house shaded an old, blocked-up well.

He parked the car, got out, mounted the three steps of the porch and knocked on the door. Professor Walters greeted him with that mixture of urgency and distractedness which had consigned most of his archaeological research papers to the less important journals. With his greyish-white hair, tortoise-shell glasses slipped forward on his nose, and slightly stooped shoulders, he gave the impression of the quintessential absent-minded academic that he was.

Walters ushered David into the den just as the phone rang from another room, and he excused himself to answer it.

David remembered very well the prominent portrait of Mrs. Walters above the mantel. The poor woman had become senile many years ago and was vegetating in an Asheboro nursing home. David recalled with some nostalgia that the professor had once seemed more dynamic, less drained than he did now. He hadn't seen him for almost a year, and the months had aged him considerably.

He took a seat on the sofa and continued his inspection of the room: two crowded but neat bookshelves, prints of hunting scenes on one wall, a coffee table with a thin layer of dust. The professor obviously seldom used this room. It was apparently only for guests.

David's gaze lingered on a series of photographs above one book shelf. A pretty, blonde girl of about twelve, smiling broadly as she sat on a pony in the backyard. The same girl at about fifteen, in a formal gown at some school function. And the last one, a beautiful young woman with the same golden hair and light blue eyes.

The photos were all of Diana Walters, the professor's daughter. David had gone to high school with Diana, had spent many hours fantasizing about this remote, almost haughty beauty who accumulated academic honors without apparent effort. Perhaps she had realized at that early age she was not the type to bury herself in a town like Clearview, content to be wife and mother. Gifted and ambitious, she had attended Brown, and then earned a doctorate in anthropology at Columbia. The last he had heard, she was an instructor at Smith.

David sighed. Thinking of Diana, who perhaps was not so much brighter or more able than he, but who was already quite successful, recalled his own less promising situation. Besides, he had had quite a long-running crush on her those short—or were they long?—years before.

Walters returned, interrupting David's reverie.

"A former student," the professor apologized. "Wanted some career advice." He lit a pipe and settled back in a chair, suddenly expansive. Old students probably did not call very often, thought David.

"Well, David, I understand that you have been conducting some sort of oral history project this summer," Walters said.

"Yes, sir," David replied, somewhat startled. He was unaware that his activities had generated any interest among the towns-people. "I've been interviewing a few of the older people in the valley. I just finished talking to Lester Hawkins. He's very interesting. Lives alone in the cabin he built over fifty years ago."

"Yes, he's an extraordinary person. I imagine he had a lot to tell you about the Depression. Probably more than you wanted to know, am I right?" Walters chuckled. David smiled in acknowledgment, surprised that the professor knew about one of the less well-known local inhabitants. Walters was not particularly gregarious.

"What do you intend to do with this material after you collect it?" he continued.

"I thought I might write a local history some day. For right now, I'm just going to keep it in the library with the other interviews."

"Well," said Walters, "I suppose you are wondering why I asked to see you, David. I certainly don't want to discourage you from your own project, but have you ever considered doing research on the Native American population in the area?"

"I wasn't aware there was a Native American population, other than a few Catawba, and their history has been pretty thoroughly covered. I don't think I could find enough to warrant a thorough oral history project."

"I'm not talking about the Catawbas," responded Walters."I'm talking about an earlier tribe. The Uwharries."

" I thought they died out years ago. All that's left of them is the name they gave to the mountains."

"Oh, yes, they are quite extinct. But let me continue. Last year I wrote a proposal to the American Indian Archaeological Institute to fund an exploratory dig at the old Spirit Rock site. It's always been thought to be a settlement of the Catawbas. But I believe it is older than that; I think it was the central village of the Uwharries. I requested a grant to do an excavation of the site.

"I've come across some journals of early traders in the area that recount meeting Indians with blue eyes and facial hair. I believe these were descendants of the survivors of the Lost Colony. Legend has it that the survivors of the Lost Colony made contact with the Uwharrie. If we could discover some artifact that would conclusively prove sixteenth century European contact with the Uwharries, it would set the historical profession on its collective ear. Might make an interesting book, too—if some energetic young writer was willing to work as a co-author."

David pondered this last statement. Walters' implication was not lost on him.

"But I don't know anything about archaeology. What possible use can I be to you?"

"We'll need further documentation to justify such a project"explained Walters. "What I had in mind was a series of interviews of the descendants of the original settlers to this area, the stories they heard about the first contacts between the whites and the Native Americans here, the legends that were repeated. You'd be surprised how many of the folktales that we mistakenly attribute to Anglo-Saxon tradition originated from Native American folklore. In cases like this, the oral traditions of an area can be accepted as evidence in lieu of written documents. The grant I received is just seed money to investigate the possiblility of a more extensive project. Your interview transcripts, combined with the artifacts uncovered, can provide that data. If nothing else, you will have compiled a valuable collection for the library."

Walters' arguments were persuasive. Perhaps here was the opportunity he was seeking; a chance to work with a man of modest but solid academic reputation on a potentially significant project. But he was hesitant, still unconvinced that he could be of genuine help to the professor. Random oral history interviews to alleviate boredom were one thing; a sophisticated, professional research project was quite different.

"Are you sure I'm the right man for you, Dr. Walters?" David said. "Surely you could find someone more experienced to assist you."

"The grant is not as munificent as you might think, David. Nor is my theory that popular among my colleagues. Besides, you're readily available, and I want to get started immediately."

David saw the twinkle in the blue eyes he remembered whenever Walters had surprised students by proposing a shocking concept to them. It was good to see some of the old fire in those eyes again.

"All right, Dr. Walters. If you want me, I'm with you. When do we start?"

"Right away. I'm putting together a survey team now. I talked over the project informally with the mayor, and I'm certain he will allow you very flexible hours at the library this summer. And my daughter will be helping me out, too."

"So Diana will be working here this summer?" David asked, trying to sound casual.

"Yes. Her teaching duties are over. She'll be in on the twelfth, staying in the garage apartment. Why don't you give her a call after she settles in? You two used to be classmates, didn't you?"

"Yes, sir, we did. And I'd like that very much," Hale answered. He felt excited at the prospect, in spite of himself. Perhaps she had changed, was not so aloof now. He really could not imagine her being interested in the company of a small-town librarian, but perhaps they could have dinner together, at any rate. He'd find out.

"Fine," said Walters, rising to shake Hale's hand "The others are already at the site. Why don't you come out to meet them?"

David walked with the older man to the door.

"I'm serious about your calling Diana," said Walters. "Life is pretty dull for her around here when she visits. It would do her good to get out with someone her own age."

"Of course," replied David. "I'd be delighted."

Yes, he'd be delighted, but he wasn't at all sure about Diana.

CHAPTER THREE

Sheriff Joe Witherspoon grimaced as he took a sip of the coffee. On his wife's urging, he was trying to give up sugar, but the experiment wasn't going very well. The black coffee tasted more like stump-water. He felt a twinge of guilt as he pulled the sugar dispenser down the counter and let the powder flow into his cup. He took another drink; now it was too sweet.

"Just another glass of water with my breakfast, all right, Millie?" he called to the waitress. It wasn't going to be a good day, he thought.

The air conditioning in Mabe's cafe sputtered in the background. It was only the middle of the morning, but already the temperature outside was above ninety, and not much cooler inside. Witherspoon wiped the back of his neck with a napkin, then balled it up and put it into his pocket.

He turned his attention to the plate of eggs and grits and began to eat, but his thoughts were elsewhere. Arthur Walters had just started digging around the old Indian mound, but already there was a disruption in the quiet and order of the town. Just last night Peter Blackwell, one of the student helpers the professor had imported from the university, had turned up, stoned half out of his senses, in the back yard of John Benjamin, falling all over himself and yelling obscenities. It wouldn't have been a major incident except Benjamin was a grumpy old character with a spinster daughter, and he was ready to sign a 'Peeping Tom' complaint, although Witherspoon doubted very much that June Rose was anything a college student would want to peep at. If Benjamin were a reasonable sort, Witherspoon could hold the boy a few days on public intoxication and then let the Professor ship him back home. But now it looked like a more complicated charge, and the boy might wind up on the county farm, depending on how Judge Harper in Ulah viewed the matter. But maybe he could talk some reason into old Benjamin when he calmed down a bit.

But the sheriff could feel the trouble and aggravation starting to build up already. Clearview was the sort of town where a few unfamiliar young people could raise everyone's blood pressure.

The sheriff wasn't bothered by high blood pressure; aggravation went straight to his stomach. He was already developing heartburn from the grits and coffee, perhaps in anticipation of a summer full of incidents like the Benjamin case. He wondered what that fool of a professor could be looking for in the dirt out at the clearing. Another batch of arrowheads and broken pots didn't seem to be worth all the trouble and expense. What else could possibly be out there? Witherspoon had no interest in digging up more trouble from the past; there was always more than enough of it in the present. College students, he thought, damn them anyway. Let them dig up junk in their own backyards.

"Here's your water, Joe." Millie set the glass down and wiped up the ring from the first glass with a rag. "How're the grits this morning? I thought they were a little on the runny side myself."

"No," he said absentmindedly. "They're all right."

"Well, you let me know if you want more toast instead. No charge. I'm not partial to watery grits myself."

"Thanks, Millie, these are okay."

The waitress started to walk away, but then said: "Joe, isn't that Mason Thomas out there?" She was looking through the plate glass at the front of the cafe. "I thought the forest ranger was out looking for him."

Witherspoon glanced out the window and saw Thomas get out of a pickup truck. The other door opened and his son Willie stepped out. From the gestures they were making, he guessed they were having an argument. The boy shouted something, then turned to storm off toward the hardware store.

The sheriff turned back to his breakfast. "I told Willie that Mason was just out on a toot. I see he's got a bandage over his ear. Probably poured off most of a bottle and fell over a stump, then slept it off and wandered back home."

"That old fool will go cooning one night and trip over his shotgun," snorted Millie, "and like as not they'll never find him."

Witherspoon nodded. That was probably the truth. Millie liked to gossip too much, but her predictions were usually accurate. "I suppose so," he told her. "But he's all right this time, anyway."

The look Millie shot Thomas as he came into the cafe made Joe glad his stomach couldn't tolerate more than a beer once in a while. He fully expected to hear a tirade from her about the college boy in Benjamin's back yard, and a prediction of what bad end was waiting for the student. He scooped up the remains of the eggs with his toast and stuffed it into his mouth, the quicker to get to the antacid he kept in his car.

Thomas plopped heavily onto a stool a few feet from the sheriff. The farmer sounded a gruff greeting, then ordered coffee. Millie took the order with her mouth pinched in disgust, then went back into the kitchen.

Witherspoon returned Thomas' nod and studied the man for a moment. He certainly looked like he was back from a binge, all right. His hair was matted, he had two or three days' growth of beard, and there was a virulent redness to his eyes. The sweat stains on his shirt had made a double white ring of salt under his arms.

Well, thought Witherspoon, he never gives *me* any trouble, anyway. Thomas might like his liquor, but he was not one of the roadhouse bunch. The sheriff never had cause to give as much as a warning to him. In fact, when he was in town, he was usually reasonably friendly and courteous, perhaps to make up for what folks had heard about him. The sheriff had been surprised to see him arguing with his son outside. But maybe he wasn't quite sober yet, or suffered from a nagging headache.

Witherspoon supposed it was his duty to ask a few questions, to clear up the missing-person report Willie had made. Then he could tell the ranger he was wasting his time searching out in the woods.

"You all right now, Mason?" he asked.

"What? Why, sure, I guess," said Mason, in a low voice.

"What happened to your head?"

"Ran into a tree limb chasing a coon." Then he added, "If it's any of your goddamn business."

Witherspoon was surprised at the outburst, and felt his stomach churn. "Now, hold on a minute, Thomas. Watch how you talk to me. I guess I have a right to ask where you've been, since your boy filed a missing-person report."

"None of his damn business where I was. Nor yours, either."

"I told you to stop sassing me, Thomas. I'm not going to take it. I figure you got drunk and slept it off in the woods. Is that the way it happened?"

Thomas nodded sullenly. Must be hung over real bad, thought Witherspoon. Never seen him act like this before. "All right then, that's what I'll put in the report." He stood up to leave. "But you lay off that stuff for a while, will you? We had to put the ranger out looking for you, and he's got better things to do. Understand?"

Witherspoon saw Thomas' hand clench around a cafe knife. He started shaking and turned to the sheriff, a scowl on his face and his eyes blood red. Then he said in a furious whisper: "Wesichau!"

With that, he sprang from the stool, the knife curving backhand toward Witherspoon's midsection. The sheriff blocked the blow with his wrist, and grabbed Thomas from behind. His left hand twisted the man's neck, and his right managed to catch his wrist. He turned the arm against itself, wrenching it up behind Thomas' back. The farmer groaned, then grew rigid in pain, and dropped the knife.

An hour later, Willie was talking in an agitated voice with Witherspoon at the jail. Mason Thomas was behind bars, and although the sheriff was still shaken by the incident, he tried to calm the boy, who understandably was upset at witnessing his father in handcuffs being manhandled into a cell.

"I just don't understand it, sheriff. Pa just hasn't been...*right* somehow since he came back out of the woods. He's always a little edgy after a binge, but he never took a swing at anyone before, much less the law."

"I know that, son. But he could have hurt me with that knife, and then your pa would be up for some serious charges. Now, I tell you what I'm going to do about this. I know you might fall behind on your mortgage and lose your land if he was put away, so as far as I'm concerned he was just drunk and disorderly out there today. There'll be a fine, but that's all.

"But I'm going to make a condition that he get examined by Doc Burke right away, and see about his head. A man his age can't drink like a fish and get banged on the head to boot, and not have it hurt him. He just can't keep up the drinking, and it'll have to be up to you to keep him sober. If he causes any more trouble, I'll have to come down hard on him, son, and he might have to go to jail the next time."

"He just was like another person after he come dragging up from the woods this morning, Sheriff. You know I was worried about him being gone so long this time. Then he came back half-starved with his head bleeding, and he'd lost his gun. It was like he was, I don't know, *different* somehow. It was like he wasn't my pa anymore. He looked at me funny too, like we were strangers or something. Even the dogs didn't come up to him like they usually do."

"Listen, Willie, the best thing you can do right now is to let him stew a while in that cell back there, and do some hard thinking. Go on down to the drug store and get a coke or something, and come back in a couple of hours. We'll know what the Doc says by then, and we'll get it straightened out. Just try to relax now, and let me handle it, okay?"

"I guess you're right, Sheriff," the boy sighed. Then he left the office.

Witherspoon put a form into the typewriter and began to make up the arrest sheet on Mason Thomas. What with the events of the last twenty-four hours, it looked as if he and the town might be in for a very long, uncomfortable summer.

CHAPTER FOUR

Joe Witherspoon was trying to give a lecture to the occupant of his squad car back seat, the Peeping Tom of the weekend, Peter Blackwell. His words were falling on deaf ears, however, and this increased Witherspoon's sense of frustration as he headed the car off a paved road onto a dirt one, in the direction of the professor's dig at Spirit Rock.

He checked the rear-view mirror and saw that Blackwell was smiling at him with a particularly vapid, arrogant smirk.

Perhaps that was because Judge Harper had accepted a fine in lieu of more jail time for the college student. The boy's father had wired the money so quickly that Witherspoon suspected he wished to avoid having to appear in person on behalf of his son. From what little the sheriff had seen of the boy, it was probably a wise move on the father's part.

"Tell me, son," Witherspoon asked the rear-view mirror, "what's a rich kid like you doing here digging for bones in the hot sun?"

Blackwell chuckled. "Hell, Marshal, I enjoy it. It's a great way to stay in shape. Besides, my mother always wanted a scientist in the family, to balance off the businessmen and lawyers."

"I told you once not to call me marshal. I'm a sheriff. Marshals are federal officers."

"Yeah, well..."

"And if you want to live long enough to be a real scientist, you'll take my advice and stay away from those drugs."

"What drugs are those, Mar...Sheriff?"

"You know what I'm talking about. You may have fooled the judge, but you don't fool me one bit. You're no Peeping Tom; you were stoned out of your mind. You're lucky I didn't shoot you as a burglar. What would your mother have thought then?"

"Oh, she might not have minded as much as you think. But I wasn't on drugs that night."

"Shit. I know you're not crazy, Blackwell. You're too much of a pain in the ass to be crazy. So why else would you be running around at three in the morning, buck naked and yelling gibberish?"

"It was a natural high, Marshal."

Witherspoon scowled into the mirror. But Blackwell didn't seem to be smirking now; he sat silently staring down at his hands. Maybe the kid *was* crazy after all. Just what I need, he thought, another crazy like Thomas. "You mean the 'full moon' got to you, or something, eh?"

"Ah, I don't know. I was walking around out near the dig and the smell of the trees gave me a blast. Like a big jolt of meth, you know? You ever had an methadrine, Sheriff?"

"No."

"Well, I got a lot of energy all of a sudden, and I started running, and I ran all the way into town. Then...I really don't know what happened after that. Must have been a flashback or something. I used to drop a little acid."

Witherspoon snorted in disgust. "You want to know what I think?"

"Sure," said Blackwell, the smirk returning to his face. "What's your analysis?"

"I think you've taken so many of those drugs that there's little tiny holes in the bottom of your skull, and your brains are leaking out, along with your good sense. If you ever come into town and cause any more trouble, I'll see to it that you do some time at the county farm, you hear? I don't care about your daddy's money."

"Well, I appreciate your concern, "Blackwell guffawed, "but don't worry about me. I manage to have a good time wherever I am. Even in a jerk water town like this."

"You really don't give a shit, do you, son?"

"No, Marshal, I really don't. About anything."

Witherspoon started to say something, but just sighed. It was pointless. He had seen kids like this before. He didn't know why they wanted to waste their lives. Maybe too much money, not enough discipline. He shook his head and concentrated on the road instead.

The dirt road was ending, and Witherspoon saw Spirit Rock rising in the distance. He turned left onto a rutted path that was beginning to show the marks of vehicles after many empty years. Probably an old wagon road, and before that a footpath. The clearing was pretty far off the beaten path. He could have let one of the professor's college kids come get Blackwell, but he wanted to have a look at the excavation for himself.

The car came to a widening of the path which led to a large open space. Witherspoon saw a group of people in a clearing where only scrubgrass grew. Several were walking carefully among roped-off grids; others emptied shovelfuls of dirt into large sieves. Off to one side, a square canvas tent stood near a porta-john.

The sheriff was surprised at how small the operation was. He had expected to see large machinery and swarms of people, like the National Geographic specials he had seen on television. Not very impressive for a 'scientific' excavation.

Walters met the car and stood by while Witherspoon let Blackwell out of the back seat.

"Are you all right, Peter?" asked the professor, noting the ugly purple welp under Blackwell's left eye.

"I'm sorry about that, Doc," said Witherspoon, "but the boy bit my deputy when we tried to arrest him. I had to lay him out with my nightstick."

"Yeah," said Blackwell, "and you enjoyed it, didn't you, Marshal?"

"Now, you be quiet, Peter," admonished Walters. "Sheriff

Witherspoon told me this morning that Mr. Benjamin agreed to drop the charges of indecent exposure. You should consider yourself fortunate that you received only a fine. And your father has agreed to let you remain on the dig."

"He's just glad to be rid of me," sneered Blackwell.

David Hale watched the scene as Blackwell, amused at the attention he was receiving, swaggered over to the equipment building, then turned to wave farewell to Witherspoon. It was obvious he enjoyed stirring up trouble. But the boy soon re-emeged, carrying a shovel. At least he did his share of the work, David thought.

Hale spit and bent over his sieve again. He'd taken a few hours off from the library to visit the site and, feeling out of place, had volunteered to help. It was in an area away from the main excavation, and he was unlikely to produce any valuable finds—or likely to ruin any artifacts as a clumsy amateur.

He didn't mind the hard work or the patronization of the more experienced students. He found it interesting and, besides, Diana was working only a short distance away. He was enjoying the view of her tight-shorted behind as she shifted the sieve back and forth. Even with the sun beginning to scorch his shoulders, this was far more pleasurable than watching Gertrude type overdue notices.

Diana swung around, and their eyes met. David was momentarily flustered, his gaze caught coming up from her inviting posterior.

"Hey," she said, "You're supposed to be trying to find dead bodies. Not ogling live ones."

She said it loud enough for Eric Blair, one of the student helpers, to hear. He gave David a knowing grin that made him feel like an adolescent. His face grew hotter than the incipient sunburn on his shoulders.

For a moment he felt like he was in high school again, with the 'Ice Bitch' staring him down, staring everyone down with her casual superiority. But he was older now; unlike the schoolboy of a decade earlier, he did not slink back inside himself. Instead, he was angry. He attacked.

"I don't have to be doing this at all, you know. I'm supposed to be the oral historian around here, not a ditch digger!" He rose and dusted off his pant knees.

"Nothing's stopping you from conducting your interviews," she came back. I'm sure you would be much more useful to the project in that capacity. Dad asked you out here because he thought you might enjoy learning more about the site. But since you'd rather watch the 'view' than work, perhaps you *had* better go."

That was too much. "Just a damn minute!" he exploded. "Your father told me you would give me the historical background on the area Indian tribes, and *that* is why I am out here. But you've been too busy parading yourself in front of me to do your job. Or let me do mine."

David knew he was being unfair, but at the moment he didn't care. He momentarily savored the anger and embarrassment on her face, then turned and stalked off, feeling avenged and ridiculous at the same time.

CHAPTER FIVE

There was no mirror in Singer's shack, but if there were it would have shown a ruggedly handsome man, in his early forties, his face weathered by cold and wind and hard times, with thick shiny black hair which he wore long and ragged at the back. His eyes were also black, the color of anthracite, complementing the swarthy tone of his skin. He had very little beard, and the only line on his face was one deep furrow crossing his brow. His nose was straight and long, his cheekbones high and prominent.

His face conveyed the classic features of his Native American forebears. He was not full-blooded by any means, but, as the shaman had said, a drop of the river is still the river. When first he arrived in Clearview, everyone assumed he was a Catawba from down south. But he was not a Catawba. Singer did not know what really was in his blood, where it came from, what tribe. He was still a stranger to himself in that regard. More so since the shaman had come.

The shack contained two wooden chairs, a cot and two wool blankets for the winter, a wood stove for heat and cooking, a washbasin, a crude board table, some shelves where he kept a few cans of food, two nails where he hung a change of jeans and several long-sleeve work shirts, some pots and pans; very little else. A motel ashtray that no one had ever used, as he had no visitors. An outhouse in the back.

Singer stepped out onto the plank porch and gazed at the moon. It was a clear night, and the moon did not have a tint of yellow or grey that sometimes appeared when the filth from the paper mill thirty miles away blew toward the mountain.

It was on nights like this that the shaman would come. Singer was apprehensive, but at the same time expectant, the same feeling he had had when he made field jumps as an army paratrooper. It was a heightened awareness of both danger and accomplishment, death and freedom. The pause before hurling oneself into space.

He looked down the mountain along the twisted, rutted path. A long jagged decline studded with dry shrub, gnarled pines, and outcroppings of rock and shale. The moonlight showed the land here barren, almost waterless. It was a dead skull overlooking the softer spread of the valley.

The night was very warm, almost hot. Singer felt the oil of his neck mix with sweat and begin to slide down his shirt collar in slow drops. He saw in the distance that the clearing in the valley was glowing again, a soft and diffused light with a reddish tint to it. From this high point it was quite evident; the moonlight intensified it as it did the snake-like ribbon of sparkling water that bordered the clearing, closing off one side of the large jagged circle where no trees grew. He felt warmer watching the glow, his throat suddenly dry, almost burning with thirst. He returned to the cabin's interior and used the hand pump to draw up water from the old well. He scooped the mineral-tasting liquid into his mouth.

When he returned to the porch, the shaman was waiting for him.

He was tall, with an aura of bone and sinew rather than flesh. And he was old, the skin of his face like cracked brown leather, streams of wrinkles and furrows which ran together at the sides of his eyes. There might have been more to know from his face, but once Singer looked into his eyes, they were all he saw. Singer's own gaze was drawn to them. The eyes were deeply alive, burning with an energy that was perhaps stolen from his immobile, stoic face and his dried-up frame.

Coals, Singer thought. Burning coals, red and glowing like embers in a fire. He did not know if they were dying or just beginning to burn.

And he was silent now, waiting for Singer to ask his questions. If John moved to the side, looked at the shaman from a sharp angle, the moonlight seemed to flow through him; he could almost make out the outlines of the doorway through his body.

But from the front, that fragile image disappeared and he appeared solid, awesomely powerful. His eyes held Singer, forced him to freeze like a rabbit sensing the hunter.

Singer was suddenly afraid; his heart raced, the moonlight whirled for a second. Then he knew he had to ask, to find out, to make sense of his doubts. The shaman had the answers. He was, in fact, the only answer Singer had ever truly known.

"You've come back," he said, finally.

"I have never been away," answered the old one. "And neither, really, have you, John Wolfe Singer. Though you come from another place, here you have always been, and here you will always be."

The voice was high but strong, and seemed to crackle, like wind blowing through a wood fire. Its sound took away some of Singer's fear. It did not soothe, but excited some element in his gut that braced him up, turned the fear into a tense anticipation.

"Why do you pursue me?" Singer asked. It was in the tone a child might ask an adult.

"No, John Singer. You are the pursuer. You are the hunter."

"If that is so, what is the prey?"

"The hunter sooner or later will stumble over himself. Slow down, John Singer. Do not lose sight of the shadow that runs in a circle back to you. For it is yourself."

"I don't understand. You talk as if I were something lost."

"And can you truly say you are not lost?"

Singer had no firm answer, so he was silent, his brow furrowing.

"John Singer, you have lost yourself. I have brought you here, and I will lead you back to yourself. There are many things you have forgotten. They are in your blood, but not in your memory. But the blood knows better. The blood is wiser than the heart or the head. If you will let your blood have its way, quickly you will discover who and what you truly are, and why you have been brought to this place, this valley."

"But I was not brought here. I came of my own will."

"You were drawn here by your blood. It is ancient blood, and if you will listen to it, it will tell you many things. The forest and the river are there inside you, whispering. They brought you back as surely as the hawk returns to the nest. I know you have felt at times in your life that you were not John Singer, but someone else, and that the place where you grew to be a man was not your true home."

Singer swallowed hard. "All right. That is true. Sometimes in the night I have had dreams where I was not myself, but someone else. I would wake up sweating and confused. And afraid."

"In these dreams, who were you?"

"I was...something wild, moving in the night. I was hungry and there was a smell that I followed. But I always woke up then. The waking was worse than the dream, because it seemed I had to pull myself out of the dream, or the nightmare. Other dreams I simply woke from; these I had to climb out of."

"You wanted to stay there, in the dream. You wished to remain the wild and free thing you became then."

"No. I don't know. The only thing I know is that the dreams disappeared for a long time, but then a few months ago they came back. And I left the place where I was and came here, and now I am not sure any more if I am awake or dreaming or gone mad. I do not know if you are real or something in my head, like the dreams."

"I am more real than anything you have known in your life before now. That is what frightens you. You know I am not a dream. You recognize me by your blood; how could I not be real?"

"I do recognize you, but I do not know who you are. You are like my great-grandfather, but you are not him. You are like the thing I was in the dreams but you are not that, either. "

"I am all these things, and your blood knows it."

"No!" Singer turned his face away. "Stop staring at me! Go away and leave me alone!"

"You know I cannot leave, just as you cannot leave this valley. Your blood tells you to stay. Why do you fight these things? Why do you not accept the truth?"

"I do not know the truth anymore."

"But you do. What is your true name, John Singer? Listen and you will hear it in your veins."

Singer buried his face in his hands, shaking his head. "No, no!" he cried.

"Listen. What is your true name?"

"Wolf-Singer."

"Yes, of course that is your name. And who am I?"

"Sparrow-in-Snow."

"And what am I?"

Singer looked out into the dark of the valley. The clearing in the distance was beginning to glow again, more brightly than he had seen it before.

"You are shaman...of...the tribe."

"And what are you?"

"I am a member of the tribe." Hot tears stung his eyes now. "I am...Uwharrie." He said it again, louder. Then he shouted it:

"I am Uwharrie!"

CHAPTER SIX

The sweltering summer heat drifted in through the library windows, undiminished by the window fan that droned monotonously. Sitting at the circulation desk, David had caught himself nodding off several times.

"Do you want me to file these pamphlets, Mr. Hale?" asked Gertrude Weatherly, peering over her reading glasses. "I had hoped I could go over to Ulah and see my sister. She just got out of the hospital and needs somebody to check in on her."

"Okay, Gertrude, I'll take care of that this afternoon. You go on, and give your sister my best regards."

Gertrude was already halfway to the back room where she kept her purse.

"Can I order any more of that black paint for you, David?" she said from the back. "I'll be going right by the hardware store."

The iron railing of the spiral stair in the old section needed a paint job badly; because of budget cuts, he'd have to come in on a Sunday and do the maintenance job himself. Four cans of special base paint already sat at the top of the stair; had been waiting for months, and probably would wait a couple of more. Paint fumes gave him a migraine and he kept putting off the job. Gertrude's offer was by way of telling him once again the stairs were still waiting.

"No," he told her. "We've got enough paint."

David sighed with relief as the rear door closed behind her; it would be more peaceful without her puttering around. Gertrude could be irritating. Unfortunately, she was a legacy of his predecesor, and the town council considered 'Miss Gertrude' an institution in her own right. So they were stuck with one another.

His gaze swept the empty room, and the old ambivalent feelings overwhelmed him again. It was a peaceful place, a secure job where he could do as much or as little work as he wanted, where he knew everyone and enjoyed their respect; he would know what he would be doing next year, and the next, and the next...

He forced himself to put those kinds of thoughts out of his mind. They only put him in a sour mood. He started stamping date due cards, then turned to see Ada Hanner advancing up the stone walk of the library. Now, David thought, there was someone who was perfectly content to have lived her whole life in the same place.

"Hello, David," she called out in a cheerful, lilting soprano. She approached him in short, mincing steps, her feet encased in those black monstrosities the elderly wear. She also wore support hose, a flowery print dress and a flat black hat.

"How are you, Miss Hanner," replied David, taking the load of books from her arms. "What can I do for you today? Some more romances? Or how about a spy thriller?"

She wrinkled up her nose. "No, thank you, young man. I've had quite enough of those potboilers with all that sex and violence. I was very disappointed in you for recommending that last novel to the Book Club. John Le Carre´ may be quite the thing in New York, but not Clearview."

"I'm sorry, Miss Hanner," said David, barely suppressing a smile. "I'll be more careful in the future."

"How about some nice Grace Livingston Hill books for the Book Club?" continued Miss Hanner. "And we certainly hope that you will come back and give us another lecture on the reference facilities of the library. We were so disappointed when you couldn't join the Book Club as a regular member."

David lied: "I'd like to join, but the library just takes up too much of my time. And there was the...the business of Linda's things." He looked away: at the desk, the clock, anything but the patronizing look on the old woman's face.

"Oh, dear," said Miss Hanner. "She was such a nice girl, too. It's too bad she decided to leave Clearview. Well, I must go, David. Shall I tell the ladies they'll be seeing you next Wednesday?"

David nodded, already formulating an excuse; but he was grateful she hadn't talked further about Linda.

Shortly the library closed, and David drove through town toward Cedar Drive and his four-room duplex. He'd kick off his shoes and drink a beer, watch some television.

Another wild night in Clearview.

CHAPTER SEVEN

"It'll be dark in an hour," Peter Blackwell wheezed as he leaned against a boulder. His hair was matted with sweat that trickled down his face and collected in the hollow of his throat. He bent over wearily to pick the cockleburrs that adhered to his bare legs. His feet burned inside the thick hiking boots.

"What's the matter?" yelled his companion fifty yards down the trail. "Can't you take it? Some outdoorsman you are." She was an attractive brunette in a halter top stretched tightly over a well-endowed bosom. Her hips were squeezed into a pair of cut-off jeans.

"Okay, okay," he said crossly, "enough of the Amazon treatment. I don't feel like taking on Woman's Lib right now."

Anne Morris and Peter Blackwell had been hiking through the mountains since early morning. Now, they were heading toward a campsite marked on the map given them by the Uwharrie State Park Ranger. There would be a cabin where they could spend the night before making the final trek back to Spirit Rock in the morning.

Anne put down her backpack and wiped the sweat from her forehead with a blue bandana. Peter lit up a joint and passed it to her.

"You'd better watch that around here,"she said. "The natives don't take kindly to our brand of cigarettes. But she took it from him and inhaled deeply.

She handed it back to him, then picked up her pack again. "Okay, my hero, the campsite should be up over the next rise."

Blackwell took another toke, then crushed out the roach on the ground. "Not that way, my love," he called out after Anne's retreating figure. "Let's take this path."

Anne looked in the direction that Peter was pointing, a narrow, overgrown footpath. It looked like it had not been used in years.

"But the forest ranger said that the campsite was this way," she said. "God knows what's up there. Why do you want to go that way?"

"Call it my 'spirit of adventure ,'" he replied, laughing. "I was up here a couple of weeks ago and found an old cabin. There's a great view of the valley from the front door. And it'll be more...private. No other campers."

"Well, if you're not afraid of the bears, neither am I," she sighed.

The shabby cabin was somewhat ominous in the rapidly approaching twilight. Glass was broken out of the two front windows and the door hung, swaying gently, on one hinge. Rotting roof timbers sagged and pine needles from untold seasons had collected in the depression.

"This is your idea of a romantic hide-away?" asked Anne, slowly sliding the backpack from her aching shoulders.

"Come on," he said, "a little fixing up and it'll be like home, sweet home. Let's go in. Unless you want to sleep out under the stars tonight."

They entered the shack and dumped their sleeping bags in the far corner. Anne swept the accumulated dirt out the door with a pine branch fashioned into a broom. Despite the heat, Peter built a small fire over which they warmed some beans and franks. Afterward, they lay in front of the fire, finishing a bottle of wine.

Peter drained the last of the wine from the bottle. "Say, you don't think the spirits of those dead Indians we've been digging up walk around these mountains at night, do you?" he said, grinning wickedly at Anne.

"Hey, shut up," she said, a shiver running down her back. She edged closer to him. "That's not funny. Not tonight."

Blackwell was enjoying her fright. "Yeah, I can just see 'em now. A cloud passes over the moon and the old Mojo rises from the mist, calling forth the Spirits of the Dead."

"Damn you!" she said, kicking out at him with her foot. He fell back, laughing.

They smoked a joint, passing it back and forth. Anne began to feel numb, a combination of the drug and alcohol. She looked over at Blackwell, who was staring into the fire. He had not said anything for some time, but sat hunched over the flames.

"Come on," Anne said. "I'd rather you tell me a ghost tale than sit there like a zombie. Tell me some more about the Indian spirits."

Blackwell slowly shook his head. "No. I shouldn't have said anything about them."

His silence irritated her; she much preferred the irreverent, sneering Peter to this brooding stranger. It had been his insolent self-assurance that had attracted her to him several weeks ago, when she had become bored with the dig and wondered if she had not made a mistake in coming to Clearview. The thought of a weekend tryst alone on the mountain had excited her, but now Peter was acting like a stranger, and it angered her.

"You're really stoned," she said, poking him in the ribs.

He gazed at her with a wild, angry stare. Then, as quickly as it had come, his anger faded, and he stood and moved toward the door.

Anne frowned as she watched him staring out into the darkness without speaking. She could not understand why he was acting so strangely; he couldn't be *that* stoned.

"Hey," she called out. "What about that 'wild weekend' you promised me? Come on over here."

Blackwell seemed not to have heard her. He turned to look at the dying fire. "It's out," he said slowly. "I'd better get more wood."

"What? Now?" Anne asked. "It's too late. Let's go to bed." She tried to entice him back to the sleeping bags with her most seductive voice, but when he did not respond, she threw up her hands. "Okay, go out if you have to," she said, "but see if you can't come back in a better mood, will ya?"

Peter left without closing the door. Anne paused to watch him walk slowly across the clearing before disappearing into the woods. Something was wrong, but she could not put it into words. She glanced around at the darkening gloom, a shudder running down her spine, and quickly shut the door.

Once away from the cabin, Peter began picking up small pieces of wood, but soon threw them down with disinterest. He circled behind the shack, peering up the trail that led farther up the mountain. The trees were so thick that, despite the full moon, he could only see a few yards up the twisted path.

Blackwell negotiated the path with slow, measured steps. He stumbled over hidden roots, but took no notice, keeping a fixed gaze above him.

Once or twice, Blackwell stopped and looked about him in sudden confusion. What was he doing in these God-forsaken woods at this time of night? he thought, wildly. He turned once to go back to the cabin, but his legs seemed not to obey his commands. Instead, he continued up the path at an almost leaden pace, oblivious to the branches that scratched his face.

In the distance, he saw a flickering light and stopped, puzzled. What could it be? A campfire? The thought of fire made him giddy and fearful.

Yet he was compelled by a powerful urge to approach it. As he came closer, he saw a thin figure hunched over the fire. Somewhere in the back of his mind, he sensed a familiarity about the place.

At the sound of his footsteps, the figure slowly rose and stared at him. It was a deeply-lined, drawn face, almost grey in appearance. Under the penetraing gaze, Blackwell stood, fearful and silent, waiting.

"You have brought the girl, as I commanded?" it asked.

"Yes," Blackwell said.

"Yes," Blackwell said.

"Good. We must go."

The tall figure moved past him, disappearing into the gloom down the trail without looking back. Blackwell silently followed him.

CHAPTER EIGHT

David knocked on the door of Walters' garage apartment. At first he knocked softly, then with more force, until the door opened and he was staring into the very pretty—and very angry—face of Diana Walters.

"Yes?"she said, with a look that could fry an egg. "What is it?" David had interrupted her in the midst of a shower; her hair was wet, and hung to one side of a hurriedly-fastened robe. "What do you want? I was in the middle of ..."

"Yes, I see that," David came back. Damn her arrogant attitude. "I'm bothering you, I know, but, frankly, I don't care very much right now. You were supposed to fill me in on the history of the Uwharrie tribe, but you always seem to be too busy doing something else. I have to know more than I do now in order to properly conduct my interviews. So..."

"So you want me to give you a history lesson, now, dripping wet, at ten o' clock at night?"

"Yes, that's right."

"Well, at least you put it a little more gentilely than the other afternoon," Diana said, her voice retaining a hard, but somewhat diminished edge to it. "I didn't come home to be insulted by crude remarks of hometown 'good ol' boys.'"

"I'm sorry about that," said David. "But you deserved it."

He pushed his way past her into the room, which was surprisingly feminine, with a floral print on the wall. Not a scholar's hideaway at all, he thought. "You can dry off if you like," he added, staring into the consternation and surprise on her face. He looked about the room nonchalantly.

The gamble worked. Diana stood for a moment with her hands on her hips, in a defiant pose, but then said, "All right, all right, wait just a minute," and went back into the bathroom.

She returned in a few minutes, rubbing the excess moisture from her hair with a fluffy white towel. She had not bothered to fasten any more buttons on her gown, and as she sat in the chair opposite him, a length of thigh was carelessly exposed. She didn't seem to mind, so David tried not to appear flustered by the sight. Perhaps because of the moisture from her bath, the room was fragrant, and pleasantly feminine. It had been some time since he had been in a room alone with a beautiful woman. Too long. But he was here for a 'history lesson,' as she had put it.

"What do you want to know about the Uwharries?" she said, throwing her towel on the sofa and shaking her hair. "I thought you were supposed to be the local history expert. Aren't you supposed to tell me things?"

"Look, Diana, you obviously have the idea that I'm some kind of enemy of yours. The truth is, my sole interest in the dig is to provide your father with the best background material I can get for him. I think I owe him that much, and you're hampering that job. I started on short notice, and I don't know a damn thing about the Uwharries. Your father wanted someone with a general history background to conduct research. I have no formal training in oral history. How am I supposed to separate truth from legend unless I know certain basic facts? You understand what I'm saying, don't you?"

Diana suddenly began to laugh. But it was a genuine laugh, with no bitterness. David was startled by her levity. "Okay, David, I guess you don't mean me any harm."

"Of course not."

"You'll have to forgive me for making you feel like a pariah the last few days. My father said you were thinking of writing a book. There was another writer, about a year ago,after I completed my research on the natives in the New Herbrides Islands. He hung around the campus, pumped me for bits of information, and then wrote several articles for professional journals without acknowledging me as his source. Since then, I've been leery of ambitious authors."

"I'm not that ambitious. I'd like to be an author, but for now I'll make do with the public library. So, do we understand each other?"

"I think so, David. I'm sure we can work together on friendly terms. After all, we're not strangers."

"I suppose we're not," David replied. "Although we didn't exactly travel in the same social circles. But let's focus on the present for the time being."

"Fine," she said, smiling. "Now, what do you want to know about the Uwharries?"

"Everything."

"All right. About 1200 A.D., permanent Native American settlements appeared in this area. These were not wandering hunters, but small tribes that settled in one place, and had at least a rudimentary social system centered on the village concept. They built permanent shelters, cleared land for the cultivation of grains, and otherwise took on the characteristics that we could call civilization. These tribes were the first inhabitants of this region. There were two main groups, the Saura and the Keyauwee.

"In 1540, the Spanish explorer Hernando de Soto encountered the Saura main camp and spent a few days as their guest. We know little of that meeting except that it took place. The coming of the white man was a bad omen for the tribes of this region. The Saura had vanished from their ancestral villages by the early 1700s, probably from a combination of white settler encroachment and a defensive war they were fighting with some Seneca raiders, northern war-like tribes of the Iroquois Nation.

"Now we get to the interesting part. I told you about the Saura's neighbors, the Keyauwee. That name has been corrupted to Uwharrie over the years. They are the tribe you want to know about; the village we are excavating might have belonged to them. They no longer exist, of course; they are extinct. In 1801, a surveyor named John Randolph recorded most of what we know about the Uwharrie tribe. That and a few obscure reports by missionaries. At that time, they numbered about five hundred souls. Probably fifty years earlier, it had been many thousands. Their main village was somewhere in this valley. All in all, it was a pretty advanced tribal culture. A well-organized social system."

"What finally happened to them?"

"In 1840 the government decided certain tribes should be relocated on reservations in the West. So they rounded up most of those tribes of Sioux lineage, and marched them on the 'Trail of Tears' to Arkansas, and then further into Indian Territory; Oklahoma, Arizona, New Mexico, and even Mexico. Now, some of the Uwharrie tribe may have fled this forced migration and intermingled with the Catawba to the South, and with the Cherokee to the West, and so stayed in the general area. Some undoubtedly intermarried with the white population and with freed slaves, but by this time their culture and way of life had been destroyed; their land had been stolen, swindled, or treatied away from them.

"So you could say the Uwharrie disappeared by being absorbed into the surrounding cultures. But my father believes there was one group that remained somehow evading the fate of the others, staying full-blooded Uwharrie, until the Civil War or a few years later, when some natural or man-made disaster wiped them completely out. And he thinks the remains of that full-blooded group, the last of the Uwharrie, may be in that patch of dirt we're digging into right now. And if he's right, there's no telling what we'll find there."

"If I know your father, he's really looking for something more interesting and important than just another obscure village and another basketful of artifacts."

Diana seemed to be startled by that remark. "You're very straightforward, David. Very different from the boy I knew ten years ago."

Something inside him bridled at her bringing up the past,

although it had been on his mind for days. "I didn't think you really remembered we were in the same class."

"I remember." Then, quickly, "I suppose we've all changed since then. It's been a long time. Anyway, yes, my father is looking for European artifacts in the ruins."

"Is he really serious about that Lost Colony business? I've heard that old wives' tale all my life. Some people say the colonists wound up with the Catawbas. Others say it was the Lumbees or even the Seminoles in Georgia or north Florida. The legend was supposed to have been started by the fact that some early traders noticed a few piedmont Indians sported mustaches and pointed Van Dyke beards in the English style."

"Yes, that's right. Somehow I think you know more about the local Indian history than you let on, David. But besides the facial hair, my father recently unearthed another trader's manuscript that suggested a chief's wife and daughter, circa 1745, were 'of a pale complexion, almost as a lady of the Continent.'"

"They could have been a form of albino, a very common phenomenon among all cultures."

"Yes, they could have been that, certainly. But then, if we knew all the answers, there wouldn't be any reason to go digging up the countryside, would there?"

David laughed. "No, I suppose not. Touche´."

Hale left shortly afterward, feeling the same mixture of attraction and envy he had experienced with Diana a decade earlier. He certainly had to give he credit, though, for scholarship. Her knowledge of local history and anthropology was impressive; more impressive because it was only a sideline with her, learned as a necessary tool to assist her father. David had followed her true professional projects in journals the library received, astute, prestigious quarterlies of anthropology and primitive culture. As many articles indicated, her main expetise lay in something very far afield from Southeastern Indian artifacts; she was a renowned expert in primitive religion and ritual. She had studied and written about topics as diverse as the pantheistic beliefs of pygmy forest dwellers in tropical Africa to the cargo cults of Micronesia. It was certainly hard to believe she had accomplished so much in so short a time—and still had those girlish good looks and heart-stopping figure...

David caught himself before he started to compare his own modest accomplishments against Diana's. He had beaten himself with that stick too many times in the past. Instead, he turned to the question of the Lost Colony, and Professor Walters' belief that relics of their disappearance would somehow turn up in the dig. It seemed a little too much for David to hope for. Walters was not the phenom his daughter was turning into. Although an excellent teacher, he had failed to set the scientific community on fire with previous research projects, and he had had over thirty years to do that, if he were going to. David hoped this theory about the Lost Colony would not wind up as a short article in one of the smaller journals—more evidence that the mystery of the Lost Colony was *not* solved.

Why then, he asked himself, was he willing to work through the next few months ferreting out old legends and handed-down stories, running around in the heat and humidity? There might be a book in it, but it certainly would not wind up on the best seller lists; the best he or Walters could expect was a university press or regional publisher to consider such a manuscript. If they even wrote it. So, why?

He was certain of one answer to this question as he returned home. Boredom, just plain boredom. The dig was at least some excitement. It was better than stamping books and collecting overdue fines most of the day.

Then he thought, who am I trying to fool? Diana still made his heart pound faster. On the dig he was able to be around her. To look at her, talk with her, get to know her better. Maybe even date her...make love to her.

Fool, he thought, *it'll never happen.*

Peter, she thought. He was still gone. What could have happened to him? The latch was still firmly secure on the door, but if he had come back he would have opened the door. No, this was no joke; he was hurt out there.

Unsure what to do, Anne waited a few more minutes, then hurriedly wrapped up her sleeping bag and prepared to go back down the trail, to find the forest ranger or summon some kind of help as quickly as possible.

She found Peter just outside the cabin, sitting beneath a tree. His back was against the trunk, and he seemed to be meditating. He was not injured in any way that she could see.

"Pete?" she called, and he raised his head. "What happened to you? How long have you been out here? I was so worried. Are you okay?"

He didn't answer immediately, gazing at her as if he had never seen her before. But then he seemed to snap out of his reverie. He smiled, and said: "Sure, I'm all right. I got lost but I found my way back a couple of hours ago. I've just been sitting out here...thinking."

"Why didn't you wake me up? I was having the most awful dream, a nightmare. You were in danger, lying in some dark place, a cavern. There was fire and heat all around..."

Her nose prickled as she bent closer to him. There was a smell of smoke, like something had been burned. A dead campfire smell of ashes and charred wood. Her imagination? The dream had seemed so real. "Are you sure you're okay?" she asked again.

He smiled at her then, and the old cockiness and arrogance danced in his eyes. "Sure," he said. "I was just lost, is all. I didn't know where I was for a while, but I do now. I know exactly where I am now."

Anne started to say something else, but her attention was diverted to the darkness just beyond the first line of trees. She strained to make out a shadowy form that was coming toward her, more gliding than walking.

"Who is that, Peter?" she said, alarmed. "Did you bring someone back with you?"

"No," Blackwell replied. "I brought *you* to meet someone."

She looked up again at the approaching form and tried to speak, but her dry throat would make no sound.

CHAPTER NINE

Sparrow-in-Snow was across from him again, and John Singer realized they were squatting on their haunches in the middle of the clearing that he could sometimes see glowing in the moonlight from the window of his cabin. He had no memory of coming here. He had lain down to sleep in his bed and woke in the clearing. Or perhaps it was not sleep at all, but something else altogether. He was becoming inured to these shifts in time and place, and his anxiety was not as great. It was being replaced by curiosity and a sense of adventure, as if he were setting out on a journey to a place he had never seen, or even imagined.

"I know this ground," he said to the shaman.

"What do you know of it?"

"Some nights it seems to glow in the dark. The town people avoid coming near it, especially at night."

"They are wise to do so."

"One of them told me at the roadhouse that it was the site of an old fort which burned down, and that was why the clearing is perfectly round, and nothing will grow here except short grass. Those who are superstitious say it is an old cemetery, and that the glow is a ghost with a lantern. And I think the scientists say it was a natural salt deposit, and the ground is sterile, and that the glow is from gas from a nearby bog."

"And do you think that is the truth?"

"Now that I am here I know that is not the truth; none of that is the truth."

"What is this place then, really?"

"A holy place. A sacred place."

"Close your eyes and smell the air. What do you smell?"

Singer did as he was told. "The smell is familiar, although I don't remember where I have encountered it before."

"It is the smell of death."

"Yes. I remember now."

"There are many smells of death in the woods, many small deaths. Birds and rabbits and squirrels die and are eaten by the air and the earth. Is this that smell, of animals rotting?"

"No. It is much more powerful. It covers the ground like a fog. The ground is seeped with it and the trees sink their roots around it. It is old and buried, black like dried blood."

"What else do you feel here?"

"I feel heat. Something which burned. Later, the fire hid in the ground. It is down there now, burning. I feel screams and death and burning. Hate and fear and revenge, all together.

"Yes. Good, John Singer."

"Somehow all of that is in me, too. I had the same feeling once when I was beside a river, and thought to jump in and sink. But I did not jump in and sink."

"Why?" asked the shaman.

"I don't know. But my great-grandfather told me I would drown in fire," said John Singer, with no emotion. "I don't know what he meant by that. It was very strange, but he would not explain the meaning to me."

Sometimes he thought he saw, in the shaman's face, the eyes and the sadness of his great-grandfather. His name had not been Singer, but Singing Wolf. The old man did not talk very much by the time John was born; he was close to eighty years old already, no one knew for sure, and he had died when John was five. Singer remembered him as a small, brittle figure, dry and fragile as the summer dust, and yet there had been an intensity to him even at that advanced age, as if the fire that had dried him out still burned deep in the old man without totally consuming him. As a boy, Singer had been alternately drawn to and repulsed by him. His silence and piercing gaze, like that of a starving hawk, had fascinated and frightened him.

There was one day, shortly before the old man died, that he had awakened John in his bed; or perhaps John had dreamed of being awakened in the middle of the night by Singing Wolf. The details were no longer clear in his mind. But the words the old man spoke to him were still fresh, seared into his memory, or his imagination, whichever was which. The elder had shaken him, then closed his gnarled hand about the boy's mouth so he would not wake the rest of the family sleeping only a few feet away. He had taken the boy's hand and silently led him outside.

At the time, they were living on the outskirts of Asheville, many miles to the west. It was early fall and the boy shivered in the night chill. His great-grandfather led him to the edge of the bare dirt yard, to a spot where, if he looked through the growth of trees, he could see mountains. It was a full moon and he could see the mountains in the middle distance. They stood out in the white light like huge slumbering animals, almost as if they were alive—and perhaps they were, so much did the familiar shapes inspire young John with awe that night. Singing Wolf stretched forth his arms to the sky and to the peaks in the distance, and began to chant. It was a slow, mournful chant in a language John had never heard, a grey dirge of a chant, and it raised the hairs on the nape of his neck. Another chill ran through him that was not caused by the wind, and he stood, mesmerized by his great-grandfather singing to the emptiness beyond the trees. The chant might have gone on for an hour or only a minute, time was so distorted that night. But when he stopped, and lowered his arms, a wolf howled from somewhere on the peak, the howl rising on the wind.

Then Singing Wolf said: "You are the last and the first of the tribe. Through you the fire will burn in a circle again, and the kings will rise and dance once more . You will return one day to the home of your ancestors, a place of fire and water. And you will drown in fire. Always it has been planned this way, though you were not yet born. Those things that are past will be your future, as morning follows night. As the river follows its banks. Now let what I say here pass from you, so that you may hear it again when your time is come."

The old man turned and they went back to the house. The wolf howled again on the mountain, and John Singer went back to sleep.

A few days later, Singing Wolf died and was buried in a pauper's grave by the county. And was quickly forgotten by John, at least for many years.

The Singer household deteriorated after his great-grandfather died. There was John, his mother and father, an uncle and an aunt, and his mother's mother, all in a small frame house. The neighborhood was mostly of white families and blacks, all of them poor.

For a time, as John grew and entered grade school, his father and uncle worked for a tree service. That was about the only decent paying job an Indian could get in the white world. It was hard work, and dangerous, topping and trimming trees. They used chainsaws, twenty, thirty or forty feet off the ground, and some of their work was done around power lines and transformers. One afternoon John's father cut off most of his left hand with the saw, and couldn't work anymore. He was too proud to do the work his wife and aunt did sometimes, copying Cherokee handicrafts such as beadwork, and Plains Indians headdresses, and selling them to a store in Asheville as souvenirs for tourists. It was not man's work. He began to drink heavily, and within a year had degenerated into a violent alcoholic. He attacked his wife while on a drunken binge, and was sent to a mental institution for a long time. When he was released, he did not return to the family, and they learned later he was killed in a barroom brawl.

Soon after that, John's uncle fell from a tree when his old harness snapped, and broke his back. He seemed to be recovering, but died of a sudden internal hemorrhage. That left only the three women. John Singer quit school, pulled a hitch in the army, then went to work for a tree service, eventually moving from one meaningless job to another. That had been twenty years ago, and now he was the only member of his family left.

"I want to know why I am here," John Singer asked the shaman.

"You know that already. The first night I appeared to you, it was as if you were waiting for me. Were you not waiting for me?"

"I was waiting...for something. I did not know what it would be."

"You were waiting for your life to begin. Not the dream in which you grew to be a white man's Indian, but your real life, your true life."

"I had a life."

"Did you?"

"I had a job putting roofs on houses. Sometimes I had another job where I climbed trees and cut off the limbs with a power saw."

"Yes. That was in the land of the Cherokee, where you were a child."

"Asheville. I lived there, in a rooming house. Sometimes I lived with a woman. Sometimes I was lonely. My family was all dead. Often I would drink whiskey for three or four days, and would have to find a new job. I worked hard. I liked to work in the trees. Especially the high trees."

"Why did you leave that place?"

"One day I was working in the trees near a river. The sun was hot, and when it was time to eat I went down by the river. I felt very empty. I realized I had felt empty for a long time, maybe all my life. I remember thinking it would be all the same to me if I jumped into the river and drowned. The sun and the trees and the water were very beautiful, but sad also, and I started to cry. I did not want the other men to see me crying, so I hid in some bushes and stayed there until it was dark. The next day I left everything I owned and got in my truck and started to drive. When I came to this town, I felt I should stop. Since then I have known there was a secret here that I must find out."

"You will know all things soon."

"Tell me...tell me why I did not jump in the river that day, and drown?"

"It was the wrong river."

CHAPTER TEN

Miss Olivia Priddy was one of the few unmarried women in Clearview, and typified the old-style spinster. At least that was what David was thinking as she invited him into her ancient, rambling two-story house where she lived alone, almost a recluse, with a number of cats that ran about untended in the parlor. David tried not to wrinkle up his nose at the scathing odor of old excrement, urine-soaked rugs and fur that permeated the room.

Walters had suggested he interview Miss Priddy. He also suggested that no time be wasted in making the interview, as the old woman was at least ninety, and frail.

"May I offer you some tea, young man?" she asked, as soon as David was seated in the parlor. Her manners were in stark contrast to her tattered appearance; but her appearance didn't bother David. He had always liked eccentrics; they were too rare in Clearview.

But he declined the offer of tea; there was no telling in what state the kitchen hygiene would be here, and any cup might have been used to feed a sick cat.

"No, thank you, ma'am," he said. "As I said over the telephone, the library is trying to update its collection of information concerning the Native American tribes which once inhabited this area. I was told that you might have some memories of these people."

"You mean, I'm so ancient I was around at the turn of the century when Indians still lived around here?" She was smiling a bit now.

"I didn't mean to infer that you were..."

"Oh pooh! I *am* old, and I don't mind admitting it. Far too old and have seen too much. But you are concerned with Indians. Yes, I can recall..." The old lady reflected for a moment, as if she were searching inside her mind for those images of long ago. "Yes," she said again, "I remember the way it was then. I guess it was about '04 or '05, somewhere along in there, because there weren't any automobiles along the road. Never had seen or heard those awful things yet. We got where we had to by wagon, or on Sundays we'd hitch up the surry. I must have been about twelve years old then, and I was quite a tomboy, you know. Back then, it was thought badly of to be a tomboy, and to climb trees and ride the mules and such as that. Mama would make my father give me a whipping sometimes because I'd rip my dress, or scuff my go-to-meeting shoes. Lord, I'd almost forgotten about all of that, it was so long ago..."

"Yes, ma'am."

"Well, Clearview was different then. The closest thing to real law was the county agent, a man called Johnson, who had taken over the job from my grandfather about the turn of the century. But that's how I got to know about the Catawbas, you see, because my grandfather still had an interest in their welfare. And sometimes he'd point out things to me I wouldn't have realized on my own. He was an unusual man, my grandfather, especially for that day and age. He was sympathetic to the Indians, you see, and always had been. That was rare even for an agent, and when he was a very young man, that attitude had got him in all kinds of trouble with the other folks hereabouts.

"Oh, some of the church women tried to help the Indians from time to time; they'd bring my grandfather food and old clothes, and he'd go out and give those goods to the few poor souls that were left out at the edge of town. They were really poor devils, maybe thirty or forty of them, no more than that, sprawled out, on a few acres still left to them. A patch of bog land, and some trees and rocks, and a little stream that ran through it. There was a couple of tarpaper shacks where ten or twelve of them would squat together when the weather got cold, but the rest of them lived out in the open, just like tramps. And they were poor, as poor as you'd ever imagine on God's earth. Grandfather would tell me the government allotment then was less than thirty dollars a year per Indian; and they were supposed to feed and clothe themselves, and buy seed to grow their own crops on that! Why, it was a scandal, and grandfather didn't mind telling folks, too.

"You'd see five or six of them coming into town early in the morning, like a line of prisoners shuffling along the dirt road that led from their land into town. That was a ten-mile walk, and they'd do it in the rain or snow, or the boiling heat, any time they had something to sell. Not that they ever had anything that was worth selling—maybe an unusual stone from the river bottom that a man could make a watch fob from, or a rabbit skin, trifles such as that. And they'd hang around the stores, wouldn't move until someone took pity and gave them a nickel or a dime for it. Then they'd walk back the ten miles to where they stayed. Next day another group would be around the store, with another trinket.

"Does this have something to do with the excavation Professor Walters is making out at the old clearing?" Miss Priddy asked suddenly.

"Why, yes, it does. I'm working with him as an oral historian. But, of course, all information I gather will be duly recorded in the library files as part of the local history collection."

"Well," the old woman said, leaning close in a conspiratorial tone, "if you want to know what I think, there's more secrets in that clearing than you could shake a stick at. I mean, if you want to know about what happened to the Uwharrie..."

David's jaw went slack. "You mean," he said slowly, "you have some evidence it was a *Uwharrie* camp?

"Why, yes. My grandfather told me. Of course it was a Uwharrie camp. Did you think it was Catawba?" She laughed dryly.

"Well, the consensus is that the mound and any surrounding areas would have to be Catawba," said David.

"Is that what the consensus says? Well, they're wrong. By 1870 or so there weren't anything but Catawba and a few Lumbees—those were the Indians I saw trekking into town as a girl. But when my grandfather was very young, when he was first hired as a county agent, that clearing was a Uwharrie camp. And if you want to know why your files, and whatever legends there are have it different, I can..."

Miss Priddy paused, but David could see she was gathering the emotion to continue, so he kept silent, afraid any interruption would silence her for good. But there were so many questions racing in his mind. Here was the very evidence that Walters was seeking!

Then the old woman's expression changed; her jaw trembled for a moment. David thought he saw tears behind her bifocals.

"I'm very tired, suddenly," she said. "Too many memories. The excitement...perhaps another time, young man, when I am rested."

David was terribly disappointed, but struggled to hide his feelings. He flicked off the tape recorder. "Perhaps tomorrow?" he asked hopefully.

"I...no, not tomorrow. I will contact you. At the library."

"But, Miss Priddy..."

He saw it was no use. Something, a memory, a secret perhaps, was holding her back.

"Yes, ma'am, I understand," he said, and left, wondering if the interview would ever be completed.

David sat at his office desk, running his hand over the tape recorder. On the drive back to the library, he had speculated on just how eccentric Miss Priddy might be. She obviously idolized her grandfather; had she exaggerated the clearing's importance? Was it even Uwharrie?

He was about to replay the tape when he was interrupted by the telephone. At first, he ignored it, expecting Gertrude to answer.

When it rang for the fifth time, he impatiently picked up the receiver. Why was his assistant always absent when he needed her?

"David?" It was Arthur Walters.

"Yes, Dr. Walters."

"I'm calling from my house, about to leave to go to the site. I'd like to pick you up on the way. We've stumbled on another implement that could be a European knife. I'm beginning to get excited at what we might be uncovering here. I'd like as many observers as possible, if you could come."

"Yes, of course."

"I'll be there in five minutes." Walters hung up.

David pushed the tape aside; it would have to wait.

CHAPTER ELEVEN

Arthur Walters' enthusiasm was unfounded, or perhaps exaggerated, at least according to Bill Schlosser, field manager of the dig. When David and Walters had arrived at the site, Walters had gone directly to the trench, spoken briefly with Schlosser, then begun examining several recently-unearthed implements.

David stayed by the large metal cooler that furnished drinking water at the site. After talking to Walters, Schlosser wandered over to the cooler and took a long drink. He was tall and had a full beard. As David watched him pour a cup of the cool water over his head, he sensed from his muscular frame and deeply-tanned skin that this was a man at home in the outdoors, confident of both his physical and intellectual prowess.

"What's the big find?" asked David.

"We've discovered a long knife which Arthur thinks is of European design."

"You sound skeptical."

"Well, I think Arthur's preoccupation with the Lost Colony is clouding his judgment. I think that the knife is of aboriginal origin, possibly something used in their religious practices. Actually, I'm more interested in the skeleton that we found yesterday. I think that is much more important."

"Why?"

"The head was crushed, as if it had received a blow from a blunt instrument. The curious thing is that we found another one in the north quadrant with the same evidence of trauma."

"What does that mean?"

"I had originally expected to find a typical burial ground. But from the random placement and condition of the remains, it's beginning to look like this may have been the site of some sort of battle or violent confrontation."

"But there's no written evidence of anything like that, is there?" asked David. "I certainly haven't heard of anything like that."

"No," replied Schlosser, "but we'll just have to see what the other remains reveal. Well, I'd better get back over to Arthur. See you later." He ambled toward several members of the dig who were clustered around Walters; the professor was still bent over the knife.

David looked around, unsuccessfully hoping to see Diana. As always, he was amazed at the complexity involved in even a small dig such as this one. It was not, as he had assumed, simply a matter of a helter-skelter unearthing of the area with a pick and shovel. There were picks and shovels, of course, but the tools more often consisted of plumb bobs, bulb syringes for air dusting, whisk brooms and magnifying glasses, down to tweezers and tooth-brushes.

There was one student who did nothing but fill out information forms for even the smallest artifact, another who took angles and measurements in constructing a topographical map of the area. The sketching of every artifact, the labeling of what was unearthed, and the voluminous record-keeping revealed what a tedious operation archaeological excavation was. Diana had once told him that a neolithic campsite in Hong Kong had been excavated entirely with whisk brooms and small trowels.

David wiped the perspiration that had collected on his forehead from the sticky heat. As he wiped, he heard a high-pitched scream coming from the southern-most quadrant, that under Roger Dawes, a graduate student. Everyone was looking in that direction. David saw Dawes clutch his chest, then collapse on the ground.

He began running with the others to where Dawes had fallen; a group had already formed around the prone figure. His eyes were vacant and glazed; his face was rapidly turning blue. Schlosser bent over him and began applying CPR.

"What happened?" asked David, his eyes searching the perplexed faces that surrounded him.

"I don't know," said Anne Morris. "One minute we were laughing and joking, the next he was staring at us with a funny look on his face. Then he grabbed his chest. His faced looked as if he were in great pain. By the time Bill got over here, he wasn't breathing."

Schlosser glared up at the impotent crowd. "Goddammit! Somebody go get a doctor! He's dying." Then he turned back to resume his efforts. For long agonizing moments, nothing happened; then some faint, pale color came back to Dawes' features. But it was a fragile flicker of life.

"Anne," snapped Walters, "the closest telephone is in the supply tent. Go over there as fast as you can and call the Rescue Squad." He looked over at one of the male students. "Bob, you go with her. Hurry."

The two students ran down the hill, jumped into the jeep and sped away down the road back toward town.

"Heart attack?" exclaimed Walters at Piedmont General Hospital, half an hour later. "That's impossible. He was only twenty-six!"

"It happens," replied the intern. "I'll have a nurse go back and collect his valuables. In the meantime, why don't you folks make yourselves comfortable?"

Walters and David looked at each other helplessly. Because there was nothing more they could do, they sat down with Diana in the brown vinyl seats that lined the lobby wall.

"That's absurd," Walters snapped. "Dawes was healthy as a bull. Every morning before he came to the dig he'd jog five miles.

It must have been something else, not his heart. Yes, it must have been something else," he added, convinced.

"Calm down, father," soothed Diana.

They sat in a tight group, hardly speaking, still in a daze. After about thirty minutes, a nurse strode toward them, with a few items—watch, wallet, ring—in a plastic bag. "Someone will have to sign for these," she said. Then: "I'm sorry, we all thought he stood a good chance. His vital signs all looked good. His pulse had stabilized and we were preparing him to go into intensive care. Then his heartbeat became irregular again and we couldn't reverse it."

Walters inspected the articles sadly. "I don't know what I'll tell his father. He's on the English faculty at the university, you know. A nice man..."

"You musn't blame yourself," Diana said. "Poor Roger could have died in his sleep at the motel. It was just one of those horrible things that happen sometimes."

"Yes," David added, "an accident. Unavoidable."

But he was thinking it was a damned odd accident, just the same. Dawes had been as stong as a horse and was an avid vitamin and health food freak. He had asked David where the nearest health food store was to Clearview and had been very disappointed David had no idea.

Yes, David thought, damned odd, all right. Especially to have made it alive to the hospital and then died.

Then Arthur Walters signed for the valuables, and they left the hospital.

Several days later, David was in the tent at the dig talking to Walters. Activity had not resumed because several of the members had wanted to drive to Raleigh to attend the funeral. Walters, who had just gotten back from the service, had thought the layoff a way of letting them come to terms with the shock rather than rushing back into work. He, however, needed to keep busy, if only with clerical work.

He was just separating some of the smaller artifacts with David and plotting out where the team should concentrate their main activities, when he looked across the clearing with a puzzled expression.

"Who's that?" he asked.

David turned and saw a tall, muscular Indian striding purposefully toward them. His hair was jet black and his features were sharp, with prominent cheekbones. He was quite handsome, but he had a forbidding expression on his face, almost a scowl.

"I think his name is Singleton, something like that," replied David. "Hasn't been in town long."

"Are you Walters?" the man asked, when he had reached the tent.

"Yes. What can I do for you?"

"My name is John Wolfe Singer. I understand you need people to work at this excavation."

"That's true."

"I want to apply for the job."

"What experience have you had in archaeological field work?" asked Walters.

"None. I will work hard, and I learn things quickly."

"Well, it's not a prerequisite," admitted Walters, "but it would facilitate our work if we didn't have to train you."

"I understand you are short-handed now."

Walters seemed somewhat startled at the callousness of Singer's remarks. "That's correct. We had a misfortune here. One of our people died suddenly."

Singer's expression did not change. "I will take his place, then," he said.

"All right," Walters finally answered. "You can start at eight o'clock tomorrow morning. You can work with..." he thought a moment, "...Peter Blackwell. He'll be in charge of Dawes' quadrant now. Report to Peter, he'll get you started."

"I will be here," Singer said. With that he turned to David; it was the first time he had looked at him during the entire conversation. He stared at him for only a second, but it made David feel distinctly uncomfortable. It seemed to him that hatred emanated from this strange, silent man. But that was ridiculous; he had never met him before.

Singer abruptly turned on his heel and strode off, back across the clearing. There was something about the man that made David uneasy and he was not sure it was wise to be too hasty in hiring him. "I didn't think Native Americans would take this kind of a job. Don't they consider it a desecration?"

"Yes, it's unusual," said Walters. "But fortunate. Without Dawes, we will be shorthanded, and I can't be overly sensitive where I get help."

"Yes," agreed David, "but how did he know about the opening so quickly?"

"I guess gossip moves pretty quickly in town," said Walters. "Bad news travels fast."

David nodded. "I hope he works out, then."

"Well, beggers can't be choosers," said Walters, and turned back to the artifacts on the table before him.

CHAPTER TWELVE

David returned to his apartment, exhausted by a day of trifles at the library.

He felt the first surges of a headache come and go. To unwind a bit, he took a cool shower and drank a beer, then sat down to watch the evening news.

He was still irritated that the mixups at work had kept him from the dig all day. He had taken to spending the early afternoons there, sometimes talking to Dr. Walters about the progress, or rather lack of it; the project had not made much headway. Two more skeletons had been found in the last week, of what seemed to be elderly males, both by the new man Singer. David found a certain fascination in watching the man work. He had a steady and fixed concentration, working the ground almost reverently. Even in the midday heat, he never took a water break as the others did, never complained. He remained aloof, refusing to socialize with the others, and tended to his work.

Thinking about the skeletons, David was reminded of Roger Dawes' heart attack once more, and this threw him into a dark mood. He was several years older than Dawes; David felt a chill at the thought he could fall over dead like that. He was bothered that it might happen to him here, in Clearview, while he remained a small-town librarian embroiled in card indexes and looking up trivia about carnations for the members of the Garden Club. That would certainly not be just. No, not just at all. He was overcome temporarily with the desire, the need, to find a way out of his predicament. After years of entropy, of sitting still like a book on the library shelf, his anxiety and impatience to get on with his life was asserting itself in a great agitated clump.

Diana must have had something to do with that, he thought. She had moved from mere toleration of him at the site, to a more equal and helpful attitude. She even smiled now and then. He had begun showing the transcriptions of his interviews to her before taking them to the professor. She put the stories he gathered into historical context, at other times advising him as to questions for follow-up interviews.

There was a knock on the door.

Mrs. Mitchell, his neighbor two doors down, peeked through the screen.

From instinct he placed the beer can out of sight; people expected schoolteachers and librarians to be teetotalers. He rose to see what the woman wanted.

"A letter for you, dear," she said, with a maternal smile. "The mailman left it by mistake." She handed him the light blue envelope. It smelled of perfume.

"Thank you, Mrs. Mitchell," he said, wondering what the hell it could be. He smiled, waiting for the woman leave before opening it. She made some comment about the heat , and the lack of rain. He knew she was curious, wanted him to open the envelope while she was standing there. He never ceased to be amazed at the capacity of the townspeople for wanting to know everyone else's business. It bespoke a monumental boredom and frustration with their everyday lives. David wondered fleetingly if he would wind up as some older man walking his dachshund for kicks, or using binoculars to invade the windows of the teenage schoolgirl across the street.

The thought made him cringe inwardly, and he cut Mrs. Mitchell off with another thank you and closed the door.

The letter was from Linda, his ex-wife. The postmark was some blurred town in Washington state; he had no idea she had traveled so far from home.

Her last letter, six months ago, was a request for money, which she called 'alimony,' ignoring the divorce decree settlement of one lump sum payment, which had emptied his savings account. She was living in Richmond then, and wanted to take some 'enlightenment' seminars. He hadn't bothered to answer the last letter. He thought she was enlightened enough.

He read the cramped writing with a mixture of nostalgia and bitterness:

> *Dear David,*
>
> *I hope you are doing well and not too mad about the last letter I wrote (I'm trying to be more independent now) and that you're doing well. I would like to hear from you sometime. We may no longer be married, but we can still be friends. I just wanted to let you know I'm married again. His name is Bernard, but I call him Bo for short. He's a computer tech. We have a nice little place here in Seattle. It rains a lot, but the springs and summers are just gorgeous.*
>
> *David, when I left Clearview, I forgot that you still had my two Neil Diamond albums. Could you plese send them to me, and I could send you the money the next time I write?*
>
> *Well, I have to go now. Please write and let me know how you're doing.*
>
> *Linda*

David balled up the letter and threw it toward the waste can in the kitchen. Damn that bitch! he thought. She knew he wasn't going to send the damn record albums; she had just wanted him to know her life was going very smoothly without him. Gloating a bit. He thought with sadness how very much she must have disliked him at the end, to still try to hurt him after all this time. Well, he thought, good luck to Linda and her 'computer tech' in beautiful, rainy Washington. And may he bring the same unhappiness to her that she had brought to me.

The letter helped David feel better somehow. He was a completely free man now. The marriage was totally over, finished, done with. He need not dwell on it or carry it around inside himself any more, like a personal failure.

Linda was indeed gone forever.

Diana, on the other hand, was as close as the phone.

Why not ask her? he thought. He had nothing to lose.

He dialed the Walters number with a mixture of hope and foreboding. Diana answered in a clipped voice. But after he blurted out the invitation to dinner, she said yes in the same no-nonsense tone.

CHAPTER THIRTEEN

By the end of the meal, David had lost most of the reticence Diana usually brought out in him. The soft lighting and plush decor helped build a romantic mood, but he was still fighting the old school feelings he had developed when she was the unapproachable, bright beauty in a short skirt and tortoise-shell glasses.

But perhaps the restaurant's ambiance was working on her as well. They had talked on a variety of topics, moving from work to a more personal level. With the second bottle of wine, she had confessed that her academic life in the Ivy League was not as glamorous or fulfilling as he might think.

"I love the teaching," she said, "but more and more of my time has to be spent researching and writing papers for publication. There's always the feeling that with so many brilliant faculty members competing for tenure, I'm afraid I'll be passed over."

"Publish or perish," David recited the axiom.

"Yes, exactly. Publish or perish. Frankly, I've felt more like perishing the last year. I suppose it's the lack of a real social life that's made me stale."

David was surprised by that statement. "What?" he said, the

old resentment rising once again. "You mean the gorgeous and brilliant Diana Walters is actually lonely sometimes?" He was immediately sorry he had said it; the look in her eyes was not anger, but one of sadness and vulnerability.

"I'm sorry," he added quickly. "I had no right to say that, no right at all. I...I probably resent your success. You were the one who got out of this town, who went into the world and made good."

"You're still thinking we're back in high school, David, and I'm the arrogant kid with the professor father. The 'Ice Bitch.' " She laughed at his surprise. "Oh, I knew that's what they called me. So my father pulled some strings and I went to Brown, and you had to settle for the state university. But you're a perfectly good librarian and doing excellent work in oral history, from what dad tells me."

"Your father is very generous. By the way, I guess you heard that the knife they found the other day proved to be of Iroquois origin, rather than European." She nodded. "I'm sorry," David continued. "I know how much your father wants his theory to be correct." He sensed that Diana did not want to talk about the dig, and he was more than glad to turn the conversation back to her. "So what have you been doing with your life since earning your Ph.D?"

"Oh, I'm grinding myself into a permanent bookworm scholar, publishing papers in learned journals that nobody cares about, except the faculty review committee considering promotions. God, David, I don't know if *I* care any more. Maybe I'd be better off at a smaller college where I taught my classes and went home and lived like the rest of the world, instead of poring over some abstract text, trying to decide if I can stand another seminar."

She allowed David to pour another glass of wine. "Anyway, that's my sob story for tonight. What's the story of your life?"

"The story of my life right now is that I'm in the company of a very beautiful woman who just coincidentally happens to be more human than I ever thought she could be."

* * * *

The drive back to Diana's apartment relaxed David. There was no need for more conversation, no more secrets to be brought out, for the moment at least. Diana leaned back against the seat, a bit drowsy, and put her arm through his. The motion was endearing to David, and later he put his arm around her, drawing her close beside him.

The garage apartment was set back from the Walters residence and shielded by tall trees. The lights in the main house were off, everything was dark. David pulled the car into the driveway with an almost furtive slowness and silence. It was almost like bringing a high school girl home from a date and parking around the corner so that you could neck without being seen by her parents. He felt a bit foolish. There was no evidence that Diana considered him anything more than a pleasant dinner companion. She had been open and vulnerable tonight, but perhaps it was the pressure of the dig, the Dawes tragedy, and not his presence that had brought out this charming weakness in her. Her perfume was making an indelible impression in his memory. He felt awkward and clumsy, very much the insecure schoolboy. But she took all that away as she said: "You can come in, if you want to..."

An hour before dawn, David lay back against the pillow, feeling the afterglow of lovemaking that is both a physical and mental release; the pleasant draining of tension, doubt and anxiety.

The nude body he had dreamed about so often years ago was beside him in the bed, her head snuggled in the crook of his shoulder. She lay, half asleep, with one arm over his chest.

David reached over, took a cigarette from the pack on the bedside table and lit it. He saw Diana's eyes were open. She smiled sleepily.

"Want one?" he asked, indicating the cigarette.

She shook her head, but took the cigarette from his fingers. He removed his arm from around her shoulders as she sat up, pulling the sheet up around her breasts. Diana took a drag from the cigarette, then handed it back to him.

"Well, you've heard my life story earlier," she said. "What about yours?"

"Not much to tell, really," he said. "I met Linda while I was in grad school. She was a philosophy major. A mutual friend introduced us at a party in January; by May I had asked her to marry me."

"A real whirlwind courtship, huh?" You must have been very much in love."

"I thought so then. We got married just before I accepted the job at the library here in Clearview. So, we set up housekeeping and settled down to 'domestic bliss.'"

"You sound bitter."

"Not really. Everything went fine for the first year-and-a-half. But Linda became bored with small-town life; she kept talking about what a mistake she had made in not completing her degree. For the next six months, it was unending arguments from the moment I came home. At first, she wanted me to take a job in a large city; then, she started talking about going back to school. Finally, I came home one day and all I found was an empty house and a note saying she was going to pick up her own life again."

"Any children?"

"Oh, no," he laughed. "Linda was quite insistent about that. I guess she had a feeling all along that she would go back to her own life. She just wasn't cut out to be a 'hausfrau'—not mine, anyway."

"How long has it been since she left?"

"A year. I got a letter from her this afternoon; she's 'found herself' as the wife of a computer tech. At any rate, it's all over for good."

"Are you sorry?"

"No. it's just ironic that Linda left because she couldn't stand being buried alive here; now, I'm the one that wants to get out. But it wouldn't have mattered where we lived, we were just too different for it to have worked out."

He sat staring at the wall for a long time. She did not say anything ; he wondered if it had been wise to tell her about his past so soon. Sad tales make bad bed partners. But then she reached to take the cigarette from his hand and tamped it out in the tray without a word. Then she brushed his cheek tenderly with the back of her hand.

He kissed her, gently at first, then more passionately. He held her tightly, neither one speaking; there was no more thought of Linda. There was only this tender, gentle woman who undemandingly gave herself to him.

CHAPTER FOURTEEN

"Do you feel stronger now, Wolf-Singer? Do you feel the weakness dropping off like the useless dead skin of a snake when it is time for the new season?"

Singer did not answer Sparrow-in-Snow. But it was true, nevertheless. He did feel stronger. He did feel something being sloughed off, away from him, dropping like excess fat. He seemed to be less confused; the stars overhead were very clear, and brighter than he remembered them.

Sparrow-in-Snow was sitting, his ankles crossed, on a log. Singer felt as if he were waking into a dream. He shook his head. It was not a dream. There was a hardness to the reality he felt. He was more aware of his body than he had ever been. He could feel the blood flow in his veins, and his heart beating slowly, with a great steady pulse.

"Yes," he said. "I do feel it. It is true. Is this some more of your magic?"

"No, Wolf-Singer. It is magic, but some magic is true and not a trick. It is not magic of my making, but of yours. Do you see what you have done to cause it?"

Singer looked at his hands. They were red, slippery, warm. At his feet was the soft carcass of a large, brown-and-white rabbit.

"Did I kill this with my hands?" he asked. He had no recollection of doing such a thing.

"Yes, with your hands. I wanted you to feel the blood of an animal. It is the blood which has made you stronger. The life power and the speed of the rabbit is in you now. You ripped open the skin and reached inside and took it. It is one of the first lessons of the Uwharrie."

Singer raised his hands to his nose, smelled the coppery odor of the blood. It was slick, like oil. He let two fingers slide across his brow so that he could feel the still-warm substance on his face. It seemed to burn there with a greater warmth. The smell had opened his nose, made him slightly woozy for a second with the acid odor of it.

He tasted the blood with the tip of his tongue. Again it burned, but the taste was pleasant; he seemed to slough off another layer of what Sparrow-in-Snow had called his dead skin. But it was not really skin, he knew. It was that part of himself which did not belong. Had never really belonged.

"This is one of the first lessons of the Uwharrie?" he asked the shaman."

"Yes. There are many. Many bloods to taste and powers to take.

"May I ask, what is the last lesson?"

"The blood of a man," said the shaman. "Of your enemy."

CHAPTER FIFTEEN

Something was going on at the dig, from the concentration of personnel around a trench in the west quadrant. David joined the loose circle, found Diana, who smiled and held up a finger to her mouth. "Maybe something important for a change," she whispered to him. "John Singer found some animal bone-and-flint knives earlier this morning—they appear to be of sacrificial use—and a little later, he hit some human bones in the same spot. Bill is down there now, brushing away some of the debris."

David had learned that the excavation of a skeleton was a fragile and tedious affair. Bones were subject to leaching in the soil and, once their outlines were delicately brushed with a whisk or forced air, they were usually taken up whole by digging around and under the bones, then lifting the squared cut-out like a piece of sod.

He peered over the heads in front of him. They kept far enough back so that their foot pressure would not cause even a clod of dirt to bounce into the trench and upset the work going on. Only Bill Schlosser, the field team leader under Walters, was experienced enough to work with a full skeleton, and he was there now in the trench, bent over the find.

Bill used the brush and whisk a while longer, then stood up in the trench. He was sweating like a pig, but smiling. "Keep back," he said. "I"m coming out now. We have to get some photos before we try to bring up this baby."

He climbed carefully out of the hole and marched off to the equipment shed, returning with a camera and tripod.

"Photographs of the skeleton *in situ* are almost as important as the bones themselves," Diana explained to David. "It's the only way the exact configuration of the body can be absolutely studied, so we can tell if it's a burial or accidental death."

Schlosser was taking pictures from all sides and angles. He used the tripod to mount and steady the camera.

"It's funny," Diana continued, "that we haven't found a single burial in this first layer of strata. We're finding bones all over the place, or rather Mr. Singer is—that man has the best instincts I've ever seen for this kind of work—but they're scattered, thrown akimbo. It's not like any tribal ceremony I've ever heard of; it's as if there was some sort of violent confrontation and the bodies were interred where they fell."

"Could there have been a battle here?" asked David.

"None that we know of," replied Diana.

David could offer no plausible explanation. He always felt a distaste when he was around the silent John Singer, who was leaning against a shovel, taciturn, hardly watching the handling of the discovery.

"Yeah," David said, "well, maybe he can smell them. If you ask me, he looks more like a gravedigger than a field worker. Have you ever tried to look him in the eye? It's impossible. It's like he's looking right through you."

"I just think you're jealous," she teased. "He is awfully handsome, you know, in a silent, dark sort of way."

"Very silent and very dark. He gives me the creeps."

Schlosser finished with the photographs, which would be developed later in a darkroom he had set up at the motel. He handed the camera to an assistant and walked over to Diana, pulling his beard in thought. "Diana," he said, "there's some sort of artifact, looks like jewelry, gold or brass, but definitely metal, near or on the phalanges of the left hand. I couldn't dust enough off to get a good look. That's why I wanted so many photos. That skeleton is leached badly and might come apart even if we take it up whole."

"Okay, Bill," she said. "We'll just have to be extra careful taking it up. You say the artifact may be jewelry?"

"Looks like a *ring* to me. What about that?"

Diana whistled. "Wow. I wish my father was back from his meeting." Walters had driven to Raleigh to see an official of the archaeological funding board. She turned to David. "This might be it. A gold ring, buried with an Indian. Maybe a prize or trinket taken from a captive or on a raid."

"Earlier, your father thought a long knife was European. But it turned out to be a hide-skinning knife, probably traded by a fur trapper. Not the Lost Colony."

Diana sighed. "Yes, I remember," she said.

The procedure for removing a skeleton whole was the spade-and-shovel equivalent of moving a patient with a broken back from a bed onto a stretcher—only the stretcher in this instance was the square of earth under the specimen.

Schlosser was preparing to re-enter the trench to make measurements for the procedure when David, from the corner of his eye, saw Anne Morris waver in the heat and fall forward to the ground. As she fell, her shoulder hit the tripod, knocking it end over end toward the trench.

Schlosser cursed as he realized what was going to happen. The point of the tripod flipped completely over and landed square on the left side of the specimen. There was a sound like twigs snapping, and the brittle, leached-out lower arm and hand of the specimen was smashed.

The damaged specimen was removed later that afternoon. No one blamed Anne Morris; it was a blisteringly hot day and the excitement could easily have caused anyone to faint. David kept what he had seen—or *thought* he had seen—to himself; after all, it was just a fleeting glimpse out of the corner of his eye. But the particularly straightforward manner in which she had fallen suggested a deliberate dive rather than a haphazard collapse.

Walters, who had returned from Raleigh, really blamed Blackwell, who had left the tripod in a position to cause trouble and not removed it, as he was told to by Schlosser. But the professor was happy enough with the existence of what turned out to be a gold ring. Very much encrusted with calcium deposit and the hard grime of centuries, Johnson took it back to Walters' house, where special solvents were available. Walters, David and Diana waited in the living room while Schlosser worked alone in the lab room with the abrasive chemicals.

"Let me pour us all another drink," Walters said in an unusually ebullient tone. He sat back down in his chair after having filled David's glass with red wine.

"What is it about the jewelry that so excites you, Dr. Walters," asked David.

"The Uwharrie and Catawba Indians did decorate their bodies and that of the dead with trinkets," replied Walters, "but it was usually the quartzite found locally. Some gold was taken from the hills, but it remained unrefined and had little value to the indians until the advent of the white man. Then they were driven off the land in the rush to mine the gold. But these were random veins that yielded little; by the late nineteenth century, they had all been played out.

"The settlers of Raleigh's colony brought a number of precious stones and jewelry with them, for what reason, God only knows; it would have better served the colonists as a means to buy additional supplies before leaving England. But they were terribly naive about the conditions they would face that first winter."

"So you are saying the skeleton we found today may not be that of an Indian?"

"Either it is the skeleton of a white man or an Indian that had taken the ring from one," answered Walters.

"You mean it could be one of the survivors of the Lost Colony?"

asked David, hardly daring to believe the old man. His excitement was obvious, but it seemed too incredible to be true.

"That would be a bit premature," cautioned Walters, setting his glass down on the coffee table in front of him and leaning forward. He clasped his hands and spoke intently to David, as if he were the only person in the room. "It could be an individual trader that had come down the Old Wagon Road. Or it could be a member of a rival tribe—the Seneca or Iroquois, for instance—caught on a raid and put to death. But," he added with an unmistakable twinkle in his blue eyes, "it could also be a member of the Colony."

"It depends on the nature of the ring and the age of the skeleton," added Diana. "If it coincides with the disappearance of the Colony, then they could have been massacred. But if it was significantly later, then it might be at least circumstantial evidence that some members survived."

"I get the impression you don't think it is the skeleton of an Indian, Dr. Walters," said David.

"You're right, David, I don't."

"Why?"

"Of course, we'll have to wait for a thorough examination, but that skeleton intrigues me. It looked significantly larger than the others we have found."

At that moment, the door leading to the lab opened and Schlosser entered the room. All eyes turned to him in anticipation, but there was a puzzled look on his face. He frowned as he slowly pulled off his rubber gloves.

"Well, what news do you have for us?" asked Walters, standing up to face Bill. Schlosser was silent for a moment, then began talking rapidly, in a scientific staccato. "The skeleton is of a young adult male, in the ground approximately 125 years, perhaps 150. The remains show evidence of trauma; demise was probably by fire, either burned alive or cremated incompletely..."

"Yes, yes," Walters interrupted, "captives were known to have been burned alive for punishment or ritual torture. Do you think the body was of a white man or an Indian? Damn waiting for a physical anthropologist to pass judgment. What's your gut feeling?"

"I think it was a Caucasian, from the dental patterns. No missing teeth or cavities. The soil of the region here is deficient in certain minerals, you know, causing much caries in the aboriginal popu..."

"The ring!" Walters burst out. "What about the ring?"

Schlosser held out a shiny golden object. "See for yourself. The solvent cleaned it up just fine."

Walters took the ring gingerly, his smile turning slowly to befuddlement, and then to disgust.

"Central High School," he read from the inscription around the stone. "Class of 1976." Then he added, with a sort of desperate despair. "It's a high school ring, for the love of God! An ordinary high school ring!"

Part II

JULY

CHAPTER SIXTEEN

It took David some time to fully comprehend how a 1976 high school ring could be found with a skeleton that was close to 150 years old.

Such an occurance was called an *intrusion*; such rarities occasionally happened at digs, especially at strata near the surface. Diana gave a famous example of a buffalo nickel dug up in what was obviously prehistoric stratum in a *tell,* or mound in Syria. A snake or rodent, or severe soil erosion or other outside agent could carry an object such as a ring from its original resting place to a much lower one. Or the ring could have been dropped, lost on a picnic or hiking trip, tumbled into a gopher hole, and wound up resting in the right hand of the skeleton, much as if he had been holding it when he was laid to rest.

The ring intrusion had shaken Dr. Walters, and his professional insecurities had surfaced; perhaps he saw the clearing as the last in a series of failures. David saw a profound change come over the professor; he seemed morose and dispirited, lacking even the will to return to the dig for several days.

A noticable pall of gloom pervaded everyone associated with

the dig, except Peter Blackwell, Anne Morris and John Singer. David himself had begun to have dreams of death, skeletons, lurking savages, and some vague sense of doom connected with the project. He now regretted having committed himself to the professor, and it was only the opportunity to be near Diana that kept him returning to the site.

David and Diana still saw each other, but her work and tending to her father made their meetings little more than occasional trysts at her apartment. He wanted more, to talk to her, to share emotions that had lain dormant for so long.

Now that love had miraculously reentered his life, he couldn't bear the thought of returning to his former vapid existence; the idea terrified him.

Bill Schlosser bent over the tray in his motel closet, which served as a makeshift darkroom. The image on the paper was starting to form as he gently shook the tray of developing fluid. He straightened up, listening. He thought he had heard a sound from the other room.

"Arthur? Diana?" he called out. No answer. Probably his imagination. The motel had pipes that rattled and doors that slammed at all hours. He shrugged and took the prints out and hung them on the line to dry.

Schlosser studied the prints in the glow of the red light bulb, frowning at the inferior quality. I should have used the 600 from the beginning, he thought; the faster film would have given a higher resolution to the phalanges.

He mentally kicked himself for not developing the pictures earlier. There was something about that ring which bothered him. Maybe the sun had played tricks with his vision, but he believed the ring had been *on* the hand before the tripod had smashed it. But surely he must be wrong; it was absurd that such a modern thing could be on a skeleton buried for 150 years. Better to get confirmation through the photographs and dispel this ridiculous impression he had. Perhaps on the next blowup, at a different camera angle. He wasn't about to mention it again, not even to Diana, without clear proof either way.

Schlosser turned and lifted another print out of the tray. This one had a much sharper definition. He picked up a magnifying glass from the counter and studied it carefully.

Yes! This one showed it, all right. An encrusted bump, and definitely *on* the third phalange. Not beside it or on top of it, but *around* the finger.

Well, he hadn't been a fool after all. Although he'd never seen an intrusion wind up on a corpse before. Certainly it was strange, almost unbelievable. But he was a field manager, not a theoretician. Let Diana or Arthur explain it if they could.

He put the enlargement in a filing cabinet in the darkroom, for the record. Then he went back to make other prints, to take over to the Walters after dinner.

That noise again.

He paused, turning to the door. He was certain now that he had heard a doorknob click. It must be Arthur or Diana coming back to check on some files. Good. He could show the photographs now, save a trip.

Schlosser hung the second print up to dry and turned off the red light before opening the door.

"Arthur?" he called, stepping out from the darkroom. "Diana? I'm glad you're here. There's something..."

He stopped and stared at the two figures standing near the door. One was Peter Blackwell, but he didn't recognize the other, older man; he was dressed like one of the farmers in the area.

"Peter," Schlosser said, "what are you doing here? Thought you stayed at the dig with the others."

"I quit," said Blackwell. "My presence is no longer required, now that Singer is there."

"What do you mean by that?" asked Schlosser "Who is this man?" He pointed to the farmer.

Neither man answered. "Shall we take him now?" asked Blackwell's companion.

"Yes," said Blackwell. "Sparrow is waiting."

"What do you want?" demanded Schlosser. "Why, the photos, of course," replied Blackwell. "Where are they, Bill?"

"What do you want with them? You must be mad."

"No matter. You'll tell us all we want to know shortly."

Schlosser felt his heart beating rapidly and sweat break out on his upper lip. What were these two talking about?

"I think the two of you better get out of here before I call the sheriff," said Schlosser, trying to keep his voice level. When neither of them moved, he edged toward the telephone. "All right, we'll just let the authorities handle this."

"Put the phone down, Bill," ordered Blackwell. Schlosser tried to lift it to his ear, but his muscles would not respond. He was suddenly weak, ennervated. What is happening? he thought, fearfully.

He stood immobile as Blackwell took the receiver from his grasp. The other man gripped him by the shoulders.

"That won't be necessary," Blackwell said to the other man. "Will it, Bill? You'll come with us now. Don't be difficult." He wagged a finger in front of Schlosser's face.

"Where are we going?" asked Schlosser in a voice he did not recognize as his own.

"You're going to meet someone. Think of it as being off to see the Wizard. Like Dorothy in Oz. A man with unimaginable power. He's waiting for us."

The deeply-lined, impassive face looked dead, the mask of a ghost; but the eyes were luminescent centers of fierce energy. They shone in the dark, two bright-red coals that bored into Schlosser's own with an intensity that paralyzed his very thoughts. They burned with anger, with rage.

The leathered face bent lower, ignoring the fear in Schlosser's eyes to concentrate on his chest; sharp, repeated pin-pricks pained his chest and abdomen. He saw Peter Blackwell's mocking smile as he approached with a lighted torch and gave it to the silent old man, who lowered it onto Schlosser's chest.

Quickly, Schlosser's chest ignited in a hundred tiny flames. The odor of burning wood and singed hair and flesh filled his nostrils. Then came the pain; a sharp, seering pain that caused every nerve ending to cry out. His face twisted grotesquely as he bared his teeth and his body writhed spasmodically in torment. He wanted to scream, but all that came was a gurgling bubble and a thick saliva that dripped from the corners of his mouth.

"Is he to be one of the chosen?" Schlosser heard someone say.

"No. He is as the dust, and as useless. Stand him up. He must dance."

Suddenly, he was dancing, a macabre parody, as he stumbled awkwardly, placing one leaden foot in front of the other, before a swirling sea of faces, hidden in the shadows. All he saw was the fire in the darkness.

His face fell, his eyes stared uncomprehendingly at the slivers of wood on fire; his whole front was a series of tiny flames scorching his flesh. The voices intoned a monotonous dirge that grew louder and louder.

At last, he could no longer stand, he could not raise his arms to brush away the torment of those little flames. He could only watch helplessly as the faces, the voices and the fire receded into a silent blackness.

He fell onto his face, twitching.

"Place the face in the tray," said Blackwell. "It must look like suicide." He brushed the hair from the unconscious Schlosser's forehead and closed the blue eyes with his thumbs so that no one would later see the death agony in them. "Now."

Thomas lowered the face into the solution while Blackwell slid a chair under the body as it heaved one final time, then sagged.

Blackwell took the strips of negative film from the darkroom. "Take down the prints. Make sure there are none left."

Soon their footsteps receded. Bill Schlosser's last sensation was the burning liquid that surrounded his face and filled his lungs.

CHAPTER SEVENTEEN

Clearview continued to suffer in the heat. Tom Jameson, the town barber and mayor, issued a 'voluntary water conservation measure' which was printed in the newspaper, *The Clearview Chronicle*. It called for a temporary cessation of washing cars and watering lawns. Residents were also asked to keep showers and baths 'to a reasonable minimum.' An editorial in the paper suggested that people stop the wasteful habit of letting the tap run while brushing teeth or washing faces. The editorial reminded citizens that the water supply for Clearview did not come from the river, which for unexplainable reasons had not dropped an inch in water volume, but instead actually seemed to rise a bit toward its banks, but from the county reservoir, some seventeen miles away, which was dropping fast for lack of rain.

Residents complained about the inability of the town council to provide an alternate water source, especially Violet Andrews, the garden club president whose immaculate lawn was beginning to turn brown in spots and whose roses were wilting. But most of the griping ran to jokes, such as the wag at the barber shop who suggested a civic award for water conservation be given to Claude Benson, who rarely bathed even in times of plentiful water.

The cafe did a brisk business in ice tea and other cold drinks, and the drug store sold a lot of salt pills and foot powder.

Some further, less noticeable events occurred as the drought wore on. Mason Thomas, whose tastes ran to illegal whiskey, had become a regular at the roadhouse, drinking beer most of the day and well into the night. He acted strangely at times, which most people attributed to his head injury. He would take a corner table, sitting alone and brooding silently. Later in the evening, he invariably began mumbling and gesticulating, holding some sort of agitated argument with himself. He had not gotten into another altercation since getting out of jail; in fact, he seemed hardly aware of the other people in the roadhouse, except for curt orders to the waitress for another round.

Peter Blackwell had quit the dig, and left town in his red sports car, presumably to return to the socialite life of his parental home in Philadelphia. But within several days he was back, his prized sports car looking like a battered wreck. He did not return to the dig, but took a room at the Oaks Motel, rarely going out in the daytime. On those occasions, he took long walks around the streets, scrutinizing each building.

Sheriff Witherspoon would have carried out his threat to arrest Blackwell, but he was preoccupied with health and professional problems. His stomach problems required ever-stronger antacid pills and frequent stops at the cafe for a glass of milk. At these times, he was forced to endure Millie's diatribe of how the heat brought out the devil in people as the explanation of the unusual run of injuries and death that summer. Surely a good thunderstorm would have to come sooner or later and wash away the dust that covered everything in town, blown in from ruined fields, and return life to normal again.

Witherspoon wasn't satisfied with Millie's heat theory, although he acknowledged the ability of prolonged heat to turn people mean. That would account for the crotchety nature of even old friends lately. Fleming, the pharmacist at the drug store, was almost surly as he filled perscriptions, and seemed to have forgotten how to operate a simple cash register, overcharging the sheriff twenty dollars on his antacid.

Yes, tempers were flaring in Clearview, and his earlier feeling of a troublesome summer were coming to pass. Then there was the suicide of Bill Schlosser. The sheriff had dropped over to Dr. Burke's to ask again what could make a man drown himself in a dish of photographic development solution.

"I've told you everything I know about that," said Burke. "I'm not a psychiatrist, and I don't try to be. But obviously he was a troubled man. He could have had a serious depressive problem, or even been a psychotic. Perhaps the stress of his work caused him to kill himself in a state of acute illness. Joe, you aren't trying to make something sinister out of that tragedy, are you? The county coroner ruled it suicide, pure and simple."

Witherspoon had to smile. "You mean like a homicide? No, it would have taken at least two strong men to hold Schlosser's head in that solution. And he'd have fought like a banshee, but there was no sign of a struggle. But I was reading over the post mortem again, and I keep wondering about those spots you found on his chest and back."

"I couldn't figure out what they were at first," said Burke, "but on closer examination they looked like very old scar tissue from a number of small burns. Like a cigarette would make. I suspect Mr. Schlosser had been an abused child, which would further account for a disturbed mental condition leading to suicide. You know as well as I do, Joe, most folks carry a lot of pain inside of them. One day, it explodes. There's just no answer to those sorts of things, no way to prevent or predict them. Like that young man who died of a heart attack at the excavation. Just twenty-six and arteries clean as a whistle. But he goes into fibrillation, and it doesn't reverse itself. Those are mysteries that neither you or I can answer, Joe."

CHAPTER EIGHTEEN

Harry Wiggins was indecisive about the shirt he had chosen for the evening. It was new and sporty, with the proper emblem over the left breast; but he was beginning to think he should wear something more conservative, this night at least. He had only been home from the hospital for a week, and hadn't seen Cindy, his girlfriend, yet. He wanted to project just the right image; it would diffuse some of the nervousness and uncertainty he felt. He had learned from a month in the hospital that the image you projected was at least as important as the substance.

He was sure Mr. and Mrs. Cavanaugh, Cindy's parents, would be eying him closely for signs that his breakdown was something more than grief over his parents' divorce, and the subsequent departure of his father to a job in Alaska. The doctors had assured Harry he was not mentally imbalanced, only temporarily overwhelmed by circumstances. He was not entirely sure of that as yet, but was trying hard to get back to his old habits, a part-time job at the gas station and, of course, Cindy.

Harry stood before the bedroom mirror and continued to agonize over the bright yellow shirt; perhaps it could be interpreted as the sort of color a nut would choose to wear. He finally asked his mother for her opinion.

"Oh, I think Cindy will like it," said Mrs. Wiggins.

"I really wasn't thinking about Cindy, mother." Harry had no doubts Cindy wouldn't care in the slightest what he wore. He felt himself extraordinarily lucky to be going with someone like her; she had been more understanding about his problems than a sister.

His mother put her arm around his shoulder. "Honey," she said, "you've got to get over this feeling that people have tagged you as some kind of freak. We've talked about this before. Your father's leaving threw me for a loop, too. You just didn't have any proper way to show your sadness and anger, so it all came out at once. It could have happened to anybody. And if I were you, I'd wear whatever I wanted to wear, and if Joe and Helen Cavanaugh don't like it, that's just too bad. After all, you're dating Cindy, not them."

"Aw, mom," he said, embarrassed at the hug his mother tried to give him. "Everybody is looking to see if I'll flip out or something."

"I know. But you have to get over this fear of a relapse. Which," she said with a confident seriousness, "just isn't going to happen, and the people in this town will realize that soon enough."

She was right, of course. Harry knew that an hour later. There had been some awkwardness when Mr. Cavanaugh asked with a bit too much interest how Harry was feeling, and Mrs. Cavanaugh had said "be careful driving" a few times more than she would have three months ago, but he now had Cindy sitting close by his side at the Ulah drive-in. Cindy had been content just to be with him at their old dating place. They had often gone there in high school, even on cold nights when Harry had to leave the motor running as they lazily petted and caressed.

Cindy began to nibble at his neck and ears soon after they pulled into one of the spots near the back of the lot. They kissed, awkwardly at first, but soon it was as if he had never been away.

"I missed you terribly," said Cindy as they paused from their first round of petting. Harry studied her face carefully, grateful to not find any traces of artificial sympathy.

"I missed you, too. That was the worst part of it. I kept thinking maybe...that maybe you'd forget about me and, you know, get interested in another guy. Out of sight, out of mind, and all that."

Cindy chuckled. "You were only gone a month, Harry. What did you think I was going to do, elope or something?"

They both laughed, Harry with a sense of great relief. The levity faded, and they kissed again for a long time.

"Are you really over your father now?" Cindy asked, her head nestled in the crook of his shoulder.

He paused before speaking. "Yes," he said simply, and knew this time he meant it. "I won't have to go away again, I know that now."

"Promise?"

"Promise," he said. They embraced again and she responded so warmly and compliantly he knew they would wind up in the back seat before the second feature began. It had been one of the fantasies he nourished during his stay at the hospital, but if that was going to happen, he needed to relieve himself. He pulled back gently. "Just give me a couple of minutes, okay? I have to go to the can."

Cindy sat up and began to straighten her hair. The night was warm and the heavy petting had made her thirsty. "Hey," she called after him, "bring me a coke, will you? A big one!"

He smiled and nodded, whistling a nameless, happy tune as he crossed the rolling mounds of each row, zigzagging around the speakerphone cables on his way to the concession stand.

It was a low, white building, very brightly lit with fluorescent bulbs, and clouds of moths and gnats swarmed around the screen door. He moved to the side of the building, where a fizzing sign signaled the men's room in green neon. Inside, he bypassed the row of urinals and opened the door to one of the stalls.

When he was through in the stall, he checked his billfold to make sure the prophylactic was still there. He replaced the billfold, smiling in anticipation of the rest of the evening, and pushed open the stall door.

It hit another young man squarely in the chest, such that the door would not completely open. Harry was startled; he hadn't heard anyone come in. And the man was smiling in a peculiar way.

He was older than Harry by several years, a college kid with long, tightly curled blonde hair, and a blazer that sported a fraternity crest.

Frightened by the man's odd grin, and his silent reluctance to move, Harry pushed on the door, slightly moving the figure back, and slipped out from the stall. He muttered, "excuse me," not wanting to offend a possible drunk. He was anxious just to get away, buy the coke, and return to Cindy.

He said "excuse me" once more and sidled past the blonde apparition. The man kept grinning and was still anchored to the same spot; his only movement was to take a drag from a cigarette and blow smoke at Harry.

"We've got the coke, Harry," he said in a voice like a garbled sound track. "It's all been taken care of."

"What?" asked Harry, turning in disbelief.

"I said we've got the coke."

Two things raised the hair on the back of Harry's neck. The man's voice modulated up and down in a wavery, almost mechanical speech; and Harry recognized the grin as being very similar to one he'd seen on psychotics being led by orderlies at the hospital. It was a mindless, purposeless grin, frightening because it had absolutely nothing to do with the real world.

"Who...who are you? How do you know my name?"

"Why, you've been chosen, of course. Just relax, Harry. Take it easy. The old man wants to see you. Come along quietly now."

"What old man?"

"*The* old man, the birdman. Bird, man! Get it? A medical man of infinite power. He wants to check you over."

"You're crazy, whoever you are!"

"Just relax, Harry. Forget about the coke, it's been taken care of."

But Harry wasn't relaxed; his mind was spinning, trying to make sense of what was happening. Coke, coke. Could it be the blonde man had mistaken him for someone else, a drug dealer, and that some deal was scheduled to go down in the men's room? But how had he known his name? Why was everything 'taken care of'? What medical man?

With mounting fear he also wondered why no other customer had entered the washroom. Usually there was a steady flow in and out.

The adrenaline surged through his chest now, and his only thought was to get away from this crazy man. He moved swiftly, lunging toward the exit in a dizzying fear that made his legs jelly.

The blonde man was suddenly in front of him, blocking the exit. The grin said: "Everything's taken care of, Harry. Why don't you cool it?"

An arm lashed out, and he was flat on his back, but with a hard bumpy surface underneath, like flat rocks. He heard water flowing nearby, too loud and sustained to be the flush of a urinal. No; he was somewhere else, near a river or a stream, with total darkness overhead. Some of his fear had been replaced by a searing heat on his abdomen and at points on his chest, as if part of him were slowly burning. The points of pain grew more intense, spread and went deeper. He felt like screaming but, somehow, didn't. An inner instinct told him that if he screamed, he would die. He bit his tongue until it bled, until it was numb with pain and warm liquid seeped out the side of his mouth.

He passed out and came to several times after that, in a swoon of pain and confusion., Always there was the sound of water, and blackness overhead. He heard the wavery voice speaking off to the side, as if to another unseen figure.

His consciousness flickered, and there was a broad Indian face bending over him. The face was impassive, more dead than alive; a small skeleton, like a bird's, hung from the Indian's earlobe. Then hands were running along his chest, and the burning eased somewhat.

The Indian made a deep sound that seemed to vibrate through his whole body, rattling his joints. It sounded like a feight train rumbling through his head, very loud. The sound reverberated through him, until his head was reeling again, and every muscle ached.

He thought he heard the wavery voice say, "Want us to make him get up and dance?"

The Indian's red eyes bored into his, and once again all was darkness.

Harry awoke, if that was what it was, on the floor of the men's room, his head throbbing. The tile floor was cold and hard against his back. Two drunk teenagers were urinating nearby, weaving on their feet, their faces turned to him in vague curiousity.

A florid face bent over him; he smelled a powerful mixture of beer and stale vomit. The mouth attached to the face said, "This guy's okay. You're okay, aren't you pal?"

"He ain't o.d.'ed?" asked one of the others, zipping up his pants.

"Naw."

"Shit. I thought he o.d.'ed, or something."

"Well, he's okay, I tell you." The florid face and the vomit smell moved away. Harry sat up, slowly getting his bearings back. An instinct made him grope to see that his wallet was still in his back pocket. It was.

The dizziness left him, and he stood up, just as the three drunks left the men's room. He felt very strange, as if part of his mind were trying to split off from the other. Then he remembered the blonde man, and the arm flashing out. He must have been knocked out by the crazy bastard. Maybe the guy had been high on animal tranquilizers; Harry had heard they could make a person wild and phenomenally strong. He must have struck his head on the floor and lost consciousness. Maybe he had a concussion.

But how long had he been out? It seemed like hours had passed since he had come in here. He left the men's room and peered at the screen; the first feature was still playing.

He decided to buy the coke for Cindy. He ordered the drink and gave a dollar to the cashier. He stared at the object she returned before realizing it was a quarter. He'd forgotten for a moment what a quarter was.

The smell of frying meat was strong in the concession stand, and he was suddenly very hungry. He bought three burgers and then left the stand, out into the starlight. Another customer nudged against him, and Harry turned sharply and hissed: "Wesichau!"

"Sorry, bud," the other said, startled, and continued through the screen door.

Harry shook his head. Now, why had he said that? He had no idea where that word had come from. Or the sudden anger that abated just as quickly as it sprang up.

By the time he returned to the car, he had eaten one of the hamburgers, rare, with the blood oozing between his lips. Physically, he felt much stronger, and the dizziness was gone. He smelled the strong scent of pines emanating from the woods behind his car. It was funny; he had never noticed before what a strong odor they put out, or how bracing it was. He took several deep breaths.

Cindy remarked how quickly he had been able to make the trip. When she saw the remaining burgers in the bag, she said, "Say, you must *really* be hungry!"

She drank part of the coke, watching the final scene of the movie. Harry ate another hamburger, savoring the drippings, and then wiped his mouth with the back of his hand. The smell of Cindy's soft skin aroused him. He felt strong and masculine, extremely powerful. He took the drink from her hand and pulled her close to him, pulling the panties down and thrusting his hand roughly between her legs.

The sound of a river was rushing inside him, and the scent of pine and the urgent smell of the woman were like living things. He had completely forgotten the blonde man with the grin, or waking up on the bathroom floor. His head felt fine; he had never felt better in his life.

He was only vaguely aware that Cindy sat very far away from him as they drove home later. Almost as if she were afraid of him.

CHAPTER NINETEEN

David was surprised to see frail Miss Priddy make her way toward the circulation desk. She walked with her head high, as if on a mission of great importance; in her right hand she held an ancient sheaf of yellowed paper, speckled with mold.

"Mr. Hale," she said, without any pleasantries, "when you visited the other week, I neglected to give you this...document. It was written by my grandfather many years ago. It concerns the excavation site. And other things."

She held out the manuscript to him; David took it gingerly. "Your grandfather? The county agent?"

Miss Priddy smiled faintly.

"My grandfather was the dearest man on earth," she began, in a delicate but proud voice, "and all his life he was a tortured soul. Not because of anything he did wrong, mind you, but because of a secret that he knew, and was afraid to tell. I think it shortened his life, having that secret with him. When he was struck with the dropsy, and knew he didn't have long to live, he called me to him—I was about sixteen at the time—and he gave me a document he had written forty years before, in 1868. He'd never shown it to a soul, not even my mother or my grandmother. I guess he gave it to me because we were a lot alike, and perhaps he thought I would keep it and one day make sure that it was passed along. So much time has passed that the retribution he was worried about, well, it's all ancient history now. But I have had the document as part of my estate. It was going to go to the local history collection here at the library anyway. I'd just as soon give it to you now, and be done with it."

"Yes, ma'am," David said, wondering now if Miss Priddy's reputation as an eccentric was well founded. What document could she have that could once have brought about 'retribution?' But he said: "I'd be proud to take the document and put it with the local collection."

"You take good care of this," she said, with a weak smile. "It will soon be all that's left of the Priddys."

David again promised to treat the packet with special care. Miss Priddy turned and walked away She stopped at the door. "It's a shame you couldn't have known my grandfather, young man. I think the two of you would have hit it off."

"Perhaps we would have at that. He must have been a fine man. And I'm anxious to know what is in this document. I'm sure if he thought it so valuable, it must have great historical significance."

"It's all dead and gone now," she said wistfully. "All ancient history, like I said. But once you read that piece of paper, I don't think you'll ever feel the same way about this town. Or maybe a few other things, too. People say I'm odd, and maybe I am, a little bit. But I'll make you a small wager that you'll never put that paper anywhere on public display."

Then she was gone.

David stared after her for a long moment. Then he turned his attention to the manuscript. He wiped the dust from the title page and spread the following sheets out on the table. They were yellowed and crumbling with age. From the faded handwriting, the top sheet looked like an inventory of supplies requisitioned for county land usage. He laid those aside and shifted through page after page of precise, neat handwriting, but at first found nothing remarkable; just some personal family reminiscences, a sort of loose diary. Miss Priddy must have been mistaken about what she thought would be in here, either that or her mind was going. Then David noticed some more tightly-written pages near the end. They came after a number of blank pages, as if intended to be separate from the rest. He turned to the first page and read:

August 31, 1868

> *May God forgive me for my helplessness on this day, and may He protect my family from the madness which overtook this town and its inhabitants; and may He mercifully spare all gentle people from such heinous sights as my eyes have witnessed this interminable, damnable morning.*

> *I hereby set down this record of the true events and happenings which I have seen, so that the villainy of those involved be preserved in some fashion, and that the truth may one day be brought to light for all to know, and benefit from the foul lesson herein.*

> *I was awakened three days previous, several hours before sunrise, by Major Caleb Simpson, late of the North Carolina 8th Cavalry, Partisan Rangers. He was in a state of great mental agitation, such as I have never before seen, and his wits were further undone by imbibation of spirits. He was mad with rage over a rumor which had swept through the tavern outside Bladenburg, concerning a young woman of the district, who said a red man had attempted to lift of her garment, and had otherwise frightened her and acted in a way which had soiled her honor as a lady. The tale was so vague, and the reputation of the 'lady' already so*

suspect, I could only dismiss the story as a bald lie, or the most fierce embellishment of a harmless incident. The Major's rage was almost insane, however, and he quickly laid the blame for the incident on the small tribe of Uwharrie who were under my jurisdiction. He further accused them of slaughtering two of his cattle.

I did not then see the Major was using me as a ploy in a grand and dastardly plot, and that the cattle and the lady's honor were a mere ruse. Instead, I considered him a dangerous drunk, who might make trouble for my charges. I warned him that the Uwharrie band would not tolerate an invasion of their hunting preserve without a savage defense and much bloodshed. Further, that it was a violation of United States law to encroach on their land, to which they still held legal title, and that I, as Couny Agent, would act as lawful arbitrator for any claims against the tribe. I then told him to the best of my knowledge I had never known the Uwharrie to touch beef, preferring deer and wild fowl.

Simpson ignored my entreaties with an impatient wave of his hand, and his cursing of the Indians was extended to me in a most brutal fashion. He demanded that I accompany him, for motives I could not gather at the time. I dressed as hurriedly as I could, while trying to calm the fears of my good wife, Kate, as to the wild goings-on in the yard. Simpson was in such a crazed state that I feared for the safety of my wife as well as myself, had I not presented myself outside in short order, and saddled my mare with shaking hands.

Together we rode about a half mile, past the crossroads and the church, which I looked to for some comfort in this mad ride, but all was dark and silent; I could not hear any sound save the beat of our horses' hooves on the road.

Simpson turned off into a grove of oaks, and suddenly we were swallowed up into the shadows. He stopped, and I heard the neighing of other horses behind the trees. There were perhaps thirty heavily armed men surrounding us. Most were strangers, but several were known to me. The deference with which they treated Major Simpson led me to believe they had served under him during the late war. I recognized at least five of my neighbors, whom I was distressed to find in the company of this sinister and inebriated band. Only two days before, I had stood in church and sang hymns with these men, but now, under the trees in the moonlight of that awful evening, it was as if they were total and horrid strangers, and not the decent souls I took them to be. May God forgive my youthful naivete´, that such men could have lulled me into complacence, and that I did not see their design over the wards of my position as County Agent.

For they quickly let it be known to me their destination was indeed the Uwharrie camp for the purpose of avenging themselves for the loss of the two cattle. Of course, the role of Major Simpson in this vigilante ride was all too obvious—if the Uwharrie were savagely driven from their land, he could add it to his own at a fraction of its true value.

I tried fruitlessly to appeal to the dormant Christianity in the hearts of these men, but was quickly threatened into silence. The Major ordered that I be bound and gagged. Helpless in the midst of these brutes, my horse was led by one of the Major's henchmen.

A ride of some quarter hour brought us to the

vicinity of the Uwharrie village, which was comprised of some twenty wooden buildings in a clearing. While at some distance from the camp, under cover of the trees, the group quickly grew silent, and even the drunkest of them took on a sober aspect as they prepared their horrid scheme. Simpson's men spread out in a large circle, their backs to a strong dawn wind that blew from the north. There was no movement in the village; in fact, the camp had a strange aspect to it, as if abandoned.

The attackers stealthily moved from the treeline to the edge of the corn and high grass that surrounded the village. At a signal from the Major, several men emptied kegs of kerosene onto the grass. I soon saw fire spring up at a dozen different points.

I prayed for the wind to change, but in a moment a swift and furious blaze engulfed the village. I was mystified at the absence of warriors in the camp. Then I recalled it was the twelfth day since the death of their chief Keyauwee Jack, and custom forbade bearing arms during the funeral ceremony. After a day of fasting, the men would imbibe a root concoction which has much the same effect as laudnum, producing a stuporous and ecstatic religious state. So this was the reason the camp was defenseless.

Screams emanated from the village as women and children, followed by men in a dazed state, ran from the huts. At this point, Simpson's men opened fire, felling those Indians not already consumed by the flames.

The Major would have been content if the blaze had continued into the timber, thus relieving him of the necessity of clearing it once the land was in his possession, but the flames turned back on themselves owing to a sudden cessation of the wind. In a very short time, all that was left of the village and surrounding cornfields was a blackened circle illuminated by an occasional smouldering ember.

Simpson's band fell upon the prostrate bodies, committing unspeakable acts of barbarism as they mutilated the bodies of their victims. The only consolation I could take in such a scene was that none of the women had survived to endure the lustful appetites of their tormentors.

I could not bear to look at the other townsmen, such was my shame for them and for myself. I made a vow to myself to never speak to these men again, nor have any dealings with them in the future, even if I should have to leave the community of my birth.

In the midst of the despicable carnage, one of the men ran up to Simpson, shouting that he had seen survivors, a man, two women and a child fleeing the village. The Major dispatched three men to hunt down these poor wretches. Although he waited for over an hour, these men did not return.

At last weary of the mayhem, Simpson led the band from the massacre. We rode back to town, drained and silent. In that hour, I lost whatever faith I possessed in my fellow man, and saw too clearly the foul state of humanity as a whole. I then perceived why Simpson had taken me on his foul mission; I, as County Agent, would give some legitimacy to his crime, should any question arise, and I would be falsely vilified as the instigator of the massacre, instead of a hapless observer. I was further threatened with death should I ever convey a true account of what took place that night.

I went into my house and, disguising my heavy heart, told some soothing fiction to calm Kate, and forced myself to take breakfast, though I could scarce hold it down. I have since gone about my business with this loathesome knowledge inside me like a slow and devious disease. I waited to see if some official inquiry would emanate from Raleigh as to the reason for my resignation. But the state government was preoccupied with tmore important matters. I suppose my small station was simply lost in a bureaucratic morass.

In the days that followed, I returned to bury what was left of the bodies. Shallow and ragged these graves were, for I had to complete this work alone, for I told no one. But to each I prayed God have mercy, and read from the Scriptures. None of my fellow townspeople gave much thought to those grim events; Major Simpson provided the suggestion that a forest fire had decimated the village and scattered its inhabitants, piling falsehood upon falsehood, and the townspeople found it convenient to accept his story. It would have been pointless to pit my word against that of a powerful landowner and war hero. And, in truth, I feared for my life, and that of my wife.

Now I commit these words to paper because of what I feel is my guilt in this tragedy, which, had I but been more faithful to the tenets of the Scriptures, the true facts concerning the final destruction of the Uwharrie might have already been brought to light. Now, I can only leave this narrative to posterity, so that history may someday know the truth. As for me, I shall spend the rest of my days in service to those poor Indians who lacked the same resolve to stand against the greed of Simpson and men of his kind. Perhaps in this endeavor, I can

atone in some manner for my shame and cowardice.
I can only commend the souls of the massacred
tribe to the mercy of our Lord Jesus Christ. And
may He have mercy on me and protect my family,
and spread His justice over the guilty and innocent
in the Last Days. World without end, Amen.

Signed,
Joseph Priddy

David closed the journal slowly. My God, he thought, so this was what Miss Priddy had hinted at. No wonder she had been so secretive about it. But what a marvelous find, tragic though the story was. How could any group of supposedly civilized people do such a thing? That Colonel Simpson must have been a real bastard.

David was anxious to show the manuscript to Dr. Walters after he left the library; he could well imagine what the professor's reaction would be. He was about to place the manuscript in a cabinet when one of the yellowed pages fluttered and he saw additional writing on the back of the last sheet. He had to peer closely at the writing to make it out. It was in Joseph Priddy's handwriting, but lacking the neat script of the journal entry, as if it were added as a hasty afterthought. There was a drawn cross, perhaps invoking the Deity, beside five names. It struck David that these names must be the five townsmen who rode with the Major.

As a good oral historian, he wrote the names down in his notepad. He'd check them out later.

* * * *

David was surprised at Dr. Walters' bland reaction to the Priddy document. "David," Walters had said, " this is irrelevant to our research. I sent you to Olivia to see if her grandfather had heard stories of the Indians regarding early European contact, not another sad account of nineteenth century Native American-white conflict." He told David that Joseph Priddy had spent his last years suffering from a condition that today would be diagnosed as Alzheimer's Disease. Eventually, he had to be committed to an asylum, where he would lie in his bed all day, clutching the Bible.

At any rate, there was no confirmation in old town records that might validate the document. David only had records in the local history collection going back to the 1870s, when the town was incorporated. There had been earlier records, but they had been tossed out during the Depression, due to lack of space before the addition to the library had been built.

David was disappointed that the fruit of his most revealing interview was so poorly received. But by then he realized that Walters was more than ever obsessed with the Lost Colony idea. It was the old man's Holy Grail, his last chance to turn a mediocre career into one that would live on in textbooks. And like the Grail, was a vague myth lost in time, receding ever backwards.

CHAPTER TWENTY

The abandoned tobacco curing shed had sides of rough boards and a tin roof; by noon the sun had heated the air inside like a sauna. John Singer found it hard to breathe. His throat was dry and parched, blistered by the heat. He had not had food or water for three days now—or was it four? The leather straps holding his hands to a rod on the hot tin wall had scraped the skin of his wrists raw; an ugly reddish-black sore oozed there now, where a large bottle-green fly lit, then lifted off to buzz around the stifling room.

Sparrow-in-Snow must have tricked him, thought Singer. The shaman wasn't going to come back, meant to leave him here to die of heat and thirst. His fatigue and the parched pain that spread through his lungs kept the rage inside him from causing any more movement.

But then his rage turned to sadness. Singer saw again in his mind's eye the beauty of the clearing as it had once been, the faces of the dark people, so strong and proud. His people, the shaman had called them. He was supposed to be their saviour; but first he had to prove that he was worthy, that he was indeed a man.

Singer didn't know if he was worthy. At this point, his body beginning to fail, his resolve had weakened almost to the breaking point. His naked chest rose and fell rapidly. His thighs and calves beneath the loincloth were streaked with dried urine, which the suffocating heat had made more rancid; he was continually nauseous from the smell. Dried excrement had formed into a hard ball between his legs. His groin was raw and burned from the filth. And now the fly had come back, bringing several friends, to crawl along his wrist wounds, tickling the pain into sharp spasms.

Sparrow-in-Snow had said he would come back only when the pain and thirst Singer endured were enough to kill a weaker, undeserving man. How much would it be, he wondered? Or perhaps when that point came he wouldn't know of it, having failed the test and died.

How much of the soft Wesichau was left in him, and how much of the hard Uwharrie? Which blood would survive? The white was death; the red was life.

Suddenly, Singer felt the hot tears; they flowed from his eyes, blinding him. He thought of his father and his early, senseless death. He thought of his great-grandfather and the night he had awakened him, of his beseeching the sky to hear his ancient language, of how the wolf replied from the valley and the strange things the old man said that night. And he thought of his death days later.

It had all been so bleak and hopeless after that, all childhood joy stifled before he was old enough to realize what was happening to him. All his heritage gone before he even knew he was a Uwharrie, that the blood of chiefs roared in his veins.

He held his head back, so that the tears would not attract the flies. Tears did no good. He could not remember the last time he cried. He had been silent and alone and full of a great bitterness for as long as he could remember; it seemed there had been nothing more to his life. *Had been nothing more.* Now came the shaman with his visions and his hypnotic power to make Singer see a lost beauty and savagery that was his true self, his true history. And Singer, in the depths of his being, was unsure. The shaman had shown him magic, had made him feel the power of his own blood. All the ways of the whites were as nothing compared to the power and the natural strength he felt at the shaman's promptings.

And here he was, being tested beyond pain. Fouled. Scared, the strength ebbed away. His energy and confidence stolen by the simple expedient of wood and tin and heat. His heritage beaten down because he was alone, and he still did not know exactly who, or what, he was becoming.

He felt weak and unworthy, no more a Uwharrie than he was a white man, a Wesichau. He would die there in the heat and stench of his own body because he was neither one nor the other. He belonged nowhere, not even to himself.

John Singer screamed in rage and frustration. The scream seared his vocal chords; he felt they had physically ripped apart. His chest heaved, the dizziness returned to torture him anew. He tried to vomit but there was nothing left in him to throw up, only a foul smell from his throat. And the burning, the heat inside and out.

He lowered his head and the tears of anger and hopeless rage fell from the bridge of his nose to the red dirt floor of the shed. Help me, shaman, he thought. Then he passed out.

Singer was no longer sure if he were dreaming, or if he were awake and in the grip of some hallucination. He was aware of being in the shed, and his pain was intense, his thirst demonic; he would have killed for water. He tried to lick the tears from his cheeks with his swollen tongue, but the salty taste only added to his misery. He could no longer scream or even whisper.

Then, in the height of his agony, he felt a part of his being rise from his body. There he was without pain, very light, aloft on the hot currents of the air in the stifling shed. A part of him was being pulled away, separated from that corpse-like human he saw shackled, unconscious, to the tin wall. He had pity for that bag of flesh, trapped in agony, but at the same time had no urge to help it or reduce its suffering.

And then he was aloft, high over the shed, moving up as if he had wings. A sparrow hawk darted past, climbing, and pulled him along in its draft, up further and faster. There were clouds above; he was being drawn into them. Then there was whiteness all around. He heard water roaring and people shouting.

He knew who the warrior was, and could even remember his name: Running Elk. His crime was that of poisoning, putting a deadly herb in the communal well. Seven Uwharrie had perished. Now he was condemned by the chief and the elders to die by ritual torture. Running Elk was not a Uwharrie, but a Tuscarora, from a village not many miles distant. The previous winter he had entered the camp, having married the widow of a Uwharrie brave killed in battle. It was permissible for a woman whose husband was dead to marry outside the tribe if no other brave offered to take her. So the Tuscarora was allowed to remain in the camp, as long as he obeyed Uwharrie custom.

But now, after the poisoning, it was known the Tuscarora was a spy, and had entered the camp with the purpose of avenging his brother, killed by a Uwharrie three snows ago. Running Elk had not tried to escape after his deed, but was taken immediately to the elders for punishment.

Singer somehow knew all this, and watched as the whole village gathered around the place where the Tuscarora was tied to a wooden pole with leather thongs. The Uwharrie braves were laughing with the anticipation of the spectacle to come. The women and some of the children took it as a festive occasion, and there was dancing and shouts of joy when the punishment was announced.

In the midst of the gathering crowd around the pole, Singer felt himself caught up in the gaiety. His wrists had been burning and his mouth and throat had been dry and raw, but now these things were forgotten. He felt himself merge with the members of the tribe as, laughing, they swept from the lodge houses into the middle of the clearing and to the doomed spy.

Sparrow-in-Snow descended from the totem house, a building raised on stilt-like foundations. When the crowd saw that he approached, their laughter subsided in reverence to this important man.

The shaman was the executioner.

He seemed to glide along through the crowd, as lower-ranking members drew back, squeezed against each other to make way. Very quickly he was at the pole, peering down at the prisoner whose upper body was bound with thongs. It was customary that the condemned man be bound sitting, so his lowly state would be all the more evident.

Without changing expression, the shaman bent over his helpless prisoner, made two circular cuts around his wrists with a long knife, and stepped back to watch as two assistants sprang from the crowd and began to pull on the skin. The Tuscarora's face went rigid with pain, but he did not cry out. The skin of each wrist gave way with a wet sucking sound, and the skin was slowly stripped off over the fingers.

With the red sinew and bloody bone of the fingers exposed, the shaman took a short heavy stick and, with the assistants immobilizing the prisoner's arms, struck each finger at the second joint with a sharp, quick blow. Then to the first joints, and the larger bones. The knuckles cracked with the sound of chicken bones being snapped. When the Tuscarora moaned, the women giggled and the children danced around in glee, stopping to watch each step of the ritual.

The Tuscarora's hands were now a mass of red pulp, almost indistinguishable as anything human. The shaman inspected his work, seemed to be pleased that the prisoner had not passed out from the pain, and motioned to the assistants to unbind the prisoner from the pole.

He had to be helped up, bodily lifted to stand woozily on his feet. His shirt was ripped off, and the shaman stepped forward again. With the assistants holding the spy tightly, the shaman drew a brace of thin sticks from his waistcoat; they were strips of pine, coated with pitch. The ends were sharpened like toothpicks. The shaman took them one by one and pushed them through the skin of the Tuscarora, who flinched but did not cry out. There were many slivers of pine and the spy was soon a living tree with thin branches piercing every muscle of his trunk.

"You will die now," the shaman said in a flat tone to the suffering captive. "If you die well, and in silence, you will be remembered as a warrior, a brave enemy. If you cry out, and are not brave, your body will be thrown to the dogs to devour. Then you will be forgotten."

Sparrow-in-Snow gestured to the assistants, who seized the Tuscarora more tightly, dragging him back to the pole where he was again bound with the thongs. The shaman motioned for a young child, a girl, to come forward. He whispered in her ear, pointed to one of the smoking communal fires that were used for cooking. The child ran giggling to the fire and brought back a faggot, a yellow flame at the black end.

"Do as I have told you," ordered the shaman.

The child took the flame and allowed it to touch the end of one of the slivers sticking from the captive's chest. The pitch caught rapidly, with a thick black smoke.

The assistants then ran to fetch other faggots from other fires. Speed was essential now; the pitch would consume the splinters in short order. The child and the assistants completed the lighting of most of the splinters. The captive was surrounded by plumes of black smoke before the smell of burning flesh rose to meet every nostril in the audience.

Still the Tuscarora had not cried out.

The laughter had subsided. This enemy was entitled to silence at the end.

"Cut him loose," ordered the shaman. The assistants cut the thongs and pulled the captive to his feet. "Now dance," Sparrow-in-Snow commanded.

The Tuscarora tried. Some of the pitch slivers had burned out in his chest and stomach, leaving gaping black wounds. but as the wounds were opened, they were cauterized, so that the loss of blood was slow. Shock and pain were slower to kill.

The captive was brave; even the shaman was pleased. When, after staggering in a confused parody of a war dance, he fell forward on his face, finally dead, the tribe dispersed in silence. They had been avenged, they had been entertained. They would go back to their meals and their chores without another thought on the incident.

Sparrow-in-Snow ordered the Tuscarora taken to the river and his wounds cleaned of dirt and mud. Then his body was placed on a raised burial platform of sticks and animal hides to be buried as a brave enemy warrior.

After the skin had been devoured by birds of prey, the small bones of the feet and hands would be given as rewards to a gifted hunter or a brave warrior. Such bones of a noble enemy who did not cry out were of value as amulets, and made the wearer proud. They would help when his own time came to cross the river.

Singer came to again as night was falling outside the shelter. The sleep, or the vision, had strengthened him, as after a night's rest. His wrists no longer pained him; it took a few seconds to realize they were freed from the shed wall and he was not sagging upright, but lay flat on his back on the earth floor.

He blinked his eyes. Sparrow-in-Snow was standing over him.

"You have passed the test well," said the shaman.

John Singer somehow already knew that. He sat up, found a jug of water at his side, which he put to his lips. A few drops seemed enough now; the raging thirst that had plagued him earlier was gone, taken away. He did not question how this could be, nor did he question how the wounds of his wrists and the sores had dried up, vanished. There was a little hunger, but not enough to trouble him now.

A sense of peace and joy was overtaking him, such that the pain of his body was only a mere inconvenience. he knew pain and fear would never destroy the serene strength he now felt. It was truly as if he had shed another skin; this one of pain and weakness.

As the shaman had said it would be.

"Wolf-Singer, you have passed the tests which make you a Uwharrie warrior. You have endured heat and thirst and binding, and have gone without food. You have done this alone. These things make you a man and a member of the tribe. Only the strong and brave are worthy of life as a warrior, which is the highest state of being on this earth. Your ancestors are pleased, and will reward you. You have not lost the blood of your great-grandfather, Singing Wolf, who was already a chief as a babe in his mother's arms. You have not lost the blood of his father, the great Chief Keyauwee Jack."

"Yes," said John Singer."now I am finally and truly a man."

He was very happy now, and all traces of thirst and hunger had fled. He wanted to walk among the pines and smell their sap, to feel the wind and hear the river as it ran by. Then he would go to sleep, lie down in the clearing where Walters and his underlings had dug their ridiculous holes, looking for bones when they should be running from ghosts.

"The tall bearded man, the one they call Schlosser, he is dead?" he asked the shaman.

"Yes, he is dead."

Singer stood up. "I recognized him in the face of the Tuscarora. He died well."

"Yes," said the shaman. "He died well."

CHAPTER TWENTY-ONE

The cafe was practically deserted as David spoke in hushed tones to Jack Rose. Rose was an old friend of the family, a big, red-faced construction worker turned farmer. David trusted him completely. The two were hunched over coffee cups at a corner table.

"I tell you, Jack, I saw John Singer walking up near Spirit Rock. I called to him, but he ignored me. When I ran to catch up with him, he had disappeared. Just like that."

Rose sat silently, hands cupped around his mug, his mouth pinched together in thought. He wore a sweat-blotched cap and a two-day's growth of beard.

"What's so unusual about that? Maybe he was just going home."

"No," countered David impatiently. "I think he lives way up near the ridge. Besides, he was coming from the dig, and he was carrying something in a sack."

"Think he was stealing?"

"I don't want to say that, at least not yet," replied David. "But he acted very strangely. I'm sure that he saw me, but he ran away from me."

"Why don't you just ask him about it next time you see him?"

"I don't want to create an embarrassing scene before I've had a chance to check it out myself. Dr. Walters is worried that some of the artifacts might disappear; it's not uncommon for thefts to plague digs like this. I just don't want anything to jeopardize the professor's work. I know how much it means to him."

"Okay, Dave," said Jack. "What can I do for you?"

"You know that area like the back of your hand. I remember you and Dad used to hunt up there when I was a kid. I'd like you to go with me to look around, just to satisfy my own curiosity. If he is taking things from the dig, he must have them hidden up there somewhere."

"Well, your daddy and me didn't hunt around Spirit Rock, exactly. Nobody has, not for years. No game. But it was close enough, I guess. Okay, I'll take you up there, but I don't want to spend all day. I'll look around with you for a couple of hours, but if we don't find anything, I'm coming home before dark. I've got chores to do. Like as not, all he's got up there is a still." Rose laughed, pushing back his chair and rising.

Twenty minutes later David parked his car at the base of a narrow, rutted path strewn with rock.

"Well, let's have a look," sighed Rose, as he opened the door. "But I don't think you'll find anything. If he has a cache hidden up here, it could be years—if ever—before you find it."

They climbed the path, peering into the thick undergrowth on both sides. In a few minutes, they came to the area where David had seen Singer disappear. The path was completely overgrown, eventually fading into the surrounding bushes. Pine trees met overhead forming a canopy of pre-dusk gloom.

"Jesus," wheezed Rose, taking his cap off and wiping the perspiration from his forehead with his sleeve. "Nobody's been around here for years. You're sure this is where you saw him?"

David nodded. "He went around the bend back there and when I reached this spot, he was gone. He was here, all right," insisted David. "And I want to find out why."

They continued to search the area, turning off the path, retracing their steps, and going first to the right, then to the left. There was no sign that Singer had been there.

The sun began to sink toward the horizon and the shadows made visibility difficult. At first, Rose had been in reasonably good humor, calling out sarcastic comments as they tramped through densely-wooded sections, but he had grown increasingly ill-tempered as the search seemed more and more futile.

"Goddamit, David," he snapped. "I don't mind walking around a little while with you, but I'll be damned if I'm gonna traipse through here into the night. I'm goin' home. If you won't give me a ride, I'll walk back."

The irritation in his voice was clearly evident. David didn't want to push an old family friendship too far. Perhaps Jack was right; Singer might have a still up here. If so, it was none of his business.

"Okay, Jack," he conceded. "But first I want to check the area behind Spirit Rock. That's the only place we haven't been. If we don't see anything, I'll give up and not mention it again."

"Well, *you* might not, but I sure as hell will, the next time you ask me for a favor."

They walked off the path to the left as the shadows grew longer. The tall pines whispered in a rising wind. Their coversation had fallen off; even Rose had stopped grumbling. At first, David had been preoccupied looking for signs of Singer and had not taken notice; but now the other man's silence struck him as peculiar. As the sun's rays shortened, he instinctively sought the comfort and mutual protection of the other's presence. He glanced behind him at the dark, lumbering figure. Rose had fallen farther and farther behind.

"Come on, Jack," he called. "Don't worry, it won't be much longer. I'm beginning to think you were right all along."

Rose's only reply was an almost-inaudible grunt. The thought of the two of them stumbling around in the brush began to strike David as absurd, and he smiled; he would have laughed at himself but for the behavior of the other man.

Rose was about twenty yards behind him, walking very slowly. He stopped and stood quite still for several minutes, then advanced slowly for a few paces before stopping again. David paused to watch him. For someone that was in a hurry to get back to town, he was certainly taking his time. Rose seemed to be listening for something. He would look up the mountain from time to time, and once or twice David thought he heard him muttering to himself.

"What's that?" he called. "Did you say something to me, Jack?" Rose did not reply, and his shout had an eerie, hollow ring as it echoed through the still forest.

David did not try to talk to Rose again. If he's that sullen, it's best to leave him alone, he thought. He'd forget all about it in a day or so. He walked ahead on the trail, which sloped on a gradual rise. The path was more rock-strewn than before and he had to concentrate to avoid stumbling. It was no time to have a twisted ankle or a broken leg.

At least on this gentle slope, Rose would have no trouble catching up with him. When they topped the next rise, he'd wait for him and turn back.

Behind him he could hear Rose's breathing, less labored now, as he closed the distance between them. The silence of his friend was beginning to unnerve him more than the gloom of the forest.

"Wesichau!" David heard the word, but it made no sense to him. Perhaps Jack was cursing at him; the voice had such venom in it. But surely Rose could not be that angry?

He turned to face Rose. He had a flash of a face so twisted in rage and hatred as to be all but unrecognizable. Rose's arm swung down in a wide arc and a heavy stick hit David in the chest with such force he was sent reeling backward. He landed hard upon the ground, the breath knocked out of him. As he lay there with his chest aching, he saw Rose standing over him with a section of a tree branch in his hand. His eyes had a crazed look; his lips curled back, baring his teeth in a snarl.

"Wesichau!" shouted Rose again. He raised the limb, intent on crushing David's skull.

David rolled aside as the limb cracked, harmless, on the ground, then clambered up the slope, desperately grabbing at overhanging branches. A hand grabbed his ankle, pulling him backward. David spun and kicked out with his right leg, catching Rose fully in the face. The older man tumbled back with a gasp. Rose was cursing him in a language that he could not understand, nonsensical words, but unmistakable in their loathing.

Rose scrambled to his feet and charged again.

David aimed a right cross at the on-rushing madman. He misjudged the distance between them and his fist hit only empty air. Rose's fist slammed into his stomach, doubling him over. Then his knee caught David's chin. His head snapped sharply upward and he reeled backward, slumping into a heap.

His eyes refused to focus, and his jaw felt like it was broken. Pain racked his body. Dimly, he could see Rose advance toward him. He towered over David as he lifted his foot to smash his face.

David grabbed the foot and twisted. Rose staggered and fell heavily to the ground. Hale jumped up, crouching low. Before Rose could attack again, he delivered a savage uppercut that sent the larger man reeling backward. Rose was on his hands and knees. David kicked him in the ribs, which sent him tumbling over the edge of the hill. David could hear the body crashing through the underbrush as it rolled into the darkness.

Hale paused, trying to halt his gasping breath, listening. Nothing. Either Rose was lying unconscious at the foot of the hill, or he had run away. He turned and stumbled down the hill, holding his aching side.

CHAPTER TWENTY-TWO

Joe Witherspoon walked up the porch steps of the Rose house. He saw a light in the front room and could hear the muffled noise of a television. He knocked on the door and stepped back.

Clara Rose opened the door and turned on the porch light.

"Why, Joe," she said, "what are you doing out here this time of night?"

"Evening, Clara. I'd like to talk to Jack when he gets back. Do you mind if I wait inside?"

"Gets back? I don't understand. You can come in if you want, but Jack's been here since shortly after supper."

"What?" said Witherspoon. "You mean to say that he hasn't been out tonight? Something's not right here. You'd better let me talk to your husband."

Clara held the door open and Witherspoon walked into the living room, removing his hat. He stopped abruptly when he saw Jack Rose sitting in a chair reading the paper.

"Jack," he said. "Are you all right?"

"Hello, Joe," replied Rose, putting down the paper and rising. "What do you mean, 'am I all right?'"

"David Hale told me that you and he had a fight out by Spirit Rock tonight. He's over at Doc Burke's getting his ribs wrapped. I've been out combing the woods over there looking for you."

"What in the hell are you talkin' about, Joe?" asked Rose, incredulous.

Witherspoon repeated what David had told him in the doctor's office. At the end, Rose just shook his head. "I don't know why he would tell you a tale like that. I talked to David at the café, all right, but we just chewed the fat about how he was getting along, and remembered some old times with me and his daddy."

"And you're saying that the two of you didn't go out to Spirit Rock and have a fight?"

"Hell, no!" roared Rose. "If he told you that, then the boy must be crazy! Why, Frank Hale and I were friends for over twenty years. I practically helped raise David. I don't know what would make him say such things."

"How did you get that?" asked Witherspoon, pointing to an abrasion on Rose's forehead.

"Oh, this? I was driving home and saw Mason Thomas' truck on the side of the road. Mason was working under the hood, so I stopped and gave him a hand. I raised up when we finished and bumped my fool head on the hood. That's the truth. Ask Mason."

"I'll do that," said Witherspoon, not looking forward to another encounter with Thomas. "If David was lying, do you want to swear out a warrant on him?"

"Good Lord, no. Why should I do that? I'll just talk to the boy some time next week. He's been working out at that excavation with that old professor and those college kids. Maybe they got him to smoking those funny cigarettes. That's the only thing I can figure that would make David tell a story like that."

"You're sure that's all there was to it?"

"Goddammit! I told you it was, didn't I?" shouted Rose. "It's David you need to be talking to!"

Rose's face was livid; his fists were clenched. Witherspoon was startled by the sudden anger. He looked from Rose to Clara, who lowered her eyes, embarrassed.

"I'm going to talk to David again," said Witherspoon, breaking the awkward silence. "You can be sure of it. Well, if you don't want to do anything else about it, I'll just say good night. I'm sorry to have disturbed you folks so late."

"Look, Joe," said Rose, suddenly calm, "I didn't mean to fly off the handle like that. It's just that for the life of me I can't figure why David would tell you such a wild thing. I'll see him later and get this mess all straightened out."

Clara followed the sheriff out to the porch.

"Does Jack get mad like that often?" he asked her.

"He never used to," she said. "But about two, three weeks ago, he went out hunting with Mason Thomas; they stayed out most of the night. Drinking, I guess. Since then, it seemed the least little thing would set him off."

"When did he start being so friendly with Mason Thomas? I thought they didn't much like each other."

"They didn't," replied Clara, speaking in a low voice and glancing periodically over her shoulder at the door. "At least, not until recently. Here lately, Mason has been calling Jack up to go out hunting or down to the roadhouse. Jack never used to like doing that kind of thing. Now he comes home drunk and sullen. I tell you the truth, Joe, it's like he is a different man. Sometimes I'm scared to even talk to him. I never know when something is going to set him off, like tonight."

"Well, I have to admit, that doesn't sound like Jack. But a lot of people have been acting differently lately. Maybe I'll come out and talk to the two of you again. Till then, you take care. Let me know if there's anything I can do for you."

Clara Rose nodded gravely. It seemed to Witherspoon that she didn't really want him to leave.

The sheriff didn't understand what was going on, but it was decidedly peculiar. He had known David Hale all of his life and he was not the sort of man to make up stories like this. He'd been hurt out there in the woods, there was no doubt about that, but it couldn't have been Jack Rose. Jack was telling the truth, Witherspoon was sure of it; he had known Jack Rose for more years than he could remember. But then, he was not the kind of man to take up with Mason Thomas and go around drinking at night. Something strange was going on, and he was going to find out what it was, one way or another.

Because of his bruised ribs, David was ordered by Dr. Burke to call someone to drive him home. David dialed Arthur Walters's number, and within a few minutes they were driving the short distance to David's duplex.

Before the professor could express his alarm over the way David looked, he told the older man about his experience, but decided to keep his suspicions about Singer to himself.

Walters shook his head. "What could have caused Jack Rose to act in such a lunatic fashion? Are you sure he hadn't been drinking?"

"No, he wasn't drunk. He seemed to go crazy momentarily. He was shouting at me, some sort of gibberish. It sounded like 'Wash-ee-cha,' or 'Wes-ee-chow,' some word like that, over and over, as he attacked me."

Walters frowned, slowing the car as it reached David's street. "Perhaps he was deranged. I suppose this heat could drive anyone 'round the bend, especially if you are out climbing—you said you were scouting a new hunting area for extending the dig, was it?"

"Yes, that's right." It was a spurious story, and from the professor's expression, David did not think he believed it.

"'Wes—eecha,' you say he shouted?"

"Yes, a word like that. Why?"

The professor shrugged. "Perhaps the heat is getting to me as well. Or else the misfortunes at the excavation have taken their toll. The word, if it was a word, sounds Siouxian, of the Sioux group of languages."

"What does it mean?"

"I don't know. Perhaps I could look it up, as a sort of fool's chore. I would imagine, though, it is Roseian for 'I'm drunk,' or something similar."

David was forced to laugh, but the sharp pain in his ribs made him stop.

Walters stopped in front of the duplex and cut off the engine. "David, one more thing. Perhaps we should keep this little episode between you and Rose from Diana, at least for the time being. We went over to Asheboro this morning, to see her mother...you know the circumstances of my wife's illness, I believe."

"Yes, sir."

"I'm afraid the visit was more depressing than usual. I, uh, Diana has been under a strain lately..."

"I wasn't planning to go into the details with her. I thought I would say that I fell off the path, or something similar. I don't think Witherspoon or Burke believe me, anyway."

The older man turned in his seat. "It has been a strange, very strange summer. But I didn't want Diana to be overly upset; I believe she cares for you, David. I suppose it's none of my business, but I hope you have similar feelings. I like you, David. And it's time Diana had some real happiness in her life."

Before David could reply, Walters opened his side door. "Here, I'll help you into your house, young man." The faint trace of a smile played over his lips as together they slowly negotiated the steps leading to the front door.

John Singer left the clearing, holding close to the tree line for several hundred feet, and then began following an almost invisible trail through the woods. There was a new moon and all the light of the world seemed to have disappeared; but he was able to follow the trail. He could smell that this path was used years ago; knew the moccasins that had pushed back the undergrowth over time, until there was a hollowed-out path beneath the small shrub and brush that had grown over it since then.

More knowledge was flowing to him now from what the shaman called 'the other side of the river.' He could feel the energy that lay over there, to his left now, beyond the trees across the water.

It was his companion, a presence, a current of energy and life. He was constantly aware of it, as a pigeon is always aware of his home over the hill.

The sack was not heavy, and he shifted it from one shoulder to the other.

He listened to the dry clack of the contents clicking together. They formed a rhythm that gave him joy. The trees were thick and close together now, and he felt completely at home covered over by them in the moonless night. His gait was rapid and straight, and silent except for the clacking as he moved his precious load from one shoulder to the other.

The bones were talking to him. They said:

You are the last stone in the wall.

You are the link that will complete the circle.

You are us. We are you.

John Singer followed the path, beginning to climb now toward Spirit Rock. He was very happy listening to the bones, walking straight and without a sound.

Climbing into the dark, he knew joy and peace.

CHAPTER TWENTY-THREE

At his office, Joe Witherspoon let still another antacid pill dissolve on his tongue. It was past six o'clock and he had spent half the afternoon tossing Peter Blackwell's motel room without success. Witherspoon had expected to find at least some sort of drug— anything at all would have been sufficient for his purposes— so he could put the smart-mouth bastard in jail. He was certain Blackwell had set up some kind of drug operation in the area; perhaps he was not the only pusher, either.

To Witherspoon, illegal drugs would do much to explain the bizarre events of the summer. He knew cocaine use could cause heart seizure, which might account for Dawes' heart attack. Blackwell had been on the scene there; to Witherspoon that was evidence in itself.

Schlosser's suicide could have been the result of drugs, even if Doc Burke's theory about psychological problems were true. Or maybe he had o.d.'ed right there in his makeshift darkroom, his head merely falling softly forward into the chemical solution. The sheriff wished he had asked for special toxicological tests on the bodies before they were sent home for burial.

His stomach growled, reminding him he was very late for supper. The thought of the bland food waiting at home depressed him. He stood up to leave. Let Ed, his deputy, run the office for a while.

The telephone rang. "Sheriff, for you on line one," Ed called out from the other room.

"Witherspoon," he said into the receiver.

"Sheriff? This is David Hale."

"Yeah, David. What can I do for you?"

"I was wondering if you had spoken to Jack Rose again."

"David, I told you there was nothing more I can do about that. Mason Thomas swears Jack was helping him fix a busted radiator hose on his truck at the very time you say the two of you were fighting."

"Mason Thomas is either lying or crazy. Or both."

"Well, maybe he is crazy. But as far as the law is concerned, I have no evidence to arrest him for assault. That's got to be the end of it, unless you can come up with some new evidence."

Hale hung up without another word. Witherspoon replaced the receiver, another dark thought running through his mind. He didn't want to believe it, but perhaps Hale was mixed up in whatever Blackwell had going. If drugs could make Blackwell run around the streets naked as a jaybird, they could certainly make David Hale bang up his ribs and hallucinate about being beaten by Jack Rose. It all kept coming back to drugs as an explanation of the weird things that had been happening.

It was only speculation, but it made a certain kind of sense. What would keep a kid like Blackwell around a small town like Clearview unless he had brought his own action? He recalled he'd never seen Blackwell without a certain wild, almost feral look in his eye. And whatever was giving him that look was spreading. Maybe he was planning to sell drugs to the kids when school started again in the fall.

Yeah, it was drugs, all right. He'd better do something about that kid right now, before anything else happened.

He rose from the desk. "I'm going out, Ed. Listen, you call Mrs.

Campbell over at the motel and tell her to let you know the minute that Blackwell kid shows up. Then you radio me. I'm going out now to try and find the bastard."

"He do something else, Sheriff?"

"I just know he's dirty, Ed. He's bound to have his stash in that car. And when I see it, I'm going to find an excuse to stop him and toss it."

Ed was already dialing the motel. "If you need some help, Joe, I could call in Walt Meade to watch the office."

"No. I'll handle this myself."

Witherspoon drove the roads and highways around Clearview until well after midnight, his gut gnawing fiercely. He drove almost to Ulah and circled back, then drove the highway in the other direction until Ed's voice on the radio was faint and full of static.

Mrs. Campbell had decided to evict her troublesome tenant, but Blackwell had not returned to the motel for several days. Maybe the pusher had gotten wind of his suspicions and was gone for good. It was just as well; he had come to feel that if he ever saw Blackwell again, one of them would not walk away.

CHAPTER TWENTY-FOUR

"Do you want me to drive?" Diana asked.

David's ribs ached each time he had to turn the steering wheel, but they were out of town now and the road would be straight for a while, until they reached Chapel Hill, where the professor had sent them to re-read an old manuscript that might provide evidence for his Lost Colony theory.

Hale had decided to tell Diana of the Rose incident, but toned it down, making it sound as if it were an accidental injury from a friendly scuffle. He did not want to see the same sort of disbelief in her eyes that he had encountered in those of others to whom he had told the story. Nor did he want to have another argument with her about Singer; she thought his suspicions about the man were based on jealousy over the respect the others had for his uncanny ability to find valuable specimens. So David had backed off. There was a lot of the scientist in her; she had to be shown hard evidence. He had the uncomfortable impression that his comments smacked of small-town provincialism to her. It was an image he was fighting against.

As he entered the gates of the university at Chapel Hill, the campus seemed strangely deserted, until David remembered that it was a Saturday. They parked in the visitors' parking area behind the administration building and walked across the brick pathways in the quad between South Building and the library.

The building harkened back to the neo-classical period of the nineteen-twenties. The entrance opened into a large foyer; at the other side was a double circular marble stairway. David wished fleetingly that he could work at a library like this, then took Diana's arm and guided her down a long hallway. An occasional student passed them, their steps reverberating down the hall; but mostly they had the library to themselves.

He opened the door to the Southern Historical Collection, and they walked up to the woman behind the desk. "We'd like to see the 1832 manuscript of Father McGill," Diana said. The library assistant had her fill out a request form, then rang a bell. A student came out of the adjoining room, took the slip and disappeared down a long hall. In five minutes, he was back carrying an old, leather-bound volume.

They sat down at one of the long tables in the main reading room. David carefully opened the book and slowly turned the brittle yellowed paper.

"Okay, what are we looking for?" he asked.

"Any evidence of a European dying in the Clearview area tribal site, any early traveler who might have been buried in the grave at the clearing. Father McGill was an early visitor. But as you know, the Clearview Library copy of Father McGill's travels in North Carolina is an edited version."

David skimmed several pages in silence. "Okay, McGill began his journey on December 28, 1832, from Charleston, South Carolina, by water to the mouth of the Santee River; followed the Santee to the Catawba River, through the land of the Congaree, Santee, and Waxhaw tribes until he came to some Southern Catawbas. From there he entered North Carolina, going as far as the 'Occaneechi' village. After spending some time there, he journeyed to the Sugeree, Saponi...here it is: he then came to the Keyauwee camp after crossing the Cape Fear and Yadkin Rivers."

Diana grabbed David's arm. "Listen to this." She read aloud:

*While remaining with these Savages, I wit-
nessed a raid by a neighboring tribe and the Cruel
and Barbaric practices by which they treat of their
Captives. The tribe all made a circle around a
great fire; the Prisoner then had pine slivers
inserted into his skin. These were lighted and He
was made to dance around the fire until he expired.
The tribe then watched to see if the Captive died
well, for therein lay the portents of the future of the
tribe."*

David read further in a hushed voice:

*The overseer of this barbaric ritual was a
powerful young Shaman named Sparrow of Snow.
he made no Secret of his dislike for me and his
disdain of all white men. I suspect he saw a threat
to his power by my bringing the Christian message
to his people. I was informed by a young brave of
a Great Prophecy that had been handed down to
the Shaman which was the Source of his great
Power.*

*Although my Ministry was favorably received
by only a few members of the tribe, this small
victory seemed to anger Sparrow of Snow. He was
determined to reveal me as a false Prophet. For my
benefit, he called for the Fire Ritual, a Loathesome
heathen practice that filled my heart with dread;
for it was a supernatural practice. I was assured
this heathen was indeed of the Devil.*

*The Shaman commanded that a huge Bonfire
be lit, which burned throughout most of the day. At
sunset, it still burned fiercely, and the faggots were
spread out in a continuous path a yard in width and*

did proceed to perform the ritual. In awe, I witnessed the spectacle whereby the Shaman walked some rods' length through the savage Fire and was unscathed. But he was most weakened by the feat, and I could have sworn there was more Ghost than flesh to the man, that some of him had been used up by the flames; though how he could burn and still live was beyond my imagination.

This put me in mind of the miracle of Shadrach, Meshach and Abednego in the fires of Nebuchadnezzar, but this Savage was surely of the Devil and not of our Lord. I crossed myself in fear for being in the presence of the Fallen One. Sparrow of Snow challenged me to perform the same feat, but I declined to engage in this Satanic ritual. At this, the members of the tribe were greatly agitated and advanced upon me. I surely would have been Killed had not the Shaman at that point raised his hand and Commanded that I be allowed to leave their village. His victory over the white man's God had been complete; he preferred that I leave the Village humiliated, but with my life. Thus he was the Victor and seen as Merciful too, though his eyes did not speak mercy, but Hate and Vengeful spite.

"That is an incredible story," said David.

"Yes," said Diana, "but there is still no mention of a death or burial. Apparently, no member of Father McGill's party was slain."

"So who could the Caucasian skeleton be that Schlosser found? Could it have been the body of a passing trader or trapper?"

"That seems unlikely, since tribal burial land would have been considered sacred, and taboo to outsiders. Anyway," she continued, "since we're here, let's go further in the manuscript and see if a stray comment explains anything." Diana had been scanning several pages as she spoke. Suddenly, she stopped. "Look, David. Here's a section where Father McGill talks about what happened on the trip back to Charleston. He mentions that a young brave of the Uwharrie tribe named Two Crows agreed to be his guide and told him about something called 'The Ceremony of the Kings.' She read:

> *The Funeral for a dead King, as the Uwharries call their Chief, is unsurpassed. Here Two Crows swore me to secrecy lest someone overhear our Conversation. To allay his fears, I walked a distance from the Campsite with him. On our walk, he told me of the Ceremony. The entire Village scatters ashes over their heads and rends their Clothing, and othewise Mourn and are in disarray for Twelve days and nights. Then the Elders, led by the Shaman, take the King's body up the Mountain in a solemn procession. A captive or prisoner of the tribe is selected to go with them. Other members of the Tribe are prevented from following by guards posted at the foot of the Mountain. When I asked Two Crows what they did with the prisoner taken thus, he became sore afraid and would not speak for quite some time.*
>
> *When at last I implored him to speak, he would only say the Ceremony was of more Secret import than any other thing he knew, and if he said more, by Necromancy he and his wife would be in danger. I let him be, having my own memory of the Medicine Man and his Dark power, and considered Two Crows a prudent man for his further silence.*

"It sounds like the Ceremony was not performed in the village," said David. "More like a secret or secluded place where it would not be observed by the members of the tribe."

"Many primitive cultures, particularly a warrior society such as the Uwharrie, would select a site that could be sealed up. Some sort of tomb. Most probably, the generations of kings would be interred in this same place. A sacred burial ground, especially since kingship was of lineal descent from father to son."

"A cave, perhaps?" asked David.

"Exactly. But it would have had to remain a deep secret not to have been discovered after all these years."

"You mean then, that the kings would not be found in the clearing with the other members of the tribe. They would have been buried somewhere else? In the mountains?"

"All except Keyauwee Jack, the last king. Remember? According to the Priddy manuscript, the vigilantes interrupted his ceremony. So the twelve days would not have expired, and the Ceremony of the Kings would not have been performed for him."

They pored through the missionary's account for several more hours, but could not discover further germane references to the clearing. Finally, David leaned back in his chair, stretching his cramped back muscles.

"I guess we've gotten everything from this that we're going to," he sighed. "Want to call it a day?"

Diana reluctantly agreed, and they collected their notes, returned the volume and left the library. They speculated on the significance of the discovery that the last king was probably buried somewhere in the current dig. Would that excite Dr. Walters, or only serve as a further depressing setback to his beloved theory?

CHAPTER TWENTY-FIVE

The face of Sparrow-in-Snow was placid and like stone, as always, but Singer could see the pleasure in his eyes. There was a reflection there like the glint of a knife in the moonlight. John Singer knew his teacher was pleased, and this made him very proud.

"Now you will tell me of the Other Side," he told the shaman.

"Yes, John Singer, now I will tell you of the Other Side. But before this mystery is made clear to you, I must give you your true name. You are now a man full grown and a warrior of the tribe. You have come late to be a man and a warrior, but this was the word of the great prophecy, and so it is good. All the things of your life come from the prophecy, and it has been known since before your birth that when you became a warrior you would be Wolf-Singer, which is your true and real name now and in the past and forever. Say your true name, man and warrior."

"Wolf-Singer is my true name now and forever."

"Good. And you are the same blood of your great-grandfather Singing Wolf, who was a chief of the Uwharries."

"Yes, I am the same blood of my great-grandfather Singing Wolf."

"And you are the same blood of your great-grandfather's father, the great Chief Keyauwee Jack."

"Yes, I am the same blood."

"Give me your hand, Wolf-Singer."

The shaman took a knife from his belt and cut a thin strip completely across the palm of his right hand. In the moonlight, the red blood gleamed black; it had a metallic smell, like burning copper. The blood coagulated rapidly, leaving a ragged trail across the palm.

"Now your blood is spilled along with your great-grandfather and the other chiefs, and your blood and pain are part of the tribe. This bond can never be broken, even as the river can never be broken."

Wolf-Singer was very proud and happy; he felt stronger for the pain and the black blood and the burning metal smell in his nostrils.

"Now," said Sparrow-in-Snow, "I will tell you of the secret of the river, and of the Other Side of the River, your true home. Where you came from and where you will go when your blood at last ceases to flow in your veins."

"My father was a shaman, and before that his father, and his father past all memory. But before us all there was a shaman named Man of Water. It was said that his mother bore him while she was bathing in the river, and that he swam out of her belly and up to the air, like a fish. Thereafter, his power came from the River, which is the source of much magic among the Uwharrie. And when he was old, he returned to the River, and drowned there to fulfill the destiny of his name.

"All shaman have the power to do magic, and to mix herbs and roots, and to heal by invoking the Great Spirit. And they are able to understand dreams, and to take from dreams the meaning of what has happened in the past, and what will come in the future. Man of Water was the greatest shaman in the understanding of dreams, such that he knew all things of the past and of the future.

"In the days when the Wesichau were few, and the tribe was thousands upon thousands, there came a drought on the land, and the hard rains did not fall for three snow seasons. The corn and grains died in the field, and even the great river, the source of the tribe's magic, became as a mere trickle over muddy rocks at the bottom. This was in the time when the great shaman Man of Water was young, and during the third snow season of the drought, Man of Water was to take the warrior test. He did this, and while he was in the sweat house, he had a dream that was a vision, and was the first of his great visions which came from the river and from the sky.

"Since there had been Time, our tribe had lived and harvested crops on this side of the river, for the other side was a raiding ground of the northern tribes when they came. Our crops would have been burned in the field and our women slaughtered had the camp been there. So it was a dangerous place, and looked upon as bad magic. Our women and boys when bathing were careful even at low points never to go beyond the middle of the river, and it was taboo to do so.

"Man of Water had a dream in the sweat house, and told it to the elders when his time there was up and he was a man and warrior. In this dream, he flew from the sweat house up so high in the air that no bird could approach him, and the river below was like a string of blue and the mountain was a small hill, like ants would make. Man of Water knew this to be magic, and at first was not afraid, but as he flew the wind of the North caught him and blew him over the river, far to the other side. He knew this to be taboo, and thought the Great Spirit had punished him for weakness in the sweat house, and that he would be dashed to the ground from the great height and be killed. But this did not happen. He did fall, but landed on the back of a hawk, who told him not to fear, and the hawk carried him at great speed far to the North, over the great mountain known as La-weh. and they went higher and faster till he could see no land or water below him at all, and it was as if the world had disappeared altogether.

"Colder and colder the air grew, darker and darker was the sky above, so that it was almost black, though the sun was still in the middle of the sky, and he saw no moon. The hawk again said not to fear, and Man of Water was brave and shook off the cold which was like ice in the winter.

"But the cold increased, and Man of Water was near frozen, and thought he would die from the cold and the dark. But the hawk let him down on a dark cloud, and disappeared. There was thunder and lightning, and man of Water again knew great fear. And then a voice came from out of the thunder that Man of Water knew was the Great Spirit.

"The Great Spirit had a voice that was like a man and a woman and an animal all at the same time, and it filled the sky and was louder than the thunder, and each word brought another lightning bolt. The Great Spirit told Man of Water not to be afraid, because he was summoned to the cloud for a purpose, and the thunder and dark and rain was to keep the face of the Great Spirit from being seen, for only those of the tribe who had died were allowed to view the Great Spirit.

"The Great Spirit told Man of Water that the drought would end, but not before half of the old men and women and half of the young children would die. But the tribe was not to grieve for the dead because they were to come to a place that was to be bright and happy and they would be with the Great Spirit and never know hunger or war or sickness ever again. Man of Water was to tell the tribe not to grieve, but to ready themselves for great changes.

"The Great Spirit said that the world of the Uwharrie was shrinking, like a hide left in the sun, and that when the tribe had shrunk to nothing, there would be another world which would come, but it would be in the sky beyond the North Wind. Fire and water would destroy the old world and the Wesichau that were evil. A fire would rage, and the river would split, and certain prophecies would come to pass, the words of which had not yet been made up. But the new world would be green and fruitful, and with game and fish and sweet berries for the Uwharrie to eat, and every member of the tribe who had ever died would be in the new world; each family united, and each brother with each brother, and father with son, and mother with child. In the new sky world there would be no Wesichau, only Uwharrie, and the tribe would be together in a circle forever under the robe of the Great Spirit, and all would rejoice when this happened.

"The Great Spirit pulled back the lightning and the thunder for a moment, and Man on Water saw a glimpse of the new world as it would be. He saw people dancing, and holding hands together, and great and powerful men who were chiefs sat in a circle in the middle of the dancers. And Man of Water saw one of the dancers was his father, who had been dead for five years; and his father was happy and still wore the mark of the shaman, and was young and strong. He also saw birds of the air that lighted on a tree, and the birds were so many the branches of the tree popped and split from their weight.

"And he saw the river flowing swiftly, and fish jumped out of the river by the thousand, so that the water looked to be boiling, there were so many fish. And he saw corn that was higher than the head of a man on horseback, and the fields were so vast he could not see the end of them. And the number of dancing people was thousands upon thousands, as it was supposed to be in the old days before the Wesichau. Then the Great Spirit pulled the thunder and lightning back, and the green land was behind the darkness again. He told Man of Water to remember what he had seen, because there would come a time when his dreams would tell him what the tribe must do so that all could live and be happy in the new world in the sky. He would have visions which would be a prophecy to follow in the bad times when the circle of the tribe shrank, and the men and women died like insects, and the blood of the tribe trickled like the river in the drought.

"And then the Great Spirit said a strange thing which Man of Water did not understand. The vision which would lead the Uwharrie to the new world would come to pass only after all the tribe was dead but one. Man of Water would dream and have the vision, and make a prophecy. But only a shaman of the future, when the Wesichau had overrun the old world, would interpret and carry out the prophecy. Only one of Uwharrie blood would be left, but through him the prophecy would be fulfilled. And this last Uwharrie, who would be in the line of a great chief, must bring the fire and water to destroy the old world of the Wesichau."

CHAPTER TWENTY-SIX

Ed handed Joe Witherspoon the teletyped message when he walked in the door from a lunch of poached eggs and milk at Mabe's cafe. It was the report of a background check on all the members of the dig that a friend of his in the State Bureau of Investigation had run for him out of Raleigh. Peter Blackwell did indeed have an arrest sheet; he was arrested two years ago for possession of cocaine at a rock concert. All charges had been dropped, probably at the instigation of his influential father.

Anne Morris, until recently a companion of Blackwell, was a sorority sister at the University of North Carolina. She was a good student, a former class sweetheart, and on the homecoming court. She had never been in trouble. Witherspoon shook his head, wondering what she saw in a punk like Blackwell.

Both Roger Dawes and Bill Schlosser had been typical, all-American boys: Boy Scouts, high school and college athletes. Schlosser had been in the army, was honorably discharged and had gone to school on the G.I. bill and an academic scholarship.

So, that was basically it. A frustrating dead end. He couldn't remember when he'd felt so confused. None of it made any sense;

even the Blackwell drug angle was finding a rough furrow in his thinking now. He had even tried to link Blackwell and Singer, the Indian who had recently joined the dig. But all he could find out suggested Singer was just a burn-out who preferred to live as a semi-recluse up in the hills.

Witherspoon began to wonder if something was wrong with his mind as well as his stomach. Maybe the heat was getting to him too, and causing him to imagine things and chase shadows. He still thought something was not right somehow, but it was a mystery to him how or even if any of the facts fit together. Unless he wanted to agree with David Hale that somebody like Jack Rose was a secret madman.

He'd keep trying, although he was beginning to think maybe John Singer had the right idea. Seclude yourself on a mountain and let the craziness in the valley below pass you by.

Harry Wiggins was jolted awake from his nap by the nightmare. Or maybe it wasn't a nightmare. It was more like a bolt of light tearing through his brain. He shook his head, trying to clear it, to get his bearings.

Wait a minute, he thought, just calm down. You're not at the hospital anymore. You're here in your own bedroom. It's broad daylight...

The center of his head seemed to be burning, like those horrible moments he woke up after shock treatments in the hospital. He could visualize those moments very clearly, although most of the rest of his hospital stay was a foggy blur.

They'd strapped him down, put needles in his arms.There was a surge of whiteness, of pain and heat, and after that, unconscious-ness. He'd wake up down the hallway on a roller bed, disoriented, always focusing on the once-familiar white ceiling of the hallway as if it were some strange and frightening place.

This room was frightening and strange now. But it was his own room. Or was it? He checked to see if the high school pennant was on the wall; yes, and in the same place. There was the bookcase with the same disordered paperbacks.

No, he wasn't in the hospital. He was in his bedroom at home. There were no orderlies or doctors in sight. He was home, safe.

We've taken care of everything, Harry.

Where had he heard that? Did an orderly say that to him one day? One orderly had been blonde; wasn't he the one with curly hair? The one that...

No. The curly-headed man was at the drive-in.

He had a headache. He stumbled to the bathroom, opened the medicine cabinet, and took down a bottle of aspirin. The two pills stuck in his throat and he bent over to drink water from the tap. He swallowed.

The sound of running water was very loud.

The blonde-headed man had been young, he had a crazy grin. He wore a sport jacket with a fraternity crest on the pocket. He was not an orderly at the hospital.

Harry turned off the spigot; his ears were ringing from the sound of water.

Overhead, it had been black, very black. There were eyes peering at him, eyes the color of fire...bending over him. Silent. Hot. Close.

The aspirin must have given him heartburn, he thought. His chest felt warm. But it wasn't inside, it was the skin. Spots of skin on his chest and his stomach. He raised his shirt to see if he were bleeding.

No blood. Just reddish marks, like healed-over blisters. They hadn't been there last night, when he'd tried to talk to Cindy; she'd begun to cry and then slammed down the phone. He couldn't understand why she was so frightened of him since...since the drive-in a week earlier. He'd been even more depressed and confused, slept all night, then wanted more sleep. Laid down for a nap. Then the dream and the bolt of light.

Want us to make him get up and dance?

The spots burned with a sharp pain.

What's happening to me? he thought. Am I going crazy again?

Why, you've been chosen, of course. Take it easy, Harry.

Shaking, Wiggins opened his closet door and got to his knees, scrambled around until he found it behind some old loafers. Yes, it was still there. He thought maybe he had dreamed going down to the basement yesterday, where his father had kept all the tools. Tools and other things. Like the corded nylon rope strong enough to pull the limb off a tree.

He'd taken eight feet of it and fashioned a makeshift noose, slipping the square knot over the other end and pulling it along the length..

I ought to use this, he thought. *Ought to use this right now.* He stared at the doorway; he could loop the straight end over the top of the door and close and lock it. It would hold, wouldn't slip. The overhead light was fastened to a strong fixture—maybe that would be even better.

But he was too scared, too confused. He didn't want to kill himself; just wanted these feelings to leave him, to go away. The nightmares, the aura that he was now something different, had gone crazy in an unfixable way. The eyes he felt inside him, the burning spots on his chest. Who am I now? he thought.

He panicked again, threw the rope back into the closet, and ran out of the house, feeling that something was after him, an invisible force chasing after him. Or maybe something *inside*, running right along with him.

A few streets in the bright sun and he was at the drug store; he looked desperately through the window, saw his mother behind the cosmetics counter. But there were three customers waiting for her. He couldn't go in there like this, crazy like this.

Then he saw Ed, the deputy, pull his patrol car up to the sheriff's office, and he ran as fast as he could toward the policeman.

CHAPTER TWENTY-SEVEN

Arthur Walters reached over to the tobacco tin and carefully filled the bowl of his pipe with the sharp, pungent tobacco. He lit it, savoring this first relaxed afternoon in over three weeks. He languidly glanced at the book that lay open on the table beside him, but felt no desire to pick it up; indeed, he felt no desire to do anything other than just sit and let his tired muscles rest. The tragic incidents had put a damper on the dig, so he had told everyone to take several days off for a long weekend. That way, they would be refreshed and could put it all behind them and be ready to return to work. Schlosser's suicide had left a pall over all of them.

Diana had certainly changed her opinion of David, a thought that both pleased and disturbed Walters. She often immersed herself too heavily in her work. It had become a protective cocoon that shielded her from life; but the cocoon could become so comfortable that she might grow into an eccentric old workaholic, much like himself. He knew, beneath her professional facade, she was lonely. She needed to get out and experience life.

He blamed himself for her predicament. When Blanche became ill enough to require her to stay in the rest home in Asheboro, he had buried himself in work, trying to cope with his loneliness. So preoccupied was he with his wife's recovery, that he had ignored Diana during her early adult years, just when she needed him the most; it hadn't occurred to him how much her mother's illness had affected her; she had seemed like such a self-possessed young girl, mature well beyond her years.

Walters was interrupted from his thoughts by a rustling in the bedroom— not his bedroom, but the room, now unused which Blanche had used as a sickroom for some time years ago. The professor was alarmed by the sound. A prowler! he thought, frightened.

He did not believe in handguns and did not have one in the house. Looking about frantically for something to defend himself with, his eye rested on the poker in front of the fireplace. He quietly moved from behind his desk to the hearth, pulled the slender but heavy iron tool from its cradle, and walked gingerly to the study door.

Blanche's bedroom was just across the hall. He opened the study door a crack, listening intently. The rustling continued. Closer, it did not sound like someone trying to get in. The rustling was not the wind from an open window or the sliding open of a screen. He recognized the sound now; someone was making up a bed, moving covers and sheets over a mattress.

Who could it be? he thought. Diana had left with David for Chapel Hill. The maid only came one day a week, was not scheduled until Tuesday. Besides, it was past noon, and she always arrived early in the morning. Had his reverie made him so unconscious of sound that Diana had returned, the trip postponed for some reason? But what would she be doing in the old bedroom? She hated to go in there, it made her depressed to think of her mother, and she avoided the room completely.

There was only one way to find out—to cross the hall and open the door. He had taken a tentative step when the rustling of bedsheets stopped and another sound began. Humming.

Humming in a woman's voice. The tune was familiar. Walters gasped in a jolt of recognition. Blanche used to hum that tune as she worked around the house, years ago. He had almost forgotten. Walters felt strange, giddy from the melody. Was this some practical joke? Who could be so cruel as to...he was flooded with nostalgia and yearning, temporarily unable to move a step closer.

The tune was moving around the room, beyond the door. It moved close to the near wall. Then in back of the door, right across from where he stood.

The humming suddenly stopped. The door opened.

"Blanche," he said.

She smiled at him. "Arthur,"she said. "I'm home."

He looked at his wife in stunned silence. It *was* Blanche, but not the empty-eyed, slack-mouthed Blanche of the nursing home. It was his wife come back to him as she used to be.

"What...how...?" he started to say. This can't be happening, he thought. Simply can't.

She must have read his thoughts. "It's true. I'm here, and we're together again."

He started to pour out a dozen questions, but she held up her hand. "Don't ask why or how," she said. "Just be happy we can be together for a little while. I've missed you so, Arthur."

"And I you," he answered, his pulse still pounding. It was like a crazy dream, and yet so real. His wife was there, healthy, alive....desirable. He had never seen her look so youthful and radiant, almost glowing. Could he touch her? He moved forward, and she crossed to meet him. They embraced. Her arms around him were strong, they held him firmly. He pulled her close, amazed at her soft, fragrant realness. It was like reaching out for a mirage and finding it solid, substantive.

Her lips pressed against his. They were warm and compliant. If he was dreaming, he didn't want to wake up. Not now, not ever.

The drive through the countryside was like a miracle to Walters. He squinted at the road ahead, having left his glasses on his desk in his excitement; but that was unimportant now. He could hardly keep his eyes on the road for sneaking glances at his wife. The transformation was so startling he could hardly believe it. Not only was she smiling, with that old vitality and bright zest that first had made him love her as a young woman; she seemed to be younger by years, perhaps decades. It was as if she *was* that young girl again from so many years earlier. Just looking at her made the professor feel younger, stronger, more vigorous. He felt like a man again instead of a stodgy drudge, the academic dustbowl of dry facts and stale knowledge he had become lately. The spectre of the past few weeks, the death of the young worker and the tragedy concerning Schlosser, all receded into triviality compared to the resurrection he was witnessing beside him.

"What shall we do?" he asked her, ready to go anywhere, do anything she might wish. "I feel extravagantly energetic today, like a young man. We can drive to Asheboro and eat at that nice restaurant we used to go to. Remember?" He was recalling the special dinners he and his wife had had, the private reaffirmation of their love after Diana had gone off to college and they were again alone as man and wife. This period had been too brief; the illness had interrupted it at its height.

The beautiful woman leaned over, put her hand up to his neck and stroked the flesh there slowly and sensuously. "Yes," she said, "we can do that. But later. Right now, I want to drive out to that spot near Spirit Rock. You know the one." He felt her body slide across the seat until her warmth was pressing against him. His heart beat wildly, stirred with a desire he had almost forgotten he posssessed.

The woman leaned to whisper into his ear, then playfully bit the tip of his earlobe.

"Blanche," he said, both surprised and pleased, and a bit frightened. He was not sure he was up to the suggestion this suddenly different woman had so sensuously murmured. But if this was a fantasy, it must be played out. The wonderful reprieve he had been given might be snatched away at any moment. The professor felt this day might be the last chance he would have for love, for passion. He did not understand, but he would go along.

"All right," he agreed.

His wife continued to tease him with playful licks at his ear lobes. Once she buried her face in his neck, sucking on a sensitive spot that only she knew. Walters nearly ran the car off the road. He thought then that this new person she had become, this wild strangeness and wantonness, might be so different as to be dangerous. But then he thought, if that is to be, it will be. But for this one afternoon there will be life again. Things will be as they were, this afternoon at least, and damn what comes afterward.

The old road was a well-known lovers' lane during the school year. It had been a lovers' lane since he was a young man, and the pathway had not changed. The cool treees hung low, scraping the top of the car as he navigated the road. Once, many years ago, he had brought Blanche here, and on a chilly fall night she had given herself to him for the first time.

The nostalgia of that memory flooded over him as he slowed the car, saw the big tree that still remained from those days, the one they had parked under out of sight of any prying eyes.

This summer afternoon there were no other cars around, and even if there had been, he wouldn't have cared. If the whole senior class of the high school had been sprawled on the grass, he would have waved and smiled proudly.

"Hurry," the woman said. Her breath was hot on his neck; the smell of her perfume was sweet and delicate. He pulled the car over behind the elm, slammed on the emergency brake, and suddenly they were in each other's arms, kissing and caressing like two teenagers.

"Darling," he said.

"Shh, don't say a word. Just take me. Now."

Walters pulled back, and gasped. The woman with the parted lips, with the entreating voice, could not be his wife. She was so young. It was his wife twenty years ago. And the eyes were wild, glittering. Her skin was darker, tight across the cheek bones.

"This is a dream," he said. "A beautiful, terrible dream. I must be going mad."

"No, this is real. I am real. I want you." She scattered the buttons of her blouse in one motion, unsnapped the restricting brassiere. Her breasts were firm, high.

He was aware of urgent hands pulling at his belt, his trousers being tugged open, the air cool on his hips and thighs, the fabric of the seat against his buttocks. He opened his shirt so that her breasts might swell against his chest. She covered his mouth with hers.

The woman's legs held him like a vise, squeezing. He arched his back as the woman moved her tongue to the side of his neck and bit, hard, very hard.

At the moment of final pleasure his heart almost stopped. His eyes closed and his breathing took several minutes to slow to a near-normal rate.

"I didn't think that I could ever feel like that again, Blanche," he said finally. "It was beautiful. You've made an old man very happy."

"Not so old," smiled the woman, gently touching his cheek.

"Shall we go to dinner now?" he asked.

"Take me back to the house, first," she sighed. "I'm tired." She opened the front door. "Do you mind terribly if I rest in the back seat, dear?" she asked sweetly. "I need to lie down for just a while."

"Of course," he said, as she climbed into the rear seat and closed the door.

Driving down Lawson Road, he hummed the same tune that he had heard Blanche humming in the bedroom; he was near-oblivious of the steep road and sharp curves.

How odd, he thought again, that she should show up here, without any word from the rest home. How had she gotten here?

Something wasn't right, but he couldn't quite place it. Then he cursed himself for questioning this miracle that had been given him. But he could not shake the ominous feeling that was slowly overtaking him. It was almost like a presence, right here in the car...

He heard Blanche rising to sit upright. How silly of him to cloud such a beautiful day with such absurd thoughts. His wife had returned and that was all that mattered. He smiled and glanced into the rear-view mirror.

What he saw was not Blanche's face. It was that of a young

maiden with tan, smooth skin and black shiny hair. She was beautiful, but her eyes flashed hatred as she sat there, immobile, glaring at him.

For an instant, he was transfixed, staring incomprehensibly into the mirror. As the car careened over the hillside, the last vision that Arthur Walters ever had was of that face; a shifting mixture of his lovely, lost Blanche and some wild, primitive thing...

The woman stood on the hill gazing down impassively at the burning machine. The smell of her perfume was offensive to her, and as she turned and began to walk through the woods, she breathed deeply of the smell of pine and earth to reduce her discomfort. She could hear the river in the distance. She ran for a while, taking pleasure in the exertion, exhilarating in the contraction of her muscles as they guided her swiftly and noiselessly though the wood.

It was late when David turned into the Walters driveway. There was a light rain falling that made visibility difficult. Diana had fallen asleep during the drive, and David was about to wake her when he saw the flashing red light of Witherspoon's car parked in front of the house.

"The ambulance has already taken the body to the morgue," Witherspoon later told David as a stricken Diana entered the house. "I thought you might want to go there in the morning and make arrangements." He looked over his shoulder at the house. "Maybe you can talk Miss Walters out of going with you. The car crashed and caught fire. The professor's body is pretty much of a mess. You know what I mean?"

"Yes, of course. Thank you, Sheriff," he mumbled, staring at the ground in shock.

Witherspoon nodded and got into his car. He closed the door and put the car in gear, then stopped, leaned his elbow on the window ledge, as if he had just thought of something. "You know what the professor would be doing out near Lovers' Lane? I just can't figure it."

"No, I don't," replied David. "Diana and I drove over to Chapel Hill this morning. We didn't expect to be getting back this late. Dr. Walters was fine when we left him. He said he was tired and meant to spend the day inside."

When Witherspoon drove off, David turned and ran up the steps and into the house, looking for Diana.

She was curled up on the sofa, crying. David felt helpless and awkward, too numbed by the tragedy to know how to comfort her. Finally, he sat down beside her and pulled her up against his chest, hugging her tightly. Her crying gradually ceased.

Soon she stood up and slowly walked over to her father's favorite reading chair beside the fireplace. She let her fingers idly trace the outlines of the opened book on the table.

David noticed the professor's glasses resting on a pile of papers. "I thought your father was nearly blind without those," he said.

She picked up the glasses. "Yes, he was. He'd have never gone out of the house without them. Not unless something happened that would make him forget."

"Well, he was working on something here," said David, bending down to peer at some scribbled notes on a pad. They seemed to be various spellings of words that made no sense to him. He picked up the book that lay face down beside the glasses. "*Lingusitic Origins of North American Indian Dialects,*" he read aloud. A sheaf of paper was protruding from the book. He pulled it loose and scanned down the page.

"What is it?" Diana asked.

David shrugged. "Nothing," he said. He waited until she turned away, then quickly folded the paper and slipped it into his shirt pocket. No, he thought, this is not the time to talk about it. Not even to himself.

Part III

August

CHAPTER TWENTY-EIGHT

The shaman's eyes caught those of Singer's and held them. It was as if they were magnets that drew and focused attention, then slowly began to pull him in.

Singer was being pulled closer, then closer still. But his fear was leaving him. The red glint in the eyes was fire, he now knew; a deep and constant burning which was timeless, imperishable; but as it destroyed, so could it cleanse.

He felt himself being pulled harder, gently but with urgency, into the vision the old man saw. And in a moment he was inside, looking out. What the shaman saw, he could see. The words the shaman now spoke were what he, Singer, had also lived and experienced. So too could he now see—and begin to understand.

"In the days when King Keyauwee Jack was newly dead and taken to the charnel house, and Singing Wolf was still a babe slung behind his mother's back, there came to the village white men who tried to buy the last of our hunting lands. Perhaps they came because the King had passed over the waters, and the tribe was not yet certain as to who would be the new king. Many of our tribe had died over the winter because of the white man's sickness of the red spots.

There were some who said the king passed over the waters because of his grief that so many brave young men had perished, and perhaps this was true. But there were only the elders left to make counsel, and these had no power to make a war council and gather the warriors. And the whites who were weak of limb but strong of mind knew this.

"A shaman does magic, and magic was needed then. Only magic could keep the circle together. So the elders called for me. What can we do? they asked me. I went to the river and stayed there three suns, without food or water. Then I went to the mountain and stayed there three more suns, and ate the bitter root. and I saw, as Man of Water had seen before me, that the spirit of the tribe would be scattered, and the circle broken, but that it would come together again many days after the elders were gone, and even the babes were gone. All this I saw, and I knew it was what the Great Spirit had set down for the Uwharrie. So I went back and told the elders. Where is your magic? they said. I told them I would not do magic against the Great Spirit, because that would only bring death, and the tribe would be scattered without hope of redemption forever.

"I knew that the whites would soon return to claim our land, and this time the whole village would be rubbed out. I saw flames and bullets, and that all there would die. I knew the braves would be in mourning, and drink the bitter root as is the custom twelve suns after the death of a king. As shaman, I could have forbidden the custom, and raised a war council; or even moved time about so that the mourning would be over before the whites came, and our braves would be ready for the attack and slaughter the whites. All this I saw, and all this I could do as shaman. But it was against the prophecy of Man of Water, and therefore against the Great Spirit.

"I could not make the elders see that the Great Spirit would allow this terrible thing to happen because it was a trail that must be followed to the end. The vision foretold of a time of separation, and of hardship and cold and starvation, and of death in a hundred ways not of the warrior. This was a dark prophecy, but the end of the prophecy would bring the tribe together again forever. But the elders said that I was a bad shaman, and was weak in magic, and other lies. They were too old and weak to know truth anymore, but only those things of the earth which all can see, and not the spirit truth, which only a shaman or a king can see, if he is wise.

"So I knew that the village must perish. All perish, except for one woman and one boy babe, for whom I had a plan. The woman was Bright Fawn, the youngest wife of King Keyauwee Jack, and the boy babe was his only surviving son. His name was Singing Wolf, your great-grandfather.

"The elders and the warriors began to prepare for the mourning ritual. I supervised the ritual bath each took in the river, to harden his body and cleanse him of all weakness and cowardice.

"I knew the whites would be many and the village would not last long. But I said nothing; the warriors were content and smeared their bodies with bear grease and berry juice, as was our custom. By dusk they had drunk the bitter root, and my work was near an end at the village. Because Bright Fawn loved one handmaiden, I ordered the woman to leave the camp and travel south; thus she was saved as well. Then I left with the widow and the babe near dawn, to travel west, to the camps of the Cherokee. When we were some distance into the woods, I heard the shots and could see with my inner eyes the flames and our people burning. And this saddened me, but it had to be. I knew also there would be three whites coming after us, and when they came I made their rifles turn against them so that their own bullets killed them.

"It was ten suns until we reached the Cherokee camp, a hard journey, but the women were strong, and so was the boy child, as befitted the son of a king. When they were taken in, my work was done, and I left to wander alone in the mountains. I did not want to stay with the Cherokee, and they would have not had me, since I was a Uwharrie shaman and therefore too powerful and dangerous in their minds.

"I went north, and two days later met a raiding party of the Seneca. I killed four of them and was killed in turn. In the fight, my ear was severed and the sparrow bone-charm fell to the ground at my side. Later that year it snowed, and the sparrow was covered by snow, as was I. This fulfilled the prophecy of my naming day, when my father held me up and saw in my birth what my end would be. For a shaman is not named for a circumstance of his birth, but of his death. So are there circles even in words, and an end even in beginnings."

CHAPTER TWENTY-NINE

After the funeral service for Arthur Walters, David drove Diana home. He offered to stay with her, but she wanted to be alone for a while; she would call him tomorrow. He had to admit he wanted some time to think as well; he had not mentioned to her the disturbing thoughts that preoccupied him; there would be time enough for that later.

David returned to the library. It was nearly noon; the place was virtually deserted. He sat down at his desk and pulled the folded piece of paper from his pocket. The professor had written a list of words, then crossed most of them out.

"'Wee-Chee-a, Wancha...waishe...,'" David read aloud.

He sighed. "'..chau.'"

Wesichau. That was the one, the word that Jack Rose had shouted out at him on the hill near Spirit Rock. He was certain of it. Dr. Walton had made an abbreviated notation. 'Saura?' 'Uwharrie?'

David read Walters' all-but-indecipherable scrawl. 'Combination of 'weash,' meaning 'white,' and 'cheaisee' meaning 'devil.' That's what Jack called me, he thought: 'white devil.' But why?

Why would Jack Rose shout out a word in an extinct language just before attacking him in a violent rage?

Walters had been working on the translation just before he died. Was there some significance there, too?

How could there *not* be, he thought grimly.

He had to get out, away from his thoughts. Saturdays were usually slow and Gertrude wouldn't need him for a while. He walked through town, not caring where he was going, until he impulsively turned into the door of the roadhouse. Maybe a beer and some inane conversation were just what he needed.

"Hey, David," shouted Ken Symmes from behind the counter. "Want a cup of coffee, or something stronger?

"I think I'll have a beer, Ken," said David, swinging a leg over the seat at the counter. "Thanks."

"What would the good ladies say about the town librarian having a beer in the middle of the day?" chided Ken, pulling at the draft stob.

"You mean 'good ladies' come in here?"

Ken laughed and pushed the frosted mug over to David.

"No one was in the library," said David. "I really didn't feel like working today, anyway. Not after the funeral."

"You ought to tie one on. Sometimes it helps."

"Yeah. Maybe I ought to get drunk. Crazy drunk."

Ken leaned close to him and said in a low voice: "I'll tell you what, though; you want to know somebody that is sure enough crazy, it's that Wiggins kid over there."

David turned in the direction of Ken's nod. He saw Harry Wiggins sitting in the corner, quietly sipping on a soft drink. "What makes you say he's crazy?"

"He was in the looney bin up at Butner. Came back a few weeks ago. Everybody wondered if he would go off the deep end again, and sure enough he did."

"Oh?"

"Sure. Ed told me he came running to the office bug-eyed last Wednesday looking for the sheriff, like he had seen a ghost or something. Grabbed Ed by the shirt and demanded he get Joe Witherspoon, quick. Something about being chased by an old Indian, crazy stuff like that.

"Joe's known the boy's mother for years. He just calmed him down and called his mama to come and get him. She seemed real embarrassed by it and promised she would keep him around home for a while. I wonder what he's doin' here? Maybe he slipped mama's noose for a couple of hours."

David turned toward Harry's table. "I think I'll go over and talk with him for a while," he said.

Ken looked surprised. "Okay, David, but watch him. If he gives you any trouble, just holler. I don't allow nobody to start anything in my place. Say, maybe he'll tell you next that he was taken up in one of those flying saucers." Ken laughed and turned back to the grill.

David walked slowly over to the corner table. He stood over Harry, who did not acknowledge his presence for several moments, then gazed at David impassively.

"Hi, I'm David Hale," he said, extending his hand. "You're Harry Wiggins, aren't you?"

The younger man did not shake his hand, but David put his beer on the table and sat down anyway. "Mind if I join you?"

Wiggins shrugged and returned to his soft drink. "Look, I know why you came over here. I heard you and that fat tub of lard bartender laughing about me."

"I wasn't laughing. I wanted to hear your side of it."

"Everybody in town thinks I'm crazy. Even my mom"

"Why don't you tell me about it? I promise you I won't laugh."

Wiggins stared down at his cup for several moments. "Why?"

"Suppose I told you I believe some pretty strange things have been going on around here, and I would be interested in talking to someone who felt the same way?"

Harry said nothing, just stared at David.

"Don't worry, you can trust me. I'll keep it confidential. I promise."

"Okay," said Harry. "But not here. Everyone in town is watching me. They're just looking for an excuse to put me away again."

"How about my house?" asked David.

"No way, man. My house, 507 Springdale."

CHAPTER THIRTY

David listened to Wiggins' account of his experiences at the drive-in without comment, intently studying the youth's face, listening to the tone of his voice. He asked him to repeat the story over and over again, trying to catch any inconsistencies; but there were none. He had interviewed many people and was good at spotting any fabrications or distortions. After hearing the story once again, he was sure of one thing: Wiggins was telling the truth; at least, what he believed to be the truth.

Reliving the nightmare had exhausted Harry.

"And you're sure about this word you blurted out after you left the concession stand?"

"Yeah. I mean, I think so. Like 'Weseecha,' something like that. I shouted it at the other fellow, a stranger. Why is that important?"

Hale sighed and said: "I'm not sure. Not yet, anyway."

He made Wiggins go over and over the description of the blonde curly-headed man, until he was certain it could have been no one but Peter Blackwell. Just a few days back from the hospital, Wiggins wouldn't have had a chance to see him around town, wouldn't have known the face.

So Peter Blackwell was involved in this...whatever it was.

Wiggins sank back into the chair, his face buried in his hands. When he looked up, his face was filled with doubt and anguish. "You do believe me, don't you, Mr. Hale?"

"I believe that there are people who are up to something pretty strange around here."

Harry smiled sardonically. "I don't know. Sometimes even I don't believe it myself. Maybe my mother is right; I left the hospital too early. It all could have been an hallucination."

"Well, don't worry," said David soothingly. "Whatever it is, we'll get to the bottom of it." He took out his car keys, and moved to the door. He turned back to Wiggins. "Listen, I have to go close up the library, but I'll be back in an hour. I want you to stay right here. I'll come back and we'll talk some more."

"Hey," said Wiggins nervously. "Talking about this has got me all spooked again. Couldn't you stay until my mom gets home? I don't want to be alone and I don't want to go back to town."

"I'll just be an hour. Hang tight, okay?"

Wiggins nodded.

Harry Wiggins waited anxiously for David to return. He had told the whole story now, everything he had seen and felt that night at the drive-in, and the strange spells he had been having since then. He didn't care anymore if it meant he would have to go back to the hospital. Perhaps he truly was out of his mind. It certainly felt that way, he thought, although the librarian seemed to believe his story, as if it might have happened, and was not craziness at all.

He waited for David in the kitchen, with the back door open. He was frightened, and sitting close to the open door in the fading sunlight, surrounded by the cheery pastel shades of the kitchen, somehow dampened his anxiety. The light had an unreal quality to it, but most things had an unreal element to them now.

Talking to David, he had felt he was talking to someone who was perfectly imitating the librarian. The mind-splits had done that to him; he himself felt at times that he was a very good imitation of Harry Wiggins, and not the real thing anymore. Another personality—no, another *thing* seemed to be residing inside Harry Wiggins. It resembled the real Harry in every way—talked, walked and looked just like good old Harry; but sometimes it would feel and do things Harry would never have done. Like that night at the drive-in, when his sex with Cindy had become so rough and violent that she was finally repulsed by it, frightened of him. The look on her face was fear, fear that he wasn't Harry anymore but a crazy wild thing that had taken over his body temporarily. And she was right. Holding her, grappling with her in the back seat, he had been aware of the blood coursing through her veins—really *felt it moving*, the heart pumping; he could even smell it. And he had with difficulty suppressed the urge to do something unspeakable to her, to tear and rip at her flesh until the blood was free, until he could reach in and feel it with his hands, smear it over his face...

If that wasn't insanity, what was? He kept going back to the fall he had taken in the drive-in washroom, the strange and powerful hallucination he had had there. The blond-headed man's face was still fresh in his mind; it seemed more real than Harry right now—and the old Indian, the one who bent over him with the blood-red eyes. Those eyes still burned him when he thought about it. When he was feeing most strange, it was like the eyes were looking at him, but from the inside; almost as if they were his own eyes somehow, the eyes of this new thing trapped inside him.

His fear had dried his mouth until he could hardly swallow. He didn't want to leave the chair and the open door, but he had to have some water. He walked across the room and turned on the tap, leaning his head to drink from the sink.

The door slammed; the kitchen was suddenly much darker. Harry choked when he heard the scuffle of feet, and he banged his head against the spigot in his panic.

He looked up, knowing already who he would see.

It was the curly-headed blonde man from the drive-in. With him was Mason Thomas, who stood close to the door as the blonde man sauntered across the kitchen.

"Wait!" said Wiggins, holding up both palms trying to stop the advance, like a ridiculous traffic cop.

Amazingly, the blonde man did stop. He smiled in that off-center way he had. "Harry," he said, his voice modulating, "you know me. We're old buddies. You're not going to give us any trouble now, are you?"

"Don't be trouble," said Thomas from the door.

Wiggins couldn't understand what Thomas had to do with this. The blonde man was crazy; but Thomas was just a farmer. His son Willie and he had played on the same sandlot baseball team. Mr. Thomas couldn't be crazy too. Or maybe it was just him, old Harry, that was crazy.

"I won't give you any trouble," he said, not knowing what else to say, trying to stall. "Mr. Thomas, what's going on here? You are Mason Thomas, aren't you? Willie's father?"

But Thomas was silent, his big frame completely blocking the door. Wiggins had a sudden impulse to run through the house the other way, and out the front. But the younger man had moved to cut off that avenue of escape.

"Didn't I tell you when we met at the drive-in that we'd take care of everything?" said the blonde. "Isn't that right, Harry?"

"We take care of everything," mimicked Thomas in a flat tone.

"That's right. Everything. Why are you fighting us? Why don't you just come along now..." He reached for Wiggins' arm; the teenager drew it back with a jerk. The blonde giggled in a wavering voice.

"Go where? I'm not going anywhere. I don't think you're real. I think you're a hallucination. I'm not going anywhere with you. I need a doctor. That's all I need, a good doctor. Get out of here and leave me alone!"

The blonde man grinned. "That's what we're here for, in a way. To take you to a...man of medicine."

"You don't have any choice, boy," said Thomas menacingly, pointing a long finger at Wiggins. "You're one of us already. He'll burn you again if you don't watch out."

This is too crazy to be real, thought Harry, his heart racing. But he pressed forward with the thought. "I'm not going anywhere with you. You're nothing but a symptom, a delusion! I'm sick, is all. Anyway, I got away the last time."

"No, you didn't," said Thomas from the doorway.

The red spots on Harry's chest were itching again; he unconsciously began to scratch at them. Then he saw his chance—the blonde was laughing again, his head thrust back—and Harry ran past him to the dining room, and then to the living room and the front door. But the bolt lock was set; he turned it several ways, up, down, but it wouldn't let loose, the door wouldn't separate from the jamb.

The blonde man paced after him, a little angry now, and bored. "Come on now, don't be such a damn coward. We've all got work to do, and the old man will be mad if we're late getting back."

"You bastards!" screamed Wiggins. He skirted around the blonde, who now had his hands on his hips, sighing, and ran back to the kitchen. With a great clatter he found a long knife in a kitchen drawer. It was the one his mother used to carve roast beef. He thought of her now with sadness.

Look what's happened to me, mom, he thought, in a fearful gloom.

Thomas had moved from the doorway. "That won't help, Harry," he said. The teenager lashed out at the big man. He could have sworn the knife blade caught him straight across the forearm; it seemed to go in, to rip flesh, but there was no blood. Thomas's shirt was torn, but there was no screech of pain, no wound.

Harry was breathing hard now, from fear and exertion. His legs were beginning to shake and an icy sweat had popped out on his face and neck. His mouth was dry again.

They wouldn't go away, just wouldn't go away.

"We're really late, Harry," the blonde man said, and his mouth was set hard. He meant business this time.

There was just one more chance, one last chance. He evaded the blonde once more, ducked under his reaching arms, and dashed into his room. He locked the door and flung open the closet, finding the noose he had fashioned a few days earlier. Pulling the desk chair to a position under the overhead light fixture, he wrapped one end of the rope around the electrical connection and made sure it was tight. *This will get rid of them,* he thought in a mad frenzy. *They'll leave me alone now, they have to.*

A finger tapped him on the shoulder. He turned and screamed. The blonde man smiled at him, his eyes red and rolling in their sockets. "See you later, Harry," he said.

Before the chair could be pulled from under him, Harry jumped off. It was only a short drop. The rope was strong and the light fixture held. A piece of plaster fell to the floor, and Harry swung back and forth gently. His neck was broken, and he knew only darkness.

CHAPTER THIRTY-ONE

David heard the siren just as he was leaving the library to return to Harry Wiggins' place. He drove toward the sound, hoping it didn't mean what he thought it did. But he rounded the corner at Springdale just as the vehicle was stopping, pulling with a skid to the curb.

He recognized the same attendants who had come such a long way for Bill Schlosser earlier. Mrs. Wiggins met them on the porch, her face contorted with grief and shock. A few minutes later the sheriff had arrived and was consoling Harry's mother as the body was rolled from the house on the gurney. The sheet was drawn up, covering the face.

"What happened?" he asked the taller attendant.

"Hanged himself," was all the man said. Then the ambulance doors shut and the vehicle drove off.

David drove straight over to Diana's. He didn't want to be alone just then. All sorts of questions were boiling in his mind. There was some hard talking they had to do; maybe she could help him figure out what was happening in Clearview.

He saw the dim outline of the Uwharrie Mountains in the distance, rising as purple monoliths on the horizon. Where once he had looked at them as majestic sentinels of by-gone eons, they now took on a more ominous and threatening visage.

David told Diana about Harry Wiggins and Blackwell, not just that the teenager was dead, but that he had been privy to the boy's strange tale; of how scared Wiggins was, the glazed fear in his eyes when he had left him at the house. The words tumbled out; he felt guilty for having left the boy alone. Perhaps he could have saved him. He told her the full story of his fight with Jack Rose, the Indian word he had yelled; the one her father had traced down as meaning 'white devil.' And that Wiggins knew it, too. He told her of his seeing Singer carrying something in a sack out near Spirit Rock.

"All right," she said, talking with a more professional tone now, with objectivity; she was fighting hard to be the detached scientist, to be cool here and not be swept away by the onrush of David's facts and suppositions. "Just a minute. There are some strange happenings here. But Harry Wiggins wasn't the most reliable witness in the world. I know it's a tragedy and I feel sad about it too, but he did have a history of psychiatric problems."

"Depression, yes. But he wasn't depressed, Diana, he was scared. Just plain scared out of his mind."

"Out of his mind. Did you hear what you just said?"

"He wasn't crazy," David said, adamantly. "He knew the word, the 'white devil' word. Like Jack Rose."

"It could have been a coincidence. Or not a word at all. Jack Rose came at you and grunted in anger; Wiggins had a psychotic delusion and spat out a nonsense obscenity at a passerby. Couldn't it have happened that way?"

"No. I know you're playing devil's advocate, Diana, and I appreciate it. But I believe someone, or something, is influencing these events. Rose, Schlosser, Dawes, Wiggins. Maybe your father..."

"Now you're talking murder, David. I don't want to believe..."

"Yes, maybe murder. Wiggins and Schlosser *both* didn't commit suicide. Wiggins was supposed to be crazy. That sounds like Doc Burke and Joe Witherspoon talking about Schlosser; that he was crazy. Hell, the sheriff thinks maybe *I'm* crazy. Either that, or a doper like Blackwell."

"But David, what could possibly be so powerful and sinister to cause all these things? It sounds like a conspiracy to...to do what? There's nothing *valuable* enough to kill for."

"Singer is evil," said David. "I could feel it when I was around him. You can laugh at that if you want to."

"I'm not laughing," she said. "But what could he, or anyone else, have as an objective?"

"I don't know yet. but I've asked around, and there are other strange things going on. Besides the deaths and 'accidents.'" Mason Thomas attacked the sheriff earlier this summer, right out of the blue. Like Jack Rose attacked me. Willie Thomas told Millie at the diner that his father just isn't the same man—like Jack Rose isn't the same. It's almost as if they have become something else, metamorphosized. Or are under the control of some force."

"Now you're beginning to get spooky. You're talking about something supernatural going on."

She took his hand and gripped it hard. "David," she said, "I'm starting to get scared now."

"Yeah," he said. "I am too." He changed the subject quickly. "If only I had some kind of real proof."

"Maybe...maybe I know a way to prove something one way or the other," said Diana.

"How?"

"You remember when Bill Schlosser brought out the 1976 high school ring that was in the same strata as the old skeleton? The white man that had been either burned or tortured by fire?"

"Yes. It was carefully explained to me how unsupernatural that was. Something about an 'intrusion,' I remember. Everybody was laughing about it."

"Except Bill," she said. "While the bones were still in the trench he told me he thought the encrustation was *on* the hand, not just in the same spot, but actually on the hand. Then the tripod smashed into it before that could be confirmed. When the ring turned out to be an 'intrusion' and not an English artifact, I forgot about the incident. Until now."

"What are you driving at?"

"Well, every angle of that excavation was photographed. You were there when Bill was taking pictures. If we could determine that the ring was actually on the hand, then...oh, this is crazy, David."

"Maybe so. But he did die in his darkroom setup. And maybe it wasn't a suicide. Just like maybe Wiggins wasn't a suicide. Where would that roll of film be?"

Diana grabbed her pocketbook. "Let's go," she said. "Several motel rooms were rented by dig members for the whole summer. Bill's was one of them."

CHAPTER THIRTY-TWO

Mrs. Campbell, owner of the motel, was frankly relieved that Diana had come to sort out what remained of Bill Schlosser's belongings; Witherspoon had sent the more personal effects to the family. Having Peter Blackwell and then a suicide for tenants was quite enough trouble for her, she said; she was thinking of closing the place and selling out.

"Sheriff said you'd be over to collect those files and things," she went on, opening the lock with a master key. She turned on the light as the closed in, musty air exchanged with that of the outside. "Hasn't anybody bothered anything. It's all here, been closed since the sheriff came that day."

David closed and locked the door carefully, making sure the dead bolt was engaged. He'd done the same careful locking of the car outside as well, although it was only a few yards away.

"You're starting to make me really paranoid," Diana told him.

"Let's hope that's all it is," he said.

"Bill kept some of the photographs locked in that tall filing cabinet in the darkroom," Diana said, crossing to the room. She felt under the top drawer, and pulled loose the piece of paper on which

Schlosser had scrawled the combination to the lock; a precaution lest he forget the combination. She tried the combination; the lock disengaged and the drawer pulled open easily.

"These files are in awful shape," Diana said, flipping through a row of folders. "They're all dated and tagged correctly so there'd be no chance of getting something out of sequence. But they're still not in any kind of order." She shrugged. "Bill was more of a field manager than an academic. I guess Dad should have overseen him more strictly," she added sadly.

The shuffling of papers and photographs went on for some time. Near the middle of the second drawer, Diana stopped, pulled out a handful of photos, and said: "Here it is, I think. Yes, there are the angle shots of the trench, and here are..." She suddenly became silent.

David took the photo from her hand. It was an enlargement of one of the trench shots, with very good resolution of the left forearm and hand of the skeleton.

"He made a blow-up," she said. "Oh, David, I thought he had made a mistake that day. I thought he was imagining things."

"It's not your fault. Who'd have believed it in a million years?"

He held the photograph to the light so that the detail, the encrusted ring, could be seen easily. It was clearly on the finger, the ring finger, of the hand.

"Then there's no mistake," he said.

"How can it be, David?" she asked in hushed tones. "A modern ring on a skeleton buried well over a hundred years ago? It's crazy."

"But it's true. Somehow a modern ring was buried with someone who died in the early or middle 1800s. Remember what Bill said? The skeleton was not that of an Indian; probably a white man. That can only mean that somehow, some way, a modern man was taken back in time and killed and buried in the Uwharrie village."

"Then it must be..."

"Magic. Indian magic. Ironic, isn't it? In earlier cultures like the Uwharrie, it was a commonplace assumption that magic held power over people's lives. But with our modern technology and worship of science and rational philosophy, we've destroyed that belief. Or rather, destroyed the people that believed it. But perhaps the magic has survived."

"What are we going to do?" she asked, struggling to control the hysteria rising within her.

"Well, we know now that Schlosser didn't commit suicide. *We* know. But even this picture isn't proof. As it is, it's just another strange event in a series of strange events. People would never believe us, especially not Witherspoon. They have taken care of that."

"You said 'they,' David? Just who are 'they'?"

"I don't know. All we have to go on are the people that we know have acted strangely: Blackwell, Wiggins, and Jack Rose. Thomas gave him an impossible alibi, so add Thomas to the list. I think they are under someone— or *something's* control, for what reason I don't know. We can't be sure if more townspeople may be involved with them. We really can't trust anybody."

Diana started to laugh, but it died in her throat when she saw the look on his face. My God, he's right, she thought. A short while ago, she would have scoffed at such an absurd idea; but not now. She couldn't be sure of anything anymore. Logic and rationality seemed out of place now.

"Then what chance do we have against them? What are they doing, and why?"

He just shook his head.

"I'm going to make copies of this print," she said.

David insisted they stick together, so they drove to his duplex. Fatigue swamped him and he fell exhausted across the bed. Diana gently covered the already-sleeping form, then lay down beside him. She was exhausted, too.

David slept fitfully, his slumber disturbed by frightening dreams. Angry faces swam around him: Blackwell, Wiggins, especially that of Jack Rose. His one-time friend was dragging him toward a stake in the ground near a crackling fire. A wraith-like Indian stood immobile before him, while all around were shadowy figures mumbling an incoherent chant. He struggled against his captor as he was relentlessly dragged toward the bloody stake. But Rose was too strong for him. He was stretched out and tied to the stake. The Indian lifted a long knife, closed his eyes, mumbling. Then he opened his red eyes wide, staring savagely down at Hale.

"David! David, wake up!" Diana shouted, shaking his shoulders.

He sat bolt upright in bed, breathing heavily, his face bathed in sweat.

"You were shouting and raving like a madman," she said. "You were having a nightmare."

"I...guess so," he stammered, trying to control his breathing. "God, it was awful! There was this group of—Rose, some others— they were trying to kill me. One of them was an old Indian with red eyes."

"Like the experience that Harry Wiggins told you about?" she asked. She put her arms around his neck.

"Yes. I suppose that was it," he sighed. He could smell the clean scent of her hair in his nostrils and it gradually calmed the rapid beating of his heart.

"Don't worry, darling," she soothed. "It was only a dream. I'm here. Don't worry." She might have been comforting a child.

He raised his head and stared at her. "Suppose it wasn't just a dream? Wiggins said he felt tortured. Perhaps he was. Maybe it all is real!"

CHAPTER THIRTY-THREE

"Wolf-Singer, you have asked me what was the final vision of Man of Water, promised him by the Great Spirit. Now I will tell you, for it is your destiny as well as mine. When Man of Water was in his last season, he dreamed he was at the top of a tall montain, looking down on the village. At that time, the village was a thousand and a thousand and a thousand Uwharrie, and each man had his own house and land, and there were storehouses of grain such that no winter was hard enough or long enough to use even half of the store.

"But from the mountain he saw the village grow smaller and smaller, until there were only a few huts, and even these were falling down. He tried to see what had caused this, and he saw that there was a giant in the North, and from the giant's mouth there came four winds. One was a hot wind, and was the color of weak blood, and there were red spots swirling in the wind. This wind took many of the tribe and blew them away, and their houses and grain stores were blown away also. The second wind was cold and blew hard, and was yellow. This wind blew many of the tribe away, and then buried itself in the ground and disappeared under the dirt. The third wind was a whirlwind, and as it came it threw out words in a strange language. At first, the words were blue and green like the grass and the sky, but then the whirlwind drew them back, and the words turned black like thunder clouds, and rained down on the tribe, driving more of them into the arms of the whirlwind, which blew them away. The fourth wind drove before it skeletons on horseback. The horses breathed fire and their eyes were a fiery color like hot coals. The horses trampled the women and children of the tribe underfoot, and the warriors were helpless against them.

"Man of Water was bent with sorrow at seeing these things happen to the tribe, and in his anguish he called out to the Great Spirit to help them, forgetting he was in a vision, and that the Great Spirit willed the vision to come to him in the first place. And the Great Spirit caused a peace to come over him, so his sight of the vision would be true and complete. For the vision was to be interpreted by a shaman not yet born, and each sign and portent must be handed down as clear and unchangeable truth.

"So Man of Water saw every man and woman and child, and even every dog of the Uwharrie swept away, until there was nothing left but a black field where nothing would grow. When all was gone, Man of Water saw there were two wolves, an old one and a young one, in the black dust that once had been the tribe, and between them was a bird, a sparrow. The old wolf howled, and suddenly it was night, and he kept howling until the howling became a song, and he was chanting in the language of the Uwharrie. Then he whispered some words to the young wolf, and died.

"Just then another whirlwind blew again in the distance, and a great army of skeletons came back, riding the wind; but these were spit out by the wind and fell to the ground.

"The sparrow then flew up squawking, and picked up a skeleton and carried it screaming to the other side of the river. The sparrow kept seizing the skeletons and carrying them across the river, and dropping them, and with each broken skeleton more of the tribe returned in the sky, back from the winds that had blown them away. And when Man of Water looked again, he saw the whole tribe as it had been on the other side of the river, and they were a thousand and a thousand, and were happy and prosperous, as they had been.

"And Man of Water was pleased, because the vision was done, and at the end he saw the tribe was again whole and in the other world, as the Great Spirit had promised. He knew it would come to pass that when he was dead, another shaman would interpret the prophecy, and carry it out.

"Tell me now, Wolf-Singer, man of the tribe and rightful heir to the kings, what the last vision of Man of Water truly means? What did I understand before the Wesichau and the Major called Simpson came to burn the village as it lay in mourning for the dead King Keyauwee Jack? What vision did I also see on the banks of the river and in the mountain? And how is it to come to pass?"

Wolf-Singer did not hesitate. The great vision of Man of Water was also in his blood and his blood would speak.

"Man of Water dreamed he was at the top of a tall mountain, which was the height of wisdom. The mountain was his magic which let him see the things to come for the tribe. He saw the village decrease and lose its greatness because of a giant from the North. The giant was Time, which conquers all things and scatters all before it. The giant blew four winds which are both the past and the future for the tribe and for you and I.

"The hot wind with the color of weak blood was the sickness of the Wesichau which took the old ones and the young ones and many in between. It was the sicknesses of the Wesichau brought with them across the seas. There was the Burning Sickness, and the Fever Which Leaves Scars, and the Winter Fever that clogged the throat and robbed the children and old ones of air. And there was the Swollen Throat Sickness which could kill in a day. These were all in the red wind.

"The yellow wind was of another fever, but it was a fever of the mind. The Wesichau Sickness. Yellow was the color of the Rock Which Made The Wesichau Crazy. White men would kill each other over a plot of ground that would not grow so much as a weed. They would go without sleep to dig up the ground and wash the ground in the river like women wash a garment. Those that were not killed carried the yellow ground in little sacks; more and more would come back to claw the ground until it was nothing but holes.

"The third wind was of words, which were the promises of the Wesichau that were never kept. The words were only paper but they killed by deceit and greed, and because soldiers would use the words to take away hunting grounds of the tribe, and many starved in long winters because of the words. At first, the word-wind was pretty like sky and grass because the words sounded true and good; but then they were broken, and became a black rain, like the lies they truly were.

"The fourth wind drove before it skeletons on horseback. These were the white devil Simpson and his men. The horses breathed fire, which was the coward's way to surround the village and kill all inside the circle, with fire. First fire, and then bullets.

"Then everything was gone, as was the village, which is now only a clearing where nothing will grow. Everything was gone except two wolves, an old one and a young one, and between them a bird. The old wolf was my great-grandfather who sang to the wolf in the valley and whispered some words in my childish ear, that I would drown in fire. I am the young wolf. And you, shaman, are the bird, which was a sparrow.

"Then Man of Water saw the whirlwind come back, and scatter skeletons over the land. These are the white devils called Schlosser, Dawes and Walters. And mixed in with them are the bones of our dead on the last day of the tribe, the ones that Walters was digging up.

"Man of Water saw that when the sparrow picked up these skeletons and dropped them screaming across the river, the promise of the Great Spirit would come forth, and fire and water would destroy the old world and the whites there, and the new world of the sky would open up and receive the bones of the last king.

"You, shaman, have taken the white devils across the river into the past, just as you took me in visions, and they were put at the stake and made to pay. Pay for the past and for the future, which will be ours once again. Have I seen the truth?"

The shaman said nothing, but he was almost smiling.

CHAPTER THIRTY-FOUR

Joe Witherspoon was already upset when Doc Burke called him. The Wiggins boy had been on his mind, another strange death so shortly after Professor Walters' car crash. The sheriff was struggling to make some sense in these apparently random and senseless events. His town was coming apart at the seams, and he felt powerless to stop it. Call it suicide or accident or heart attack, there just had been too many unexplained deaths.

He felt guilty about the Wiggins kid. He should have sent him straight back to the hospital that day he came to him, ranting and raving, instead of letting Mrs. Wiggins try to handle it. What could she really do, a working woman whose husband had run out on her?

Yeah, he should have shipped him straight back to the hospital. Too late now, though. Hell, he thought, maybe I'm going crazy, too.

That morning he'd seen Mason Thomas stopping for gas at Benson's service station. There was another man in the truck, and as Witherspoon drove by in the squad car he thought he recognized the profile of Peter Blackwell. Witherspoon had wheeled the car around and slammed to a stop in front of Thomas' truck, and advanced with his hand to his holster.

But it hadn't been Blackwell at all, just a young Catawba hitchhiking south. There was a resemblance to Blackwell only in a slightly wild and arrogant look to the boy. The incident had shaken the sheriff; he'd been so sure it was Blackwell. Perhaps the heat and the pain in his stomach had triggered some imbalance that was affecting his eyesight—at least he hoped it was his eyesight and not his mind, that he had not started to fantasize things out of thin air.

Then the phone call from Burke, and his mind was reeling again, causing his stomach to churn further.

"Joe, I've got some rather unusual news about the Wiggins boy's suicide."

"Doc, lately there hasn't been anything that isn't unusual. Let me have it."

"Well, I got a call from a pathologist at the county morgue. He called me because I was listed as Wiggins' family physician. And he was asking me what in the hell they'd done to the boy up at the mental hospital, that he'd already called them and couldn't get any answers. He thought someone had been torturing the boy. There were burns and scar tissue, like a cigarette might make, some old and some new, mostly on the chest and the back."

Witherspoon cursed. "You mean like were on Schlosser?"

"I'm afraid so. And I told him there weren't any burns, because I had been there when the EMTs cut him down and opened his shirt to give him a shot of epinephrin, trying to restore some heart action. You were there, Joe; did you notice any burns or scars?"

"No. It was just a skinny teenager's chest. No hair that could cover up a wound of any kind."

"That's what I told the pathologist. Then I remembered how Schlosser's body had looked, his burns. So I'm going over to Ulah with Wiggins' complete file to consult with that pathologist."

"What do you think it all means, Doc?"

"I don't have any idea, Joe. I think the answer to that question will have to come from you."

"Can you see that Wiggins' body gets a complete tox screen?"

"Oh, it already has. Except for a tranquilizer I prescribed, it was clean. No other drugs, no poison. Nothing."

"Okay, Doc. Thanks for the call."

They hung up. After a moment, Witherspoon cursed again and banged his fist on the top of his desk.

CHAPTER THIRTY-FIVE

Although the trench photograph strengthened David's conviction that some as yet unexplained plot was unraveling, there was still nothing he could present to Sheriff Witherspoon. The sheriff was still touchy about the Jack Rose incident, and David believed Witherspoon suspected *he* was somehow mixed up with Peter Blackwell.

The mysteries of the photo did ease David's anxiety about one thing, however. He had been silently worried that, after her father's death, Diana would pack her suitcase and return to Smith, and put an end to their affair. But by now she was as caught up as he in finding an answer.

The excavation, on Diana's instructions, had been discontinued, at least for the summer. That meant paying off the last of the students and arranging equipment at the site. This took two hectic days, and David helped as much as time allowed. The activity diverted Diana's grief over her father's death.

When the students had gone, Diana sat heavily in a chair in the field shed, exhausted. David fixed her a glass of instant tea from the cooler in the cramped shed that was filled with tools, papers, and an assortment of artifacts in plastic bags and boxes. The bulk of the artifacts were in heavy cardboard containers which contained the bones of the disinterred specimens. There were a dozen or so that hadn't been sent to the university; a truck would pick them up later in the week.

The boxes gave David a sense of foreboding. Death was all too real to him now. The clearing where they stood was obviously the scene of the massacre the Priddy manuscript had depicted; the configuration of the bones, scattered all about as they were, argued against any sort of ceremonial burial. The clearing was not a graveyard but a battlefield, although Professor Walters had ignored that fact in his quest for evidence of the Lost Colony survivors.

The massacre had happened so long ago. But something similar was happening now—a sort of massacre of dig workers, a mind-death of some townspeople. The bodies and pesonalities were mounting up.

Two massacres, of very different kinds, over a century apart.

Very different. But so close in space. Major Simpson had come over from Clearview. You might say that the town had killed the Uwharries.

And now Clearview was being ravaged.

"Diana," he said suddenly, "maybe we've been looking at this thing all wrong. All these deaths, we've been seeing them as either accidents or perhaps murders for some unknown criminal purpose, by men of the present. But suppose that's not right at all. What if we're on the wrong track?"

"I don't understand," she said.

"Maybe the key to this thing isn't in the present at all. Perhaps it's in the past."

"You mean some sort of revenge thing? Indian spirits rising from the grave to pay back Major Simpson? Surely you don't believe in ghosts, do you, David?" She came to him, and put her hand on his face. "Believe me," she said, with a serious gaze, "if I could attribute my father's death to spirits, I would. It would simplify things. I'd just call it supernatural and go on with my life. There does seem to be a 'curse' operating here, but I think it's just bad luck. There was supposed to be a curse on Tutankhamen's tomb, and many members of the team that excavated the tomb did die in close proximity to each other, and in bizarre ways. But a scientific analysis of the deaths showed it was due only to chance and natural causes. No curse, no supernatural."

David sighed. "But think about the Uwharrie tribe for a moment, how very savage they could be with enemies. You're the expert. Explain to me the reason for such torture as was described by Father McGill."

Diana frowned, as if trying to put a complicated explanation into layman's terms. "You have to remember, David, that these tribes had a much different value system from ours. For instance, the revenge element. In tribal societies, 'an eye for an eye' is a literal term. It was a form of quick and easily understood justice."

"All right, I can understand that. But why make a ceremony of it? Why have the shaman perform it as a rite?"

"It *was* a rite, almost a sacred duty. In a warrior society like the Uwharrie, power and strength were paramount. A powerful enemy was respected for his strength and courage. The purpose of torture was to take that power from him, almost as if it were a physical thing that could be transferred to the victor. Sometimes prisoners were sacrificed to be servants to a brave warrior or a chief in the after-life, what popular fiction calls the 'happy hunting ground.' The Egyptians had a similar belief, which is why they sealed up members of the court in the tombs of dead pharaohs."

"What if a Uwharrie warrior were alive today?" asked David. "What do you think he would do?"

"Revenge," said Diana, slowly. "Against whites, and the 'village' that sent Simpson—Clearview. Perhaps against the members of the raiding party. But they would all be dead."

"And how would he exact his revenge?"

Diana didn't need to say it. But they were both thinking: *Fire.*

David shook his head. Suddenly very tired, he tried to find a place to sit down in the crowded room. There were three crates stacked one atop the other, the last of the skeletal remains to be shipped. He settled for leaning against the crates while Diana prepared to leave for the day. As he did so, he felt the crates give; not to the side, but straight down. There was a crackling of pine board and the two top crates were suddenly lower.

Diana immediately was down inspecting the splintered remains of the bottom crate. "Help me move these top crates off. Something's not right here."

David moved the two boxes to reveal a broken, empty crate. "That was artifact group number C-43. It's gone, missing. See here, how the end boards were pried out and then replaced? The nails were bent and pounded back in crookedly."

He asked which skeleton it was.

"The one found away from the others, beside the river. Elderly male. Position of the bones indicated ceremonial burial. Now why would somebody want to steal that? It has no value except to a museum, and a museum would never buy from a thief."

"I don't know why he would steal it," David scowled, "but now I can just about guarantee you what was in that sack that Singer was carrying.

CHAPTER THIRTY-SIX

David tried unsuccesfully to quell the feelings of paranoia as he worked the next morning in the library. He tried to busy himself with routine, but halfway through the morning he quit the pretense altogether, and sat in his office staring out the window that bordered on Commerce Street.

Finally, he could put it off no longer and left the library, walked the short distance to the town hall, and asked clerk Walt Meade to use the record room.

It was not an unusual request; many times he had used the birth and death records of the township to document some minor point or other in his oral history activities. But this trip caused his hands to shake as he dug into the large ledger books, the pages crackling with age.

He worked forward from the oldest files, using the five scrawled surnames at the end of the Priddy manuscript as guides.

In 1868 there were only about two hundred residents of the township; however, the large number of children in families made tracing single individuals a chore.

William Hadley, the first of Priddy's town nightriders, had been a prosperous storekeeper. He had five children by his first wife; after she died, he married her younger sister and proceeded to have five more. Of these, three died in childhood from various diseases. So only seven survived to adulthood; one was a spinster and one a lifelong batchelor. But that left five others.

It was laborious work, tracing the lineage of William Hadley through marriage, birth and death certificates, and tax records. The family continued into the thirties, when the record books no longer carried the name. Hadley's grandson, James Willis, had a daughter, Thelma, who married a preacher named Wilfred Thomas. They had one son in 1926, who seemed to have left the area at maturity. and another son in 1928: Mason Rutherford Thomas.

David felt a chill when he came across that entry. It confirmed— or started to confirm—a feeling which had been growing inside him for some time. The lifeline of William Hadley, the storekeeper who participated in the massacre at the clearing, stopped with Mason Thomas. And Willie, of course. But David wasn't concerned with Willie.

Tracing Hadley's genealogy had taken all morning. David's eyes were burning from reading faded handwriting, and his nose was irritated from the dust and disintegrating paper of the old ledgers. But he felt he couldn't stop. He plunged ahead into the descendants of the second name.

Paul Bryant was less prodigious than Hadley, and the work went faster. The last surviving member of the family was Jack Rose. An older brother had died last year from a stroke, and there were some distant cousins living in Ulah.

The end of the line of Robert Dowdy was Harold Wiggins, Sr., an engineer who had moved to Alaska. And Harold Wiggins, Jr., known as Harry, now deceased.

Marcus C. Juvenal, M.D., the town physician in 1868, had a son John, whose daughter Edna married a young school teacher named Edward Walters in 1921. They had a son who grew up to be a college professor and sired a daughter, Diana.

David had started on the descendants of Major Simpson when Walt tapped him on the shoulder. "David," he said, "give me a break. It's six o'clock. Eloise is waiting supper for me."

David sighed, then realized Meade was right. The records would still be there in the morning. He had little doubt as to what he would find, anyway: another townsperson who had been acting strangely. Or perhaps the endline would be Dawes or Schlosser, although he thought they were from other parts of the country.

But maybe there was an easier way.

"Miss Priddy, I hate to bother you, but I thought you could answer a question for me. About your grandfather's manuscript."

The elderly woman laughed dryly. "Somehow I thought you'd be calling, young man."

"Yes, ma'am. I've been looking through the county records concerning the Simpson man, and..."

"And you want to know what happened to him—if Simpson got away with it?"

David was taken aback by her guess. "Why, yes," he said, surprised. "That's exactly what I want to know. What happened to the Simpsons?"

The old woman invited him into the parlor. She scooted a cat off a chair, motioned for David to have a seat, and sat in her customary chair in the corner.

"Well, Simpson got the Uwharrie land, or at least most of it, But it was heavy rains and snow in the mountains for years after that, and it kept flooding. So he sold it off, to the county, I believe. Or so my grandfather said. That was before I was born, of course. When I was a young girl, I remember being told something about a scandal. Apparently, the old goat got another man's wife with child; I don't recall who now. But he was shot getting off a train up around Greensboro, on a business trip, and he died of the gangrene that came from it. And that's what he deserved, all right, though they never found out who did it, and I guess they didn't try very hard, either. He had no family here by then, so he was buried up there."

"I see. Well, do you remember if he had any legitimate children?"

"He had a son, Jason. He was a ne'er-do-well, always getting into trouble and became an alcoholic. Simpson was so disgusted with the boy that he disowned him. Some folks think Jason was the one that shot him, but nobody could prove it. He later died of drink over in Ulah Memorial Hospital. He had married some girl over there, and his daughter married the youngest Fleming boy."

"You mean the druggist Eugene Fleming's family?"

"Yes. Eugene Sr. was the father."

"So... Eugene Fleming would be Major Simpson's great-grandson."

"I suppose he is, young man. But I doubt he'd admit it to your face. That was one reason I held onto my grandfather's manuscript so long, because the Fleming family were such good people, you know, and Eugene Jr. is a pretty good man, I guess. Although the last time I got my sciatica pills, he was not very polite. But that may have been because of the heat. It was so hot that day I near fainted on the way home."

"Yes, ma'am, I see."

"I don't believe we can visit the sins of the father on the son, or even the great-grandson, do you? At least, that's what the Good Book says, doesn't it?"

"Yes," said David. "I guess that's what it says, all right."

CHAPTER THIRTY-SEVEN

Chief George Cloud sat impassively on his front porch as the white man and woman walked across the lawn and stood awkwardly at the bottom of the front steps. He saw the pity in their eyes for the shabby condition of his house—a shack, really—with its torn shingle siding, the faded, peeling paint of the porch and steps; but he had long ago learned to ignore the condescension or contempt he saw in whites' eyes for how the Indian lived.

"Are you Chief George Cloud?" asked the attractive young woman. "I am Diana Walters and this is David Hale, from Clearview. We'd like to talk to you,"

The old Indian nodded in acknowledgement. He knew who she was. She was the daughter of the teacher who was digging in the ground of the ancient Uwharries. He disliked the intrusion of sacred ground, but it was not that of the Catawbas, so he said nothing against it. He waited silently for the woman to continue.

The elder waved a hand in the direction of a rocking chair to his right. The Walters woman took the chair while the white man sat on the top step.

"I understand that you are the most knowledgable man about

the Indian tribes in this area," the woman said. "We would like to ask you about the legends of the Uwharries. We know you do not usually talk to outsiders, but we believe our errand is very important. Urgent, really."

Urgent? he thought. Some more white people doing a study of the quaint tribal customs of the Indians. Would they never tire of seeking to learn about the societies they had so recently destroyed? Why were not more young Native American men and women as interested in their heritage as the whites?

At first, he resisted, but then thought if his own people would not save the old legends and tales, then it was better to have them collected by the well-meaning, if naive, whites than to let them die with old men such as himself.

"What do you wish to know?" he asked slowly, in a dignified voice.

"What became of the Uwharrie tribe?" the white man spoke for the first time. "The history books have no answers. We have evidence the last village, near Clearview, was destroyed by mercenary soldiers."

George Cloud saw they did not have a tape recorder, nor did the woman write on a pad, as had all the rest. Their manner was different, too; more urgent. He detected something behind their eyes: perhaps fear?

"Yes, they were rubbed out, after the war of the Blue Soldiers and the Gray Soldiers. Before that, we Catawbas took some in— when the camps were split in what the books call the Trail of Tears. That was when the soldiers took many Indians from many tribes to the West. Some hid; others, like the Catawbas, were allowed to remain; the price was land—and pride." His eyes flickered and his tanned-leather, wrinkled face hardened, but he would not show further emotion to these whites. He knew it did little good to spew forth hatred over the past.

"What became of the Uwharries that were taken into the Catawbas?"

"At first, they remained apart and kept their own ways. But we would not allow that; we had taken them in, they must become

Catawbas if they wanted to stay with us. There was some trouble and bad blood, but eventually they intermarried into our tribe and accepted our ways."

"What about their customs and legends?" asked the white man. "Did they die out as well?"

"Most of the legends passed away or became a part of our common heritage," intoned the old man. "But some of their customs we could not accept. We are a proud people, but not warlike; when we fought, it was because we had to. Revenge was not in our nature."

"Revenge?" questioned the white woman.

"If anything was done to a Uwharrie, even the least and most unworthy of them, the whole tribe would avenge them, wiping out every one of the enemy, or the other tribe. The Uwharries were once a strong and mighty tribe, but they became less and less. Not even their magic could stop it."

"Magic?" asked the white man. George Cloud saw him glance quickly over at the woman. Could they know? Or was it just more of the white man's curiosity?

"Many believed that it was their magic that made them so strong. Their shamans were widely respected in their tribe and greatly feared by all others. The most powerful was called Sparrow-in-Snow; when he disappeared, their power left them for good, and then they were no more."

"Tell us about Sparrow-in-Snow," asked the white woman.

"He was the last great shaman. His magic made the braves victorious in battle, and great hunters. But as he grew older, he turned to prophecy. Some say that he knew the tribe would pass from the land, and sought knowledge from the Great Spirit on how to avenge the Uwharrie. His magic caused great fear among its neighbors; even members of the tribe became frightened of him. The war powers of the tribe grew weaker as he continued to seek ways to avenge the forces that would one day destroy the tribe. This made the elders very angry, but as long as Sparrow-in-Snow had the ear of the King, they could do nothing against him. He controlled the Burial of the Kings and no one could challenge him."

"The Burial of the Kings?" asked the white man, as if surprised. But George Cloud could see he knew more about it than he pretended. "What was that?"

"The kings were mourned with fasts and ritual after they died. After twelve days, the body of the king was taken from the charnel house into the mountains. There a secret ceremony would take place. All tribal kings from the first one were taken to a secret place and buried together."

"Do you know where that might have taken place?" asked the white man, a little too urgently. George Cloud paused before answering him, trying to ascertain what it was they were seeking.

"No, I do not. The Uwharries were very secretive about that, and it was not our custom to ask. The only witnesses were the king's most trusted warriors. But it must surely have been near what is now called Spirit Rock. The legend speaks of a cave in a mountain, and of water."

Both of the whites paused, looking at each other in disappointment. They were groping, trying clumsily to draw him out. "Was there ever any indication in the legend about what Sparrow-in-Snow would do to avenge the tribe?"

At that point, the old man's wife spoke from where she had been silently standing just inside the screen door. "Be quiet, old man," she hissed in Catawban.

George Cloud looked closely at the whites to see if they had understood her, but he could see they had not. "Leave me. I will decide what is best to do," he said curtly to the woman, watching to see that she obeyed him. Only after she had closed the door did he return to the whites.

"As I said, Sparrow-in-Snow was a very powerful shaman, but even he could not save the tribe after the Great Spirit had turned his back on it. All he could do was try to avenge the tribe on its enemies. More and more of his magical powers were devoted to this. It was rumored that at last he had found a way. One day the kings would return and avenge the tribe of its enemies. But this would only come about when the last of the tribe would return to perform the sacred rite that would bring back the kings."

"The last of the tribe?" asked the white man. "What does that mean?"

"The Great Spirit would not allow all to die. One man would carry the Uwharrie spirit on. When this man walked again on the land of his forefathers, then it would be time for the Return of the Kings."

"Was there anything known about where or how this would come about?" persisted the white man.

"Nothing was known, other than that it must be in the presence of the old kings. It was to be in the place where their bones rested."

Even the whites, with all of their cursed curiosity could see that he could tell them little more; that he was tired and that he did not want to impart any more of the old legends to them.

"We want to thank you for your willingness to talk to us," said the white woman, rising and extending her hand.

George Cloud did not take it, but made a slight nod of his head in acknowledgment

"It does not please me that you are disturbing the sacred resting place of the dead. But that is the Uwharries, not the Catawbas; it does not concern us." said George Cloud, impassively.

"But we did not intend it as a desecration," interjected the white woman."We only wanted to discover your heritage and try to prevent it from being destroyed. I understand your feelings, but others feel differently. Why, one of your tribe members has been very helpful to us."

"Who is that?" asked the old man.

"Why, John Wolfe Singer."

The old man tried to keep the flash of amazement from showing on his face. What were these young whites really doing here? Why were they asking questions of things even he had almost forgotten?

"You say this man calls himself Wolf-Singer? That he understands the cry of the wolf? No, this is no man of our people."

The distinction eluded the white man. "John Wolfe Singer is not a Catawba?" he asked, surprised.

"I will say this and nothing more, because I do not know what this question you are asking really means. I have only heard the name of Singing Wolf—that in time gone by would have been Wolf That Sings—once, and that was many years ago.

"When I was a boy there was an old woman in the camp who had no husband and no sons. It was said she came from the land of the Cherokee and had Uwharrie blood. She was not right in the head, and we children listened to her only to laugh. This woman who had never had a man of her own said that when she was young she was the handmaiden of the wife of a great chief, and her infant son. But she was sent away from her tribe, and it perished. We children thought it was her madness talking, and perhaps it was. I do not remember all of her tale; but the boy child, the infant king, was named Singing Wolf. That I remember."

"I guess we can put it all together now," said Diana, as the couple drove back toward Clearview. "John Singer is the descendant of the infant king Singing-Wolf. And somehow now he's come back—for some kind of revenge, because of Major Simpson and his band razing the village."

"Right, some kind of revenge. What, we don't know."

"But you said the descendants of Simpson and the others had been, I don't know, *changed*—Mason Thomas, Jack Rose, Fleming, Harry Wiggins..." Diana stopped. "My father was killed. Isn't that enough? What more could they want? What else could Singer and, and whoever he's with, possibly do?"

David laughed bitterly. "It's all madness, of course. But I just thought of something. Wiggins said that Blackwell was taking him to the 'old man.' And once he referred to him as 'the birdman. A medical man of infinite power,' he said."

"You don't think..."

"Why not? Magic. Revenge. High school rings on corpses 150 years old. Suicides and murders, or maybe just murders. This Sparrow shaman was one powerful guy, even Father McGill says that."

"Chief George Cloud said that when the kings were all together again, the revenge would begin." she said. "Do you remember the bones of an elderly male we found outside the massacre site, off by himself? Maybe he was the old King Keyauwee Jack. The massacre took place before he could be taken to the mountain, where all the other kings were buried."

"But Singer stole the bones and disapeared with them near Spirit Rock. So now they *are* all together—their bones are all in the same place, and the rest of the prophecy can come about. The revenge part."

"But all the kings *aren't* in the same place."

"What do you mean?"

"Well, John Singer. He is a descendant of Singing-Wolf, the son of King Keyauwee Jack. By lineage, that makes him the last king, really. And as far as we know, he is not dead. The legend said 'bones of the kings.' He'd have to die first."

"Maybe he will. Perhaps that's part of the plan. But I think he wants to take a lot of people with him. You remember Chief George Cloud said revenge for the Uwharrie meant that every last one of their enemies had to be killed. Well, maybe they do want an eye for an eye. A village for a....a town. Clearview."

"What do we do now?"

"We take what we have to Witherspoon. He can believe it or not. It doesn't really matter much. If we're right, a sheriff won't provide much protection."

"I meant, what do *we* do, David."

He could tell by her eyes she already knew. "We go to Spirit Rock to hunt some ghosts."

Then Diana cried, "Ohmigod! David?"

"What's wrong?"

"What day is today?"

"Why, the 23rd..." Then he knew why she was upset.

"Yeah," he said. "Joseph Priddy wrote the massacre took place on the 25th. Day after tomorrow."

He pushed harder on the accelerator along the empty, dusk-laden road.

CHAPTER THIRTY-EIGHT

Sheriff Joe Witherspoon had believed just enough of David's fantastic story to at least check out John Wolfe Singer. Perhaps he was Blackwell's front now, or vice versa. Hale was obviously taking drugs, but he could deal with him later; right now, he wanted Blackwell and Singer. He had been meaning to visit Singer's shack up in the hills. Singer was a stranger in town, and strangers caused trouble. Now he had all the proof he needed.

The rough, rocky road increased in incline and finally ran out altogether, into a sort of rutted path. Witherspoon was glad he had decided to take the jeep for the trip.

Although he had spent most of his life in and around these mountains, the blue-black hills brooding on the horizon always gave him a strange sensation, as if he were suddenly a bit lightheaded. They seemed to draw you to them, especially at dusk. Almost as if the low, rounded peaks were a giant slumbering animal that shortly would wake, shake itself, and rise to a terrible height. There was a power to the mountains that was not benevolent; they were standing in wait for the proper moment to reveal their ancient, ominous secrets.

Witherspoon shook off the superstitious thoughts with a shudder of his shoulders, and concentrated on navigating the narrow trail to Singer's shack. Any of these sharp rocks might strike a tire at the wrong angle, and even the four-wheel drive would be useless. Witherspoon didn't relish the thought of being stuck out here so far from town. The shack, the outline of which was just barely visible now against the dying sun, looked as lonely and forlorn a structure as he had ever seen. God, he thought, what kind of man would voluntarily choose to live in a wasteland like this, miles from the nearest real road, with nothing but yellow-eyed owls and weasels for company?

When he had first taken the job as sheriff twenty years ago, there were a few old codgers, hermits who lived in such rugged isolation. But those men were true eccentrics, as solitary and independent as pack rats. Harmless, stubborn creatures who sooner or later were found after a hard winter by the circling buzzards above their lean-tos, dead for months, leaving this earth as outcasts, the way they had lived. Singer, on the other hand, at least had a history of living and working in the world, but very suddenly had abandoned his job and the comforts of society to stay in a shack on the side of this barren foothill. Witherspoon was enough of a psychologist to know such drastic alterations were the product of the mind, of some great inner turmoil. Singer could be crazy, or dangerous, or both. The sheriff unconsciously reached to stroke the butt of his revolver.

Witherspoon parked the vehicle around a bend in the path; trees would block any view from the shack. It was probably an unncessary precaution, he thought, as he trekked slowly through the brush. Besides, if Singer was as much of an Indian as he looked, he would have heard the whining, straining low gear half a mile away. But the sheriff had a bad feeling about this trip, which grew stronger as he approached the shack. The place was dark, no light and no sound. It looked not only empty, but deserted, uninhabited, as if no one had lived there at all since the last prospector died on the mountain.

Witherspoon was taking no chances, however. His revolver was already drawn; he held it at shoulder height, ready to defend himself if need be. The sense of danger had grown with the altitude. He had always prided himself on his instincts, and this was one of those rare times when every fiber of his system was on full alert. If he could have seen something, anything, he would have felt better. Or heard human sounds from the shack. Anything at all. But the absolute silence and the darkness through the cabin window unnerved him. It was always the things you couldn't hear, couldn't see that could kill you.

He continued, crouching now, toward the building.

Then a voice sounded from behind. One word. The same word Thomas had yelled at him two months before.

He froze, trying to get a fix on the origin of the voice. Was it straight behind? Slightly to the left? To the right? Close, he knew. Then he thought, straight behind, and wheeled around, held the revolver to chest height, hollering "Stop! Halt!"

The figure was almost invisible, black on a field of black, but he saw the eyes. Red, glowing like the eyes of a cougar. And it was springing at him; he heard the push of the feet off the rocky soil, the parting of the wind as it hurtled toward him.

He fired at point- black range, a foot below the eyes darting straight at him. Once, twice, three times the muzzle exploded. Then the eyes were on him. He was hit hard in the chest, a great force knocked him sprawling, and he was rolling, end over end, down the slope, rocks and dirt clods ripping his back and chest.

He stopped rolling and lay motionless, just before blacking out, wondering why three shots at point-blank range didn't stop the thing, whatever it was.

Impossible. Couldn't have missed.

Then the eyes were over him; he managed to make out a human

shape below them, moving down the hill. He passed out before Wolf-Singer reached him. This very probably saved his life.

Wolf-Singer was a Uwharrie brave now, and it was against custom to kill a man who could not watch you as you took his life from him. He placed the knife back in its sheath, and with one motion hoisted Witherspoon on his back. The lawman seemed to weigh less than straw. Singer took off at a trot down the mountain side.

The clearing was glowing very brightly in the distance. He used it as a landmark as he moved over the rough ground with his quarry, toward Spirit Rock.

CHAPTER THIRTY-NINE

David's volkswagen was able to negotiate the rutted path to the clearing and beyond, then along the river in a rough and rock-strewn path that led close to the spire that was called Spirit Rock. It was something of a local landmark but seldom visited; it was considered dangerous. The rock jutted up in a phallic projection some fifty or sixty feet and was next to a small mountainous hill of shale and grey slate rock, difficult and treacherous to climb. Over the years, two backpackers had been severely injured in falls from the mountain, and an out-of-state spelunker, looking for a cave in the region, had been found floating in the river, missing most of his face after an obvious misadventure.

The car finally began to encounter a series of undulating mounds of earth that threatened to tear out the differential or damage the axle, so David thought it prudent to abandon the car and proceed by foot.

The afternoon sun was waning. "It's going to be dark soon. And even if we find the cave before then, what can we do inside in the dark?"

"I have a flashlight," David said, realizing how silly it sounded. That was all the equipment he had, a flashlight from the glove compartment, and a rapid pulse. Not much to go fighting magic with, if indeed there was magic about. He was more concerned with another Rose-like attack, perhaps from Blackwell. Or worse, from Singer.

For these two, or any other flesh-and-blood creature, he had a .22 target pistol that had been his father's, long kept on a closet shelf. The ammunition was old and might misfire .It was more for bluff than actual use; he was no gunman, and could just as easily shoot Diana or himself as an attacker. But he would use it if it came to that.

"Are you scared?" he asked.

Diana shivered a bit, either from fear or a sudden breeze that rose off the river. "Yes," she said.

"You'd be crazy if you weren't. I'm scared, too. But listen, I told you before, I'd feel better if you stayed here with the car."

"Uh-uh. We're in this together."

"If I did get in trouble, hurt myself or something, you could go for help from here."

"No. If you get in trouble, I want to be in trouble, too. Besides, I really don't know where I could get help. We seem to be pretty much on our own in this thing, whatever it is."

That was true enough, he thought. The sheriff had told them to go home and stay there. There was no use trying to convince him or Ed of a hundred-year-old-plus deadline of revenge.

They started out, following the river along the bank. The undergrowth grew heavier and thicker and higher as they neared the spire of the Rock.

David had no real plan except to find the same spot where Singer had disappeared. The cave, if there was one, would be around there. Where else could Singer have gone?

They climbed over a hillock, and David recognized the surroundings. It was near here that he had first noticed Jack Rose acting oddly. Could it be that proximity to the site of the Uwharrie ritual had altered Jack's mind? Perhaps they were near the cave.

Then he saw something strange, a slab of stone, roughly square, a foot or so taller than a man and about five feet wide, a foot thick. It had been removed from the rock and lay across part of the trail.

It was not a natural formation and seemed almost like a door removed from its hinges and laid to one side. With Rose, he had walked right by this spot and seen only sheer, solid stone. But now there was a jagged hole.

"Over here," he told Diana. They squeezed behind a slate wall and then through a fissure in the stone. There was a sudden drop-off, almost like earthen steps, leading down to the base of the cliff. And at the base, an opening.

The opening of the cave was small and low, and there was a cold breeze blowing out of the entrance, as if a wind were generated from some cooler area inside.

Once inside, however, they saw that the cave was high-ceilinged. The flashlight lost its beam before quite reaching the vault of the roof.

"My God," said David. "It's like a cathedral."

A cathedral it might have resembled in height, but the other aspects were more of the Underworld. The flashlight played over the side walls, wet and black; water was seeping slowly from either overhead or up from further underground. The air was wet and fetid, chill, a tubercular coldness. Spots of dark green and brown moss grew in fissures and cracks in the wall.

From the entranceway, where the late afternoon sun quickly was absorbed, a slightly concave rut led on a gentle slope into the interior of the huge cavern. It was like a path; but one which the two hesitated to follow. The absence of light here, the change of elements from warm dusk to a sudden, sepulchral chill, gave David goosebumps and raised the hair on his neck.

"I suppose we have to go forward," said Diana. Her voice echoed softly two or three times and then was absorbed by the blackness.

David nodded, touched her on the forearm as if not to fear. It was as much a gesture for himself. He took a deep breath of the damp air and started down the slope.

The main cave extended for what must have been several hundred feet, always downward. As they drew lower, the damp of the cave walls changed to a mossy slickness. From somewhere deeper, the sound of rushing water was evident. David cursed himself for not bringing a stronger flashlight. The beam was almost swallowed up in the inky darkness, such that he had to train it carefully on the sloping path.

At the end of the huge cavern was a fissure in the rock leading to the right; the sound of rushing water was stronger from that direction. The two moved sideways through the cleft. The flashlight wavered as David grabbed a handhold to pull himself along. Suddenly, his wrist was grasped in a powerful grip. He was pulled through to the other side, his feet almost leaving the ground from the strength of the pull.

"Welcome," said Peter Blackwell, as Anne Morris grabbed Diana when she emerged, putting her in a chokehold. "We've been waiting for you, Dave," he laughed.

The pressure from Blackwell's hand on David's wrist felt as if it would crush the bone. For inexplicable reasons, the thin, unathletic Blackwell had become immensely strong.

"What...what are you two doing? Leave her alone!" David managed to yell over the pain.

Anne Morris, hair disheveled and face smudged, but otherwise recognizable, loosened her grip on Diana's throat.

There was a soft light in this new chamber. It was like an alcove outside a larger cavern from where reddish-yellow light issued. A good-sized break in the rock must be the entranceway; the sound of water was very strong from there.

Blackwell took the gun from David and tossed it clattering into the darkness. "Wouldn't have done you any good, anyway," he said.

He lossened his grip and let go of David's wrist. "Hurts, doesn't it?" he laughed.

Anne Morris moved away from Diana to stand woodenly near the entrance to the cave room. Blackwell, on the other hand, had become more animated and cheerful.

"You think we ought to tie these two up?" he asked Anne. There was no reply. Blackwell chattered on, to David: "She doesn't have much to say any more. She's even worse than Thomas. But no, I don't think we'll have to tie you up."

He thumped David on the shoulder with his forefinger, like someone would thump a melon in a supermarket. The effect was like being hit with a brick. David groaned under the pain.

"See what I mean?" grinned Blackwell. "That was just to show you there's no reason to try and get away. You ever see anything like that, Dave?" He wiggled his finger. "As long as old Sparrow's in town, I could beat the shit out of Superman. Why, I could literally tear your arm out of its socket. Just reach over and pluck it off."

For a moment, David thought he was going to do just that, but Blackwell was studying his finger again. "Yeah, damndest thing I ever saw. Wish my father was around; he always thought I was a wimp. Imagine that!"

"What is all this about?" asked Diana,her eyes widened by David's continuing pain. "Why were you waiting for us here?"

"What? Why, so old Sparrow can carry out his plan, of course."

"Who's Sparrow?" asked David. "What sort of plan?" He thought it best to pretend ignorance; it seemed to keep Blackwell preoccupied. He was pleased to find that he could still move his aching shoulder.

"Why, the shaman, of course. I thought you knew that already, Dave. The Uwharrie boogie man. Big medicine man, lots of power. Magic, you know?"

"You're crazy!" yelled Diana. "The whole lot of you are crazy!"

"No," said David. "I'm afraid he's not crazy, Diana." He looked at Blackwell. "It has something to do with the clearing, doesn't it? The bones that were missing, they belong here in the cave, don't they?"

"Keyauwee Jack? Oh yeah, he's in the next room over there, with the others. In the river, all the kings' bones in the river. Getting ready to go over to the Other Side, like the rest of us."

David tried to ignore the last statement. "You did something to Dawes, didn't you? Killed him so Singer could work at the dig and find the skeleton of the last king, the one that wasn't brought here because of the massacre."

"Something like that. Sparrow, he doesn't have to explain, not to me, anyway. He's got all the power; he only gives me a little, but that's enough. When we cross over the river he's going to make me assistant shaman, something like that, you know? You ever rode on a cloud, David? You ever fly through thunder? Well, I have! It's like an acid trip, except it's *real,* Dave. I mean, I stumbled onto the mother lode when I got lost in the woods that night. Met up with the guru of all time, the birdman, the ultimate Mojo."

"And Schlosser? You killed him too, didn't you?"

"Sure. And the Professor. Sorry about that, Diana, but it was absolutely necessary. Anne did it. I can promise you, the old fellow went out in a blaze of glory. Pardon the pun."

"Harry Wiggins. What about him?"

"Wiggins? Yeah, him too, but it was a mistake, a bad move. He thought what was happening to him was another sort of breakdown. He fought it too hard, couldn't let himself feel the power the shaman gives you. He couldn't realize it was all *real,* wasn't a dream. And it freaked him out. By that time you were getting close, so we moved him here."

Blackwell escorted them through the hewn rock opening as if he were a tour guide to the Underworld. "And this, folks, is the inner chamber. The sanctum sanctorum, if you will. You'll recognize on your right..."—and there was Joe Witherspoon, tied with leather thongs to an outcropping of jagged rock—"the law in our neighborhood," Blackwell continued.

The Sheriff had welts on his face and a huge gash over his right eyebrow that had run blood, coagulated now, over that side of his face so that it was a grotesque reddish-black.

But more gruesome was the rest of his body. Diana choked back a scream when she saw it, and David drew in a sharp breath. Witherspoon's shirt had been ripped from his chest and hung in shards. There were long slivers of wood piercing the muscles of his chest and arms. The odor of singed hair and flesh floated in the dampness of the room; David saw that some of the slivers were shorter than the others, and blackened. Where they met the flesh, open burns the size of quarters dotted the Sheriff's trunk.

"You son-of-a-bitch," Witherspoon spat at Blackwell. But his tongue was thick and he looked as if he were about to pass out.

"Shut the brave lawman up, sweetie," snapped Blackwell. Anne Morris ran across the black rock and stuffed a piece of cloth in Witherspoon's mouth.

David couldn't quite believe the scene he was witnessing. It was all too much like a nightmare, or a horror movie.

The subterranean room was small, not much larger than the main room of the library, and very wet, with water dripping here and there, seeping down the black rock that made up its walls and overhead. A cave within a cave, and very cool, almost cold. The rushing water was from an underground stream, probably part of the larger river. The stream rushed at the back of the chamber, only a foot or so beneath a low ledge, open and visible and roaring along. The kings' bones must be under the water there, thought David.

The fire burned with an occasional snap of twig or log in the center of the room. It cast an orange glow to the spectral figures on the other side beyond the fire.

Harry Wiggins shivered and alternately stared ahead in a catatonic-like, fixed gaze at the fire, only to look up with startled eyes at the newcomers. But there was no recognition there.

He's dead, thought David. *Dead and buried.*

But he was here, just the same.

What David saw next sent a further shiver of fear down his spine. The old Indian with the burning eyes squatted behind the fire, like something out of a drawing in the Father McGill history.

Sparrow-in-Snow, the shaman.

Beside him stood John Singer, barechested, his upper body gleaming with either sweat or grease, David couldn't tell. He knew it was Singer, although he also had on facial pigment, white with a black circle around his right eye. His arms were crossed over his chest and his face was impassive; he seemed to be waiting for the old Indian to come to life, to move from his meditative state. Or was it meditation? David wondered. He seemed to be in a trance, merging mentally with the crackling flames before him.

If Sparrow were a ghost, David was thinking, he was the most impressive ghost he had ever seen. Even squatting, the Indian seemed to be enormous, and his shadow on the wall of the cave was immense. The flickering firelight cast an ominous, unreal quality to the undergound structure, but the shaman seemed to carry his own light within him. There was a surreal glow to the garment he wore, and his eyes burned with a reddish glow, like the coals of a long-simmering fire.

But he was not quite solid, either. Some of the firelight passed through him and played against his shadow on the wall.

This is not happening, thought David, seeing the other inhabitants of the room.

The professor, Diana's father, stood like a zombie against the side of the cave. His face and neck were covered with burns.

Diana wavered on her feet when she saw him, too shocked to do anything but groan.

Schlosser stood upright , but with his eyes puffed and blue like a drowned man pulled out of water—or photographic developing fluid.

Dawes sat with his mouth contorted and his neck and face blackish-blue, like someone in the throes of a heart attack.

"It's a trick," David mumbled, more to hold onto his reason than to explain anything. It was all unexplainable.

"Magic," countered Blackwell.

Peter Blackwell had pulled his shirt off, and was smiling and grinning, obviously enjoying himself. He stepped to lay another piece of wood on the fire from a pile in a dark recess of the room. In the brighter light, David saw he had a streak of red pigment across his forehead, with two black streaks down his cheeks parallel to his nose.

He winked at Diana and giggled. The fire roared higher.

Anne Morris moved closer to the fire, naked now except for a cloth around her loins. Her skin was very dark, the nipples almost black. She sat and crossed her legs yoga-style on the cold rock floor. She was silent, and peered straight at David with such hatred, almost a rage, that he could not look her in the face.

Blackwell snapped his fingers at the girl. "Cut the Marshal loose and prepare him for the dance."

Witherspoon had passed out; he looked near death. Anne

obediently rose, crossed the floor and began to cut the thongs with a bone knife.

"Magic," Blackwell said again. "Much mojo."

David shook his head. "Those people are dead. Either buried in the ground or in a morgue in Ulah. They aren't real. It's hypnotism, or voodoo, mumbo jumbo—not real, no, not real." He shook his head again savagely, trying to clear away the evidence of his own eyes.

Blackwell smiled, the face paint turning his grin into a malignant leer. "Think what you want, Dave. Doesn't matter in the least. But you're right, in a way. They're not the people you knew. Sparrow took them over. You might say they took a trip into the past, and we borrowed their—how can I say it—borrowed their *essence* while they were gone. And some of the tribe, the essence of the tribe, inhabited the shells."

"Like Jack Rose? And Mason Thomas?"

"Right, Dave. Boy, you're analytical today."

"But you're not through with them yet."

Blackwell laughed. "Right. We're not through with them yet."

David's mouth was suddenly filled with the taste of bile. "The shaman, why does he just sit there? Why doesn't the bastard say something?"

Blackwell wagged a finger in David's face. "He doesn't really *talk* to anybody but Singer. All the rest is through the eyes. When the time comes, Dave, just stare straight into his eyes. It'll be quicker that way, and I guarantee you won't feel a thing. Well, yes, you will too, since you look so much like Major Simpson, and Sparrow might want to slow it down a bit..."

"What the hell do you mean by that?" David shouted. His crazy theory was coming true before his eyes. But he wasn't supposed to be part of it. It was all too cruelly real and sinister.

Witherspoon groaned as Anne Morris pushed a fresh pine splinter into the flesh of his bicep.

"I've got nothing to do with Simpson," shouted David, really scared now. "The druggist, Eugene Fleming, he's the descendant." Then he forced himself to lower his voice, to control the panic.

"Hell, you must know that. He's different; he must be one of you already."

"You're the one, David," said Blackwell. "The old man wanted to save you for last."

And then he understood, or thought he did. Miss Priddy had said something about Simpson having an illegitimate child. It could have been any local girl, she said...

Blackwell read his mind. "That's right. Your great-grand-mother conceived a bastard child, a boy, by our Major. But she was sent to live with an aunt in Virginia, posed as a widow, had the baby and got married there later to a man named Robert Hale. He worked as a switchman for the railroad and got careless one day, and that was it for him. So Mrs. Hale moved back to Clearview, as a real widow this time, and there have been little Hales running around here ever since. At least one male in each generation. Your grandfather, your father, and now—isn't history fascinating, Dave?— you're the last one. The last lineal male descendant of Major Simpson. Just as Wolf-Singer is the last of the line of King Keyauwee Jack." Blackwell giggled. "Going to burn, Dave. First Diana and then you. Try to die well, will you? It's a much better omen that way."

David pushed down the panic again.

Something wasn't jelling in all this, he thought frantically. Wiggins was certainly dead—but now he was alive; or was he really? Maybe he was someplace in-between. And was it really Wiggins? It was his face, but the bone structure was somehow different, the cheekbones more prominent, the skin more sallow, darker...

Hale gambled, swallowing hard so that his voice wouldn't tremble. "Blackwell," he said.

Peter was studying his index finger again. "Yeah, Dave?" he answered, not looking up.

"When Sparrow first met you, when he showed you the power he had, what happened? I mean, how did you feel?"

"That's a silly question for somebody who's about to be burned alive, Dave. But I'll tell you. It was like he did with Anne and the others later, I guess. He sort of grabbed me with his eyes and then he reached out...and I kind of dissolved for a moment—I told you it was like acid, Dave— and then I was riding in the sky high over a river, and I had this new power myself, and I was different."

"Different, you say."

"Yeah, different. Peter Blackwell, but not Peter Blackwell. Stronger, freer. No longer the neurotic rich kid, but a...a natural animal, you know?"

"You know what I think, Pete? I think you're dead. I think you're already dead, and you just don't know it."

Blackwell giggled.

"Don't you see?" David continued. "You killed Dawes, Schlosser and Wiggins. Anne Morris killed Professor Walters. But you said yourself they were 'borrowed' by Sparrow."

"So?"

"Well, why couldn't you be borrowed, too? Just being used temporarily. Your essence ripped out and the spirit of the tribe put into your shell. I think that's what you are now, a shell."

"You think I'm an Indian?" said Blackell. But it was partly a real question, not a smirking comment.

"Yeah, Pete, and a damn good Indian at that. Cause you're sure a dead one."

"Keep silent!" barked Singer from the back.

"No, Wolf, it's okay, he doesn't bother me..."

"Wesichau! White devils! All of you keep silent."

Blackwell laughed, then abruptly cut it short. "Look, Wolf," he said to the hate-filled face, "I know you're the new king and all that, but I'm part of this too, and Sparrow promised me plenty if I played my part. I kept the hicks in Clearview complacent, ran a false trail for the marshal, stole and killed to make sure the prophecy would go smoothly. So there wouldn't be a panic, so the hicks wouldn't run away. Now, I did all that so you can have your fun tonight. I shouldn't be treated as one of them. I've got rights in this deal, and my own power too, from Sparrow, and..."

Singer turned to the spectre of Sparrow-in-Snow. Their eyes met, and Singer nodded once. They had agreed on something. The shaman seemed to disperse in thin air and then coalesce again next to Backwell.

He was suddenly firghtened. "Hey! What's going on?"

"You wished for your reward. Now you will receive it," said Singer.

"But..."

A translucent hand reached out and touched Blackwell; a quick burst of flame enveloped him, then smouldering bones fell to the floor where he had stood.

In quick order, the others were also touched. Dr. Walters, Dawes, Schlosser. Anne Morris was last. Her scream was cut in half by the sudden transformation of seeming flesh into dry bones that broke as they hit the rock floor.

The shock of that scene might have caused Diana to faint, except that just then Witherspoon, with a horrified look on his face, suddenly lurched to his feet. He was out of his mind with pain, but his muscular body was trying on its own to escape, to get out somehow. He ran crazily across the rock toward Singer. He fell heavily onto the Indian, a blow that, from sheer weight, would have put down many men; but Singer brushed him aside like an insect. His face splattered against the rock wall of the cavern, and he fell back down in a heap. He had stopped breathing.

David saw the opportunity, a split second where the attention of both Singer and the old shaman had strayed. "Now," he whispered fiercely to Diana, and, half scuttling over the floor and dragging her by the arm, he dashed for the underground stream. There was a wild chance it might emerge outside the cave; but even if it didn't, he'd rather drown than be turned into a pile of bones by that ghoul Sparrow.

He jumped into the swirling water, pulling Diana with him.

The cold water hit him like a brick wall; his body was immediately thrown into a clench, his muscles jerking in spasms and the air forced out of his chest. It was like ice; they had jumped into liquid ice.

Somehow he held onto Diana's hand, and his other arm began to work. He pulled in a half-crawl a few feet. He heard either Singer or Sparrow cry out. Then the water swept him fast toward a rock tunnel and he dove, taking Diana under with him.

There was no need to try to swim, the water sucked them along at high speed. David had gulped air before the rock passed over him, but the cold and the fear was using it up at an accelerated rate. He felt his chest begin to burn, hot inside and freezing without. The swirling current battered him against unseen walls of stone; a jagged edge ripped into his arm. He wanted to scream, but managed to keep his mouth closed. *We're dying,* he thought, as lights danced in his head. He was turning over and over now, spun by the current. He lost his hold on Diana.

In desperation, he clawed out, trying to catch hold of some edge or corner of the mad whirlpool. He did succeed in stopping his revolutions, and was being swept along now on his back.

His air was gone and he had to breathe, the burning in his chest was indescribable. He clawed again, felt a scant inch or two of air above the water. Between the top of the river and the rocks overhead.

The tunnel took a turn, and he was able to push his face above the water, breathed and gulped the precious air. Water ran down his nose and throat and he coughed, spat and breathed again. Diana bumped into him from behind. He reached around her, somehow found her head, pushed it toward the space of air. And they were both breathing. Then the tunnel straightened out and he was turned over again on his stomach.

His whole body was numb, frozen. The burning was in his chest again and the cold tightened the diaphragm there like an iron band. He clawed again, found another few inches of air as they were swept along. He pushed himself up, and got his nose above the water line. Everything was dark, they were like blind drowning fish in a cold, dead tunnel.

David felt dead; maybe he was dead and just didn't know it yet, like the others. He was floating more slowly now, unable to feel his fingers or his legs. He didn't know if he was breathing or not. But the rush of water was slower. Yes, he was floating on his back. It was air, not water going into his mouth and nose. The river had widened, the space of air was larger. Three inches. Then five, eight. A foot. He saw light, a dim white light. Then his head hit a great slab of rock, and he was in darkness again.

David regained consciousness minutes, or pehaps only seconds later. When he came to, he was coughing up a volume of cold water. With each expulsion it seemed he would black out again; but he didn't, and finally was able to take long, deep breaths of air.

When his vision cleared completely, he saw he was lying half in and half out of the water. A root sticking out from the bank had halted his progress. He was in weak sunlight, near dusk. The bank was sloping and low; he pulled himself up and peered over the grass at the bank's edge, trying to get a fix on his location. From his prone position he could see the spire of the Baptist church, and reckoned he was only a mile or so from town, in a creek that was used primarily for sewage disposal. The children of the town called it Stinking Creek for that reason. But there were no children playing around there now; there was only he and...

Where was Diana? The blow on the head had temporarily blocked her from his thoughts. The last thing he remembered was her bumping into his body in the river tunnel. Perhaps she had been swept along further downstream. Maybe drowned, submerged now in the slimy water, gone forever. But she had been breathing when he last was conscious of her; he had heared her gasps for air just before the rock struck his head.

He climbed up the top of the bank, looking for any sign of her. The eddies and swirls of water were much slower here, not swift and broiling as in the cave. She couldn't be too far away, either dead or alive.

At first glance her body was not evident in the low channel. He looked farther upstream, toward the mountain. It was several miles away; the underground tunnel must have shot them through at an incredible speed to get him this far from the cave on the other side of the mountain. Either that or...or he had been unconscious for a long time. If that were the case, Diana could be many hundreds of yards away in either direction. Perhaps, he thought, she had never made it out of the cave altogether, was caught by a protuberance, a jagged edge of tunnel wall, caught and held there to drown...

He sat down heavily, exhausted and heartsick. He thought with spent emotion that surely the shaman and Singer would be even now on their way to get him, to retrieve their captive. He was just too tired and numb to fathom that danger now.

Diana, he thought, remembering her soft flesh next to him on their nights of love.

Then he saw her.

She was moving, struggling to regain her feet as she pushed at a clump of matted, rusty-colored weeds and refuse. Completely out of the water, her body had been hidden from him by the thick foliage which had stopped her progress downstream.

His energy returned, he ran to her, slogging and splashing across the creek. "You're alive!" he said, with a rush of joy and gratitude in his heart.

He helped her stand on the sloping bank. She was muddy, her arms and neck were cut and bruised by the buffeting in the tunnel, her hair was wild and matted and she smelled of the sewage of the creek. She was still beautiful.

"I think I'm alive," she said, managing a half smile. Then they grabbed each other and held tight, shivering in the near dark.

CHAPTER FORTY

Mason Thomas crouched behind a line of shrubbery in a residential lawn, three staves of gasoline-soaked wood under his arm and a throw-away cigarette lighter in his pocket.

For some moments he was confused, not really understanding what he was doing here; why he had bolted up from his kitchen table at about dusk, and fled the house, knowing only that he must come to town. His son Willie had chased after him, tried to stop him from starting the truck; Thomas had struck out with an arm that no longer seemed to be under his control. The powerful blow knocked the boy off his feet. He had scrambled up, and managed to jump in the bed of the pickup as Thomas slowed to exit his rutted driveway and turn left toward Clearview. The truck swerved along the highway in great arcs, finally throwing the boy out of the bed and onto the roadside shoulder a mile or so back.

Thomas remembered these incidents as if seeing someone else doing them. He recalled his arm slashing out with a will of its own, the hard blow cracking against Willie's face, but the impact was not transmitted up his arm. It was as if he had hit the boy with a piece of wood or a crowbar. His whole body felt like that now, full of a foreign yet powerful energy and strength. And there was a great insensate rage within him, as yet with no definite object. The odor of the gasoline in his nostrils merged with other odors, very strong, of blood and fire and a damp smell like flooded ground.

The smells had driven him to stop the truck at the gas station, swerving the vehicle into a broadside. Then he had jumped out of the cab, looking for something or someone to attack.

Claude Benson, the owner, had seen him barreling from the truck and tried futilely to run; but Thomas brought his arm down on the back of Benson's neck. The sound of breaking bone had given him a brief ecstatic joy, almost like an orgasm. He let loose from his throat a shrieking sound that was more animal than human, crowing over his fallen and motionless victim.

Then he had found the staves in the junkpile in back of the empty station, pumped out gasoline over the pieces, and set out on foot in the early dark, his footsteps light and rapid over the ground. His speed seemed incredible to him.

Jack Rose drove the backhoe along route 8 and into Clearview. He saw Mason Thomas club Claude Benson to the ground, but this had nothing to do with his particular mission, and he ignored the scene. The occasional pedestrian along Commerce Street turned to look in curiosity at the machine as it made its way down the street at ten miles an hour; there was no new construction around town. A few people who knew Jack waved to him, wanted Rose to stop and explain why he was driving a backhoe down the main street of town, but he kept staring straight ahead, rounding the corner at Elm Street and then passing over the railroad siding.

Rose pulled the backhoe to an idling stop where Elm intersected with Market. He then put the machine into reverse, stopped again a few feet off the asphalt. He pulled another switch and a set of pneumatic braces lowered from the body of the machine and anchored it to the spot.

Jack paused to light a cigar and then selected the controls that would lower the digging blade of the backhoe to the ground. It had been some ten years since he had operated such a machine, but the controls were still familiar to him. He felt the blade bite deeply into the earth. Another lever caused it to scoop up another yard of hard-packed earth. Still another moved the scoop a few feet sideways and dropped the load. Then back again.

By the time a few curious shopkeepers had been drawn by the noise of the digging, the backhoe had excavated a short trench some six feet or more under the surface.

Jack Rose felt the blade strike and stall momentarily. Smiling, he tossed his cigar toward a sign a few feet away, the one that said, DANGER: GAS MAIN. Then he revved the powerful engine and gave the blade control another nudge, and was lost in the explosion that followed.

The fire had seemed to start everywhere at once. The row of stately oaks along Market street ignited one by one like a row of towering candles. The roof of the drug store was crackling, having caught from the orange flames that now could be seen through the windows. A sign saying SPECIAL—COSMETICS SALE curled into a black shard, as did a picture of a smiling, tanned girl on a sun lotion display. Then the window exploded from the heat, sending a shower of hot glass into the street. Along with Helen Wiggins, the counter clerk and druggist Eugene Fleming.

The explosion had caught Deputy Ed Molton literally with his pants down—he was in the office john, reading the sports section of the newspaper. When he heard the boom, he'd pulled up his pants and ran, gathering his holster belt around his middle, just as the smell of smoke reached his nostrils.

He was stunned, shocked at what he saw up and down the main street. The drug store, the post office, and the cafe were on fire, and a broiling cloud of black smoke wavered over the town like a tornado. Molton ran back into the office, tried to dial Ulah and the volunteer fire department there. But before he could finish the number, the line went dead. The main telephone cable was just then crashing with its pole into the roof of a two-story frame house on Commerce Street. He tried the radio, really scared now, and sensing an omen in Witherspoon's earlier failure to call back. "Sheriff, Sheriff, come in, come in!" he cried over and over, until he felt the heat at the back of his neck and realized the jail was on fire, too. Ed ran into the street again, trying to make some sense of all this sudden smoke and flame. But even the trees down by the highway turnoff were on fire. In fact, the whole stand of pines that encircled the town was being consumed. *Oh my god*, he thought, his mouth going dry with fear: *forest fire.*

But why hadn't the ranger spotted it, called in, and got an evacuation going? No, there must be some nearby source, some touchstone that had sparked the blazes. But what, and where?

Then he saw Mason Thomas, a crazed grin on his face, running from the real estate office; he was waving two torches that gave off an oily smoke as he ran. The deputy shook himself loose from his panic when he realized what Thomas was doing. Molton was a good shot, and a single bullet hit the farmer in the middle of the back. He went down like a sack of corn meal, like dead weight. One of the torches touched his shirt, and he exploded into flame. It burned out in a second, like flash paper. When Molton got to the body, it was nothing but a skeleton; white bone gleaming among grey ashes and the still-smouldering torch.

David and Diana, having failed to rouse the town in time, were caught in the open, at the end of Commerce. The fire was spreading incredibly fast around them, leaping from rooftop to rooftop and from tree to tree as a sudden wind grew stronger, then swirled furiously in a fiery circle around the main street. They were trapped now, their safety only temporary. David feared the billows of smoke that were looming lower and lower as much as the orange and yellow flames dancing on every side. They both were drenched with sweat, and the air was hard to breathe. David felt his lungs work harder, his heart pump more furiously, but he could not get a full breath. He remembered with a panic reading about firestorms in World War II, how whole populations of European cities like Dresden had perished not by fire or smoke but from suffocation, the oxygen jerked up to feed the flames in greater and greater fury.

But he saw there was no way to get out of the town, into the serene countryside beyond the circle of trees that was visible through the conflagration.

The mayor was dancing in the street. His clothes were on fire and the flames climbed upward to his face, where his mouth was open in an interminable scream.

Wolf-Singer stood in the middle of Commerce Street, watching the chaos impassively, and feeling an inner peace. A charred section of the collapsing roof of the cafe landed with a thump beside him and rolled harmlessly past. Cinders landed on his shoulders and he brushed them away calmly. It took more fire than that to harm a Uwharrie whose power came from the river.

He listened to the screams of Millie Mabe and her husband inside the cafe. They would stop soon, he knew. He was not bothered by screams anymore. The fat woman and her drone were enemies to him, worth only slight notice. They had not died well. No, not died well at all.

Another person was propelled from a house by an explosion. The figure was swathed in fire, orange with black underneath. It crumpled and seemed to melt in the brown lawn that here and there was beginning to smoulder. Wolf-Singer smiled at the absence of screams from this one. He tried breiefly to recall who it could be— but it was no matter. One Wesichau was the same as another now.

No, it really did not matter. They all would die, without names or faces, as the village had died. Brother fire would do the work.

The screams of the dying Wesichau did not move him. But he heard the trees in their pain, felt their sap-blood vaporize with a savage whisper, a sighing scream. The houses that cracked, their groans were real. The wood was alive, the flames were alive and sang to him. they sucked up the air to feed their roaring melody. The wind blew; the whirlwind danced overhead. It was happy, just as he was happy.

Wolf-Singer watched the townspeople burning, and watched them fall in the street, but he also saw something else. He saw this with his new eyes, his Uwharrie eyes. He saw the shadow of a huge bird, a giant sparrow, come down from out of the wind and pluck up each Wesichau as it fell, gripping the body that was now only flame and bone, and swoop upward with it in its claws. In a second, the bird was high and far away, toward the river. The claws would let go, the skeleton would drop, then disappear. The great bird would make a wide circle and come back from the North, its shadow once again over the town, ready for the next Wesichau to fall.

David searched frantically for some place to escape the heat and the suffocating smoke. He saw that although the new addition of the library was going up like tinder, the older stone section was free of the flames.

And probably would stay that way, he thought. Stone , brick and ironwork didn't burn. He and Diana might suffocate from smoke inhalation, but at least the flames wouldn't get them. They woudn't go like Witherspoon at the hands of the old Indian and his ghouls.

As they gained the shelter of the arched doorway, he turned, hearing a particularly loud scream, and saw Gertrude near the smoking ruins of what had been the real estate office. She was blackened all over, her clothes singed into her skin. She fell heavily on the sidewalk. Then it seemed there was a large shadow that swooped down, a flutter like huge wings, and she was gone.

Diana screamed beside him, and he pulled her into the shelter under the arch. The smoke had cleared a bit on the street and he saw John Singer standing in the middle of the street. The Indian was smiling at him. It was a hideous grin, an animal watching its prey; a rage of teeth and nostril and the red orb of an eye.

Then, from above, a frantic scraping on the library roof, like claws. The shadow and the flutter again, and brief darkness as the shape cut off the light through high windows.

David knew it must be the shaman, metamorphasized. Come to get him and Diana. Or at least him, anyway. Come to get Major Simpson's heir. The smoke burned his lungs and he was very afraid, but somehow he would have made a bargain if he could. He'd go if Diana were spared.

He was holding her and pulling one step, and then two, up the spiral staircase. He looked up, wondering if the heat would dislodge the stone of the roof and send it tumbling down on them. But no, it was holding so far.

The shadow again; and then it was gone. And he saw the shaman, a man-image again, through the open archway.

Whatever his power, it must not be limitless, David thought. The claws could not get through the roof.

The apparition at the bottom of the stairs must be part man and part spirit, ghost and man, part real and part unreal. And there must be a weakness to him somewhere. A flaw, some part he could fight off.

The old Indian had simply flown here, over the flames. Perhaps he is part of the flames, David thought. And he was here. Now. At the bottom of the steps, coming straight up. Slowly but determined, his face a fierce bright mask.

Coming after me, David knew.

"Get back," he yelled at Diana, although she was now moving up the stairs on her own. She stumbled and he caught her. They climbed backward, feeling each rung with their heels. David kept saying to himself, *don't look at the eyes, don't look at the eyes.* But it was like trying not to look at a naked woman, or at an automobile crash.

The eyes held him, and suddenly he saw it all, the whole thing in a flash. Not his life flashing before his eyes, not any of the millions of moments that had made up his life. The eyes showed him...

...another fire burning in a circle. Yes, and the river was

screaming in the background. Dawn, grey men along the tree line, the flames racing through the cornstalks...and he saw the women running from the huts and the children running, the shots ringing out...a bullet ripped through the breast of a squaw caught nursing her child, the baby biting, trying to hold on, getting blood instead of milk...and they fell in a heap.

...and he saw an arm that was like his arm somehow but different, clothed in a gray uniform, and the arm came down in a wide arc and in the hand was a sabre...a charred head rolled away from its body, came to a stop on the black grass...

David tore his gaze from the Indian's eyes, and the flashes vanished. He turned to climb further, and saw there were only three more steps. The smoke was rising, leaving the building through a hole where a part of the roof had now fallen in; smoke was being sucked up into the sky. The flames were closer now, and had eaten into all the wood and molding near the staircase; the stairs and the third story landing were isolated now. David's feet were blistering through his shoes. Diana was sagging, half-conscious from the stale air and the heat. He held her up with his right arm, climbing another step.

The heat had affected his mind. The old Indian seemed to be rising a bit with each deliberate step, to leave the ground for a split second. David shuffled another step up—and from that angle he could see the archway below, through the Indian's chest.

Something clicked in his mind, a phrase from one of the books, something that...yes: *I witnessed a feat whereby the shaman walked some rods' length through a savage fire and was unscathed. But he was most weakened by the feat, and I could have sworn there was more ghost than flesh to the man, that some of him had been used up by the flames, though how he could burn and still live was beyond my imagination...*

Then he stumbled over the paint cans, the containers of special base for the ironwork. The job he'd been putting off so long.

He reached down, grabbed a can, and pried the flat top off with his fingernails; pulled so hard it felt he was ripping the nails out by the root. But the lid moved; there was a soft sigh as it came open.

Then the other cans, three more of them, with bloody fingers as he tried to keep his gaze away from the shaman and the almost magnetic effect the seamed, hate-ravaged face exerted on him. It was as if the Indian were tugging at David's soul, trying to twist it into submission. He knew if he turned to face the shaman, his power would be too strong.

Hale forced himself to concentrate on his task as the shape, more like a heavy cloud than a form, crept up the stair like a fog. He turned one can over, then another, then the third. The black liquid glided over the slick metal and stone, following the curved contour rapidly at first and then slower as it reached the first landing, until the whole of the stairwell below them was a black oily slick.

It seemed crazy to light a cigarette in the midst of a firestorm but, with trembling fingers, David pulled one from his pocket and lit it. He puffed once, twice, very deeply so that the orange glow was strong. Then he pulled Diana up one more step and dropped the cigarette at his feet.

The stairwell erupted in a curved corridor of fire, burning and dripping down, the flames gaining height above the pool of paint near the first landing. The shaman was caught there, hovering a bit as the orange wall covered him.

David didn't know what he expected to happen. He didn't expect a scream, exactly, or any other human sound. But the silence unnerved him more than any scream could. He still felt the tugging at him from the shape, the pulling of his eyes up to meet those of the Indian. Incredibly, it was stronger now. He felt his will weaken, his resolve diminish, his fear turning into something like despair.

He was going to have to look into the shaman's eyes. He felt his head raising, his neck turning against its will, the muscles straining...

And then the sound came. Not a scream, not a groan or a cry—but a wet, small sound. Like a teakettle at first, a faint whistle of wet air rushing. A stream, a whistling. Then a flatter sizzle, a slow boiling sound.

The pressure on David's head and neck diminished. The tugging inside him slackened. His muscles stopped fighting themselves.

The shape did not loom now as it had. It was still there, but with each second the sound of steam, of vapor being freed, was louder, and the shape grew lighter, less solid.

David felt he could look now. The flames were covering the shape; it was moving backward, flowing down the landing to the archway. Then it was free of the flame. A white shadow flowed through the arch and to the outside.

Then the sound of wings again, but small ones, and a slow, wounded ascent. A crippled flutter and flap.

Then gone.

Wolf-Singer walked through the smoke and the remaining bits of flame, the small blazes that would finish the job. When he was out of the ash that sifted down, and breathed the cool air beyond the encircled town, he began to run. A short-strided run first, as he would use to chase a wounded deer who might run for hours. A hunting trot. But then he shouted in his joy, raised his arms to the sky, and saw the black night with its bank of stars. And he began to sprint, his feet like wings skimming the ground. He smelled the river in his blood now, very strong. The underground river, in the cave.

The campfire had almost gone out. The bones of the river had moved closer together.

Sparrow-in-Snow was not standing as much as floating, there in the glow of the fire. Singer could see the rock wall through him; he was like mist now, or steam after a rain. His voice was very high and no louder than a whisper.

"The seed of Simpson escaped," Singer said.

"Something always escapes," said the ancient one; his whisper echoed in the cave like wind. "Fire does not burn all of a log, nor does water cover every rock in the river."

"Yes, I understand. We will be with him just the same. As death is always there even when the child laughs. He escaped but did not escape."

"It is a small thing, and does not matter." The voice of the shaman was much dimmer now; he floated higher, the rock wall behind him was blacker. He was an outline with no real substance. Only the voice and the dampness, the mist remained. It moved over the dying fire.

"Our duty is done," it said. "The vision is true. The prophecy has come to pass. You have done well, Wolf-Singer. You are a true chief of the Uwharrie." Then it said: "We must go now."

"I am ready," said Wolf-Singer.

With that the mist hovered nearer to the fire, and was consumed down to the merest wisp. Singer could not tell if it was vapor or smoke—or perhaps it was both. Two coals from the fire glowed red, grew hotter. The wisp dove into the fire. There was a hiss and a pop as a log rolled over.

The coals were the eyes of Sparrow-in-Snow, glowing with his final power.

Singer bent over the fire and picked up the two coals. They seemed to smile at him; he felt his own eyes grow hot, as with tears that burn back into the head. Tears of joy that are held back, or of sorrow that must not be shed.

The embers were hot in his hands, but he was not burned by them. He took them to the rushing water.

The white bones of his ancestors were in a heap now, finally together forever. Singer thought of the Other Side, of the green grass there and the trees so heavy with fowl that the branches snapped from their weight. He could see his great-grandfather in the circle with the other kings, laughing.

The water of the river opened before him, swirling in an eddy that widened into a whirlpool. At the bottom of the pool lay the heap of bones.

He yelled for joy and leaped into the water. The whirlpool grabbed him up. Another skeleton joined the heap at the bottom.

The the bones began to move, tumbling in the current. They went down and around, and stuck tight in the cave tunnel. With nowhere to go, the water began to rise swiftly in the cave. The lingering fire was quickly extinguished. Black emptiness was filled with black water. The chamber filled and the river climbed into the large room that Hale had called a cathedral. This space too was finally filled, and clear water poured out the opening at the back of Spirit Rock.

The pressure on the cave wall grew. Late in the night it collapsed, one whole side of the mountain shuddered, the rumble of rocks and earth shook the surrounding land. Then the rumble stopped. Spirit Rock had collapsed into the opening, and the cave was sealed.

When clouds no longer covered the moon, the river ran by the clearing again as it had for ages past. The banks were quiet. Animal sounds returned.

Anyone watching would have noticed that the clearing no longer seemed to glow. But there was no one, at least from the town side of the river, to see it.

EPILOGUE

Dawn over Clearview.

The sense of fear and danger in David had worn down to a numbed aftershock. He sat, unmoving, on the second floor landing of what had been the library. The stone and ironwork staircase was the only part that hadn't been consumed. Every few minutes a contraction of his stomach reminded him that his body needed to eat something, and he would look across the street, almost expecting to see the cafe still standing, with customers going in and coming out, a few pickup trucks in the slanted parking slots. Millie and George calling out orders from the counter to the kitchen.

The only shouts he heard now were the occasional orders barked by the fire captains from Ulah and other towns, directing their men from the three trucks that had arrived too late to do anything but douse spots of fire rekindled from one or another of the burnt-out shells that used to be homes and businesses. They were simply stirring the rubbish. The paramedics had arrived shortly after the fire trucks, in time to attend to the few burn victims that miraculously were still alive; alarms and sirens still sounded down the highway to the hospital in Ulah. They had wanted to take David along too, for possible smoke inhalation and shock, but he, as well as Diana, was not ready to leave yet. Whatever damage had been done to them was only peripherally of the body.

She was beside him now. They held hands in mute support and watched as still another ambulance pulled away; this one moved slowly, no sirens; it was bearing another corpse to the morgue.

Several wire service reporters had been rooting about the remains of the town, and a camera truck with 'eyewitness' written on it was rolling in from the highway. Diana motioned to the truck and said, "Come on, let's get out of here before those vultures start asking questions."

"Yeah, okay," he said, and they got up, walking slowly down the skeleton of a staircase, arm in arm.

He was thinking more clearly now. He turned to her and asked, "Where can we go?" It was the first time he had thought about it; his duplex was a heap of cinders, along with everything else. He didn't have a job anymore; there was no longer a library.

"I don't know," she said. "I'm sure the apartment is gone. Even if it isn't, I wouldn't want to go back there. Somewhere else. Anywhere else."

"Yes." That sounded like a good idea, the only idea. "Anywhere else," he repeated.

One of the wire reporters rushed over to them. He had been trying to interview anyone that moved. "Won't you give me a statement now?" he asked David. "How did the forest fire start? Do you know how it could have been confined to this one area and not spread? Doctor Burke said something about a whirlwind or a tornado before he left for the hospital. Could you elaborate about that?"

"I have nothing to say." David said. "I'm just happy to be alive. I'm a survivor and that's it."

The reporter turned to Diana. "How about you? Aren't you Diana Walters, one of the people in charge of the archaeological dig near here? You're a scientist, can you explain what happened here last night? Do either of you know the whereabouts of Sheriff Witherspoon? What about...?"

David stopped and grabbed the reporter by the shirt collar. "Listen," he rasped, "if you really want to know the story, go over to that white house the other reporters have surrounded. The Priddy house, the one that wasn't even touched by the fire, and ask the woman there."

"Hey, no reason to get violent," the reporter said, pulling away to straighten his collar. "The old lady's crazy. All she'll say is some garbage about a debt being paid. Drivel about her grandfather. I'm a newsman, dammit! I want to know, in a town of five hundred or more why only a little over a third of the residents have been accounted for? Where are they? What happened to them?"

David sighed. "They're gone," he said simply.

"But where?"

"Across the river," David said.

The reporter just stood there with a puzzled expression on his face. David saw him shake his head, then turn to find another interview.

Dan Causey, the forest ranger, yelled to David and Diana.

David tried to smile. The ranger's jeep was hauling his volkswagen with a chain. The old bug was muddied but seemed to be still alive.

"This is yours, isn't it, Dave?" Causey asked.

"Yeah, it's mine."

"I thought so. Why did you leave it out in that clearing?" The question was rhetorical. Causey peered at the smoking ruins and shook his head. "Jesus," he said. "Looks even worse in the daylight, doesn't it? All my years around here, I've seen some fires, but nothing like this. I was in the tower last night when it started. I couldn't believe something could blaze up and then disappear like that. Must have been like hell, eh?"

"More than you'll ever know."

The ranger nodded, then changed the subject. "Let's unhook this thing, huh? It was up to its hubcaps out near Spirit Rock. There was a cave-in there, the river must have surged up over its banks because of it. That excavation site is pretty near washed away, Miss Walters."

"It's all right," answered Diana. "It doesn't matter now."

While Causey and David were unhooking the volkswagen from the jeep, the wire reporter rushed over again. He offered David three thousand dollars for an exclusive interview about how the two of them were saved from the flames.

David just shook his head. Finding his mud-caked car keys still in his pocket, he tried to crank the engine. It sputtered and then caught. He called for Diana to get in the car.

The reporter yelled another offer at them as David drove off, turning at the end of Commerce Street, past the wreckage of the service station, and out to the highway. He paused at the stoplight, although it was not functioning.

"Which way?" he asked.

Diana put her hand around his on the steering wheel. "I want to see my mother in Asheboro, but not right now. Just drive, okay? I want to go somewhere and be alone with you, and start forgetting all this nightmare."

"Yeah. So do I. But we'll have to come back, you know. There'll be insurance papers to file, your father's estate to settle, and..."

"I don't want to think about that. I just want to get away right now."

"Me too," Actually he was thinking, *Now I'll never get away from this place, not ever. It'll burn in my head till I'm in the ground, too.* He sighed, then turned to look at Diana. Even with the streaks of dirt and soot on her face, her hair in tangles, blouse torn—still she was beautiful. He was very much in love with her. Despite all the horror, he still could feel love. Perhaps now more than ever.

The feeling was good; he would try to hang onto it, hard.

The remains of the town were still visible in the rear-view mirror.

I can live with it, he said to himself. *I can live with all of it now, if I have to.*

He pressed down on the accelerator, but the engine started to skip. Something was lodged on the floor board, had worked its way beneath the pedal. He leaned to pick it up, held it up above the steering wheel. It was a round piece of charred wood, the type of coal that remains from a dead campfire.

It was wet and cold, completely gone out. No danger. He chucked it out the window, and the engine roared again.

The car turned right, which to the best of David's recollection was north. He figured they could stop when the car ran out of gas.

That ought to be far enough, he thought. The first day, at least.